F HOW
Howard, Heather H.
Chore whore.

$23.95

05/05

Chore Whore

Heather H. Howard

Adventures of a Celebrity Personal Assistant

 HarperEntertainment | *An Imprint of* HarperCollins*Publishers*

This novel is a work of fiction. Any references to real people, events, establishments, organizations, or locales are intended only to give the fiction a sense of reality and authenticity, and are used fictitiously. All other names, characters, and places, and all dialogue and incidents portrayed in this book, are the product of the author's imagination.

HarperCollins books may be purchased for educational, business, or sales promotional use. For information please write: Special Markets Department, HarperCollins Publishers Inc., 10 East 53rd Street, New York, NY 10022.

FIRST EDITION

Designed by Judith Stagnitto Abbate

Printed on acid-free paper

Library of Congress Cataloging-in-Publication Data
Howard, Heather H.
    Chore whore : adventures of a celebrity personal assistant / by Heather H. Howard—1st ed.
        p.   cm.
    ISBN 0-06-072391-2 (acid-free paper)
    1. Hollywood (Los Angeles, Calif.)—Fiction. 2. Administrative assistants—Fiction. 3. Motion picture industry—Fiction. 4. Celebrities—Fiction. I. Title.
PS3608.O923C48 2005
813'.6—dc22
                                                    2004054177

05   06   07   08   09   WBC/RRD   10   9   8   7   6   5   4   3   2   1

For my son, Cayman, you are my spark and light.

And to my precious mother, Patti Howard,
my wise sister, Melissa Howard,
and my big sis, Laura Caplan,
I love you and appreciate you all.

I have been used, abused, lied about and cheated. I have been blamed, shamed, screamed at and ridiculed. I have been stabbed, robbed, followed and sprayed with tear gas. I have been rammed, scammed and damned. I have been jacked over, run over and flipped over. I've had my ass kissed, my reputation dissed, my foot pissed on, my leg come on and my face spat on. All in the name of working as a celebrity's personal assistant . . . *a chore whore.*

Chapter One

Today is December 18, Steven Spielberg's birthday. Although not formally declared a national holiday, in Hollywood, California, and its environs, it is celebrated as one. A wicked form of paralysis cripples the movie industry. Celebrities, producers, directors and musicians—in fact, anyone who is or wants to be indebted to Steven—is at wits' end. Fingernails are being chewed, hair is being torn out and smokers who have quit, resume.

I prepare all year for this day, taking notes every time a brilliant gift idea presents itself. However, with so many requests from my clients, I still get caught short.

The week leading up to his birthday I can't sleep due to the spinning wheels in my brain working overtime.

The stars who employ me typically procrastinate, waiting until the morning of December 18 to call, desperate for ideas on what present to give Steven that will make *them* stand out amongst all his other gift-givers. What *do* you get someone who has everything?

Call me practical, but I always first suggest that they donate to his favorite charity, the Shoah Foundation, which his former assistant, Bonnie, who has since climbed the rungs of Amblin Entertainment's ladder to procure a loftier title, personally told me he prefers.

"Fuck that!" my clients say. They want theirs to be exceptional, not just another donation. Forget that Shoah documents the stories of surviving Holocaust victims and all that dribble, they want to give him something he'll *never* forget . . . a present of such extreme uniqueness that it will stick in his mind when he's casting his next big feature, something guaranteed to set them apart from the crowd.

Combine the usual holiday madness with Steven's birthday and December becomes a time worthy of heart attacks and drug overdoses.

Every one of my clients has a long Christmas gift list of what to get other celebrities, agents, publicists, household staff and assistants, not to mention families and friends. They know their yearly limit of creativity will be spent on Spielberg's birthday present, so they allow themselves to fall into the "rut" of giving charity donations to all the other folks on their holiday gift list.

Giving to charities makes the stars feel good once a year, it's a tax deduction (so everyone gets into the act), it benefits the downtrodden and it's a cure-all for what to give the person who *has* everything.

It just won't do for Steven.

To avoid additional pressure and stress in December, I descend upon my stationer in October and have the Christmas/Hanukkah/Kwanzaa cards done early. I also start calling everyone in my clients' Rolodexes to confirm addresses, names, spelling, babies born, birthdays, etc. This time of the year, it is not uncommon for me to come home to messages from Eric Clapton, Rod Stewart, Tom Cruise, Elizabeth Taylor, Don Johnson, Garry Shandling and Pamela Anderson—all confirming or giving a change of address. By mid-October the cards are printed in raised gold lettering with envelopes lined in silk. By Thanksgiving, several thousand envelopes have been carefully addressed. I hit the post office on December 1, hauling boxes of cards to be mailed out to addresses across the globe.

A typical preprinted gift card reads: "The [insert almost any last name in Hollywood] family is celebrating this holiday season [not "joyous season" because one wouldn't want to offend Hollywood's depressed] by donating a financial gift to [pick your charity—preferably one dealing with disease, children or the Democratic Party, if it's an election year] in your name [never specify whose]. We wish you bliss and peace in the upcoming year. All our love, [insert celebrity name].

The recipient of the card feels warm and fuzzy for three seconds, never suspecting the giver has donated $500 *total* to the charity, spent $2,200 on the preprinted gilded cards and has sent them to 1,000 people, donating exactly 50 cents per person. Now, *that's* a gift!

Eight days before Christmas, the busiest time of the year for me, and Lucy Bennett, a two-time Academy Award–winning actress, called last night wondering if I might be "available" to whip up a meal for a small, intimate dinner party she plans on having . . . tonight.

The small, intimate part doesn't bother me. The cooking on such short notice bugs me only slightly. It blends in with all the other anxiety I'm feeling right now. The guest list is the intimidating part. Cooking is a job requirement. All my clients know I love to cook, so over the years it has been incorporated as an aspect of my personal assistant job, just like taking their dog to the vet, answering their fan mail or doing their grocery shopping.

I've been Lucy's personal assistant for twenty years—way before her first Academy Award score and way before she had most of the friends she's now inviting over for dinner.

To celebrate Christmas and the upcoming Academy Award nominations, she wants to entertain ten of her closest pals—John Travolta and his wife, actress Kelly Preston; Melissa Etheridge; Courteney Cox Arquette and David Arquette; Meg Ryan; Laura Dern and her rock star honey, Ben Harper; director David Lynch and his woman, Mary.

To complicate the dinner and my life, Lucy has given me a list of what her friends will eat, won't eat, can eat and what they would prefer to eat. Meg doesn't like salmon and she's on a diet that dictates food according to her blood type. John and Kelly lead a preservative-free life. Laura's no vegetarian but she doesn't do red meat or dairy, and Ben likes chocolate. No, scratch that, loves chocolate, especially chocolate cake. Melissa is giving the Atkins Diet a try, Mary's on the Zone, and both Davids are sold on the South Beach. Courteney doesn't eat anything that "pumps, thinks, filters or scavenges"—in other words, no hearts, brains, liver, kidneys or crab. I think every last one of them should abandon their programs for one meal so I can figure out a menu without short-circuiting my brain cells.

I ask Lucy if it would be permissible to perhaps cater the dinner, or at least part of it, what with the short notice and all.

"No, sweetheart. We've done all the restaurants. Now we want feel-good food. Corki food."

So, Corki-style food is what they're going to get.

I hit the 24/7 grocery store in West Hollywood at four-thirty in the morning to do my shopping for tonight's get-together. Even though Santa Monica Seafood typically opens at nine, I called my favorite fishmonger and he agreed to let me come in at six A.M. Bless him.

My son, Blaise, however, doesn't feel the same way. He prefers to sleep in. If we need to leave for school at seven forty-five A.M., he wants to be awakened at seven-thirty. Waking him up at four o'clock in the morning to go grocery shopping, of all things, is akin to the worst torture humanly possible. He informs me that sleep deprivation may be a tactic allowed by the Geneva Convention for prisoners of war, but this is our home and it's a peaceful one at that, so can he please get some more sleep?

Blaise is ten years old with an I.Q. higher than mine. At five foot seven he is only one inch shorter than me and on a good day is mistaken for my little brother rather than my son. He is the duplicate of his father, with caramel-colored skin and light curly hair that is as unruly as he.

Amidst his blond starter-kit dreadlocks is a patch of even blonder hair smack dab on the back of his head. His brown features are exquisite topped off by piercing blue eyes—an oddity in "half-castes," as an Israeli friend of mine stated. I can only wonder what relative amongst our antecedents had the piercing baby blues—his father's Eastern Caribbean background or my Jamaican and English background?

As I squeeze clementine tangerines for the juice, in which I will cook the salmon (sorry, Meg) and lobster (sorry, Courteney), I am on the phone with Pasquale Shoe Repair, the creators of Dorothy's ruby slippers, asking when Nicolas Cage's rattlesnake jacket will be deemed water-resistant.

I don't work for Nic but my celebs love to "loan me out" to their friends. "You need what? That little doohickey that takes the bubbles out of champagne? And your assistant can't find it? Let me call Corki. She's been with me for twenty years. Corki can find anything." I still secretly revel in the fact that Tommy Lee Jones and folk singer Leonard Cohen called me a genius on the same day for securing hard-to-find items for them—during pre-Internet days.

The call-waiting tone beeps. I hang up with Pasquale after arranging to pick up the jacket later.

"Hello, this is Corki."

"Hi," comes the husky British trademark voice of rock and roll music on the other end of the line, "this is . . ." He doesn't need to say. I know who it is.

"How can I help you?"

"I just did a song for Spielberg's latest film and am struggling with what to get him for his special day. I spoke with Slash—you know him, right?"

"Of course!" I say as I continue to squeeze clementines.

"Well, he obviously knows you, too. He recommended that I call. Said you'd know what to do. I need something today!"

"Yeah, this is a yearly problem. How much are you looking to spend?"

"Doesn't matter. Whatever will do the job," he says.

"Knowing that all you get as a tax write-off is twenty-five dollars?" I ask.

"I don't give a fuck if I can only write off one dollar."

"Okay! You're aware that I don't give out my services for free, right? Did Slash tell you my fee?" I inquire as I wash my hands.

"No, and I don't care. I just want something memorable given to him as a gift."

"Fine, I'll come up with something memorable. Now, I hate to say this, but you have a reputation amongst assistants for not paying your bills, so I'll have to be paid up front. I can include my fee on the credit card you'll be using to pay for the gift. It will be sixty dollars."

The line is silent. I still hear him breathing, so I know he hasn't hung up, he's just been insulted, is all.

"You still there?" I ask.

"Yes," he says after a long pause.

"Don't be offended, it's just that I'm a working woman. I'm a widow with a ten-year-old to feed and I've been screwed over before. I just can't afford for that to happen anymore. Would you still like to use my services?'

"Yes. That's fine."

He gives me his credit card number, his formal name as it appears on his card, and the expiration date. He also tells me how the gift card should read and gives me a return number to tell him the amount and delivery time.

As I prepare to cut the leeks for tonight's gratin, I glance at the lobsters in the pail on my kitchen floor trying, in vain, to escape. This gives birth to an idea. I dial the number to Almor Liquor on Sunset Boulevard in the heart of Hollywood.

"Mary? It's Corki! Merry Christmas!"

"To you as well!" she says.

"Mary, I know this is last minute, as always, but is it possible to get a gift over to Universal Studios today by five?" I inquire.

"For Spielberg's birthday?" she asks.

"Gee, how did you know?"

"During his birthday week I sell and deliver a ton of champagne. In fact, I only sell more on New Year's Eve."

"Well, here's my idea. Can you do an All-Clad lobster pot with two live, banded lobsters, a fabulous wine, some clarified butter and decorated with maybe netting, lemons, limes, the like?" I inquire, crossing my fingers.

"Hmmm. Nice idea. I just got in a great vintage, a '95 white burgundy. It's a Chassagne-Montrachet. The wine alone, though, will be a couple hundred."

"Doesn't matter," I state emphatically. "And when you're done calculating, will you add sixty dollars to the credit card so I can be paid? I told him I'd bill him that way and he said it was fine."

I give Mary all the pertinent information and it is done. I can almost bet that Steven has never received live lobsters before. I ponder for a moment, wondering if he'll even eat lobster, since they don't have fins or scales and he is Jewish. Then I think of the rumor I heard that he doesn't drink . . . even wine. But, I decide, it's not the gift that matters; it's the *uniqueness* of the gift. This is what my caller wanted, after all—something that would stand out—and he got it.

I'm due at Lucy's house to start cooking at five-thirty. My friend Shelly said she'd watch Blaise for the evening if I'd agree to pick up her daughter, Star, and niece, Eden, from school along with him. Fortunately, they're all in the fifth grade together and the best of friends. It is ten-thirty now and before I pick them up I have so many errands to run, I don't know how I can possibly finish them all. First, I have to go Los Angeles International Airport to clear a shipment of perfume through customs.

Daisy Colette, film star and now director/producer, has designed her own individual perfume line to give as one-of-a-kind Christmas gifts. The shipment was delayed in Paris, and unless I personally go down today and clear it, the perfume will not arrive in time to wrap and deliver before half her friends leave for a week of skiing in Aspen. And then I have to pick up Nic's coat and grocery shop, another last-minute request from actor Jock Straupman.

I'm starting to feel a cold coming on from lack of sleep.

As I pull out of my driveway, I dial my doctor's phone number.

"Dr. Trabulus, please. This is Corki Brown." I ask for him knowing good and well he'll be busy and not able to come to the phone.

"Hi, Corki! What can I do for you?"

Surprise, surprise!

"Is this Dr. Trabulus live or a recording?" I ask.

"It's a recording," he says, deadpan.

"I hate to ask for this, because I don't want you to think I'm a pill popper, but I desperately need some sleeping pills. Just to get me through Christmas. I have seven days of shopping left and I'm starting to get sick from lack of sleep. Can you hook me up?"

"Have the pharmacy call me. I'll prescribe Ambien."

I have the pharmacy call and he does indeed prescribe Ambien. Eight of them. That's it. He's so careful to give only what is needed that I could never become a drug addict. One more errand—pick up my pills.

Dr. Trabulus is *the* doctor to the stars, a title that would never come out of his mouth. However, his name graces the tabloids at least monthly, and he's listed in so many album cover "Thanks to" paragraphs that the albums' printers don't even bother asking how to spell it. They know it because he's their doctor, too. Everyone shares him. He was Rebecca DeMornay's doctor. She told Lucy Bennett who raved about him to Tracey Ullman then suggested him to Veronique LeMay. She recommended him to me. In the waiting room I'll likely sit next to Ken Olin, Courteney Cox Arquette or Axl Rose, who also shares my dermatologist along with Courtney Love.

Twenty years ago my peers were getting their master and doctorate degrees with visions of contributing something meaningful to the world. I, however, couldn't suffer through the embarrassment of returning to UCLA after what happened.

I was the only one left standing in line at graduation with my cap, gown and class ring, waiting anxiously to hear my name called so I could walk up onstage and receive my diploma. But my name was never called.

I had sent out invitations. Mom and Dad had traveled hundreds of miles after rearranging work schedules to be there in the audience.

I didn't know what went wrong, but three weeks after I'd cried an unending flow of tears, the grad-check department called to tell me there was a mistake. I was twelve units—three classes—short, and I would not be receiving my bachelor's degree.

I sent back all the checks well-wishers had sent to start my new life as a grad. Rather than tuck my tail between my legs and hightail it back to school, I put on a false bravado and said "Screw it" to the world of higher education.

I took an assortment of horrifying jobs. I scrubbed bugs off small crop-dusting aircraft at the local airport, packed nectarines in shipping cartons and cleaned toilets. So when I found that newspaper ad in the bathroom trash can I was cleaning and actually got hired as a celebrity's personal assistant, I thought I had it made.

The hours were long, seventy to eighty per week, but I was young and energetic and I earned enough money to travel. I didn't mind not having the comfies of a nine-to-five job, a 401(k), a pension plan. Travel was more important than the future. I was living in the present, a young woman desperate to see the world. And fortunately, being a celebrity's assistant enabled me to do just that.

When one of my stars got a three-month film in Italy, I traveled ahead to make sure the housing was perfect and set up to her specifications. I was the one who made sure the twelve Louis Vuitton trunks were delivered to the proper airline. I got them cleared through customs—and "Yes, sir, I *was* the one who packed every last one of these, and trust me, they have *not* been out of my sight." I passed out tips left and right to every soul who had to move the trunks.

I was also the one unpacking them—the one who could complain in six different languages (an asset in my line of work) that no, ordinary 310-thread-count cotton sheets would not do. Pratesi or Frette sheets only. And no, she doesn't want San Pellegrino, she wants Fonte Tavina, in glass, at room temperature, *grazie mille.*

In Paris, in November, I had the pleasure of Christmas shopping with my client's credit card. She was busy shooting her movie, but had the intention of making it look as if she carefully chose each gift for the people back home. In the pouring rain, I combed the Marais, Saint-Germain, Saint-Honoré and the Champs Élysées, carrying multiple shopping bags while fending off pickpockets.

Loaded down, I approached a taxi stand when a man walked up to me and in perfect English said, "You rich! You are nothing but whores!" and spit in my face.

To add insult to injury, he stole my cab.

In London, I arrived to personally cater to another client's every whim. Without the language barrier, I swept the city for organic produce and wild Scottish salmon. I chopped veggies and fruit to his specifications, in exact one-half-inch cubes. The salmon had to be steamed, and no oil could touch *anything*. All food had to be put in individual Tupperware bowls, brought from home. I called these his troughs. I stocked every fridge within arm's reach for his consumption. While he dined with a half-moon of troughs in front of him, I dined with my London-based friend Marla, eating the best fish and chips ever at Wheelers in Piccadilly.

If a production company shot a movie on location and decided to pay for a local to assist my stars, I was left at home. Time for my vacation! No special sheets or water or Tupperware. Just a toothbrush, sunscreen, camera and clothes in my own affordable, sturdy, green 1960s Samsonite luggage.

I went to the Caribbean, right in America's backyard.

Antigua, a small dot on the map in the Eastern Caribbean, has 365 white, perfect sand beaches. The water lapping at the shore is warm, shallow and decorated with every color of blue and green imaginable. Tropical reef fish swam between my fingers and slumber came easily in the balmy night air. The scents of fresh coconuts, mangoes and ginger lilies wafted through the air. I was hooked.

I learned to snorkel and scuba dive and even went deep-sea fishing. And that was where I met Basil . . . the captain of the ship.

I heard the deep bellow of his laugh first. When I saw his sea-bleached blond dreadlocks and his tall, gorgeous body with its skin like caramel candy, I wanted to taste it. I found him addictive. Basil would tell fisherman tales with his deep West Indian accent and swear they were true: nights at sea, legendary ocean monsters, fighting off Colombian pirates and reeling in tuna by hand in the South Seas. He showed scars from encounters with sharks and emotional scars from past loves.

His father, a doctor, had insisted Basil return to England to finish his medical residency, but Basil wanted to fish. He wanted to be free out on the Caribbean. After we met, he considered coming to Los Angeles to finish his residency. After a year of long-distance phone calls and occasionally seeing each other, I went to Antigua and impulsively married him with the promise that he'd return home with me.

Basil and I were in what he called "young stupid amounts of love." For our honeymoon, we went sailing in his fishing boat. We explored small, uninhabited islands by day and made love on deck every night. We sailed up the island chain to St. Martin, where we docked and explored.

As I shopped in the small French seaside town of Marigot, Basil went out to sea to catch our dinner. I went to the dock at the agreed-upon time with a bottle of wine, cheese, cornichons, boiled eggs, tomatoes and a baguette.

I waited at the marina until sundown.

Basil didn't return. I sat through the night nibbling on the bread while mosquitoes nibbled on me. I waited some more. I waited until I felt sick to my stomach. I called his mother in Antigua. Basil hadn't come back.

He was pronounced lost at sea.

Three weeks later, I went home to L.A., a married, pregnant woman with no husband to be found. I was in yet another situation where I was embarrassed to admit what I'd done. While my friends were getting married (to men who were here and could be supportive), pregnant and prequalified for mortgages, I was alone and raising my son, Blaise, in a small apartment I rented in West Hollywood. We lived only two miles from my clients' multimillion-dollar homes in the hills, but light-years away from their lifestyles.

Ten years later, I struggle to balance being a good mom who's there for my son and a good employee who's there for my other children—my clients—who need mothering almost as much as Blaise.

My oldest "kid" is Jock Straupman. At fifty-four, he needs me to supply his creature comforts. I need him in order to pay my rent, make car payments and cover medical insurance premiums.

I'm not qualified to do most types of work, and other jobs I've had don't pay enough to live on. In the dog-eat-dog environment of Hollywood, I have to fight to keep my job. As I do Jock's fan mail, I'm constantly throwing away eight-by-ten-inch headshots and resumés from young beautiful women who would give anything to be the assistant to a movie star.

In December I'm overwhelmed by eighteen-hour days, but when January arrives, work slows down to a mere trickle because celebs meet with their accountants for a reality check on how much the holidays truly cost them. They try desperately to regain control of their spending. Their good behavior lasts sixty days tops, then I'm back to work as usual.

Jock Straupman called early this morning needing more groceries than the ones I buy him twice a week. Any other time of the year this would be an easy request, but the groceries he needs are from three different specialty stores, all in different directions, fifteen miles apart. This one errand combined with traffic being a bear becomes a two-hour affair even after I've called the stores and had the items bagged and prepaid.

I have the fantasy of telling Jock I can't do it, it's physically impossible to be in all the places I'm needed, but A-list movie stars don't take that kind of news well. If his assistant of fifteen years isn't available, he might get the idea that I don't need the job. He may entertain the notion of getting himself a younger, more nubile assistant, one who doesn't have a ten-year-old boy with twice-a-week swim lessons, one who never gets sick and will work twice the hours for half the pay and throw in a few goodies on the side whenever she feels so inclined.

As I pick up at the last grocery store, my cell phone rings. I transfer the grocery bags to one hand and dig my cell out of my purse to answer it.

"Corki Brown?"

"Yes, this is she."

"This is Dr. Castillo."

Oh shit, Blaise's principal. It must be bad if she's on the phone personally. She's only done this twice before: once when he needed stitches and once when he broke his arm.

"Hi, Dr. Castillo. How are you? Merry Christmas!"

I pelt her with good wishes before she accosts me with the real reason for phoning.

"Thank you, to you, too, but that's not the reason I'm calling. Blaise is fine, he's not hurt or anything. However, I can't say as much for our school."

"What do you mean?" I ask.

"He set off the school's fire alarm system. By law, we had to evacuate all eight hundred students and it was an enormous disruption. He is presently in my office and I'd like for you to come pick him up. Now!"

"Dr. Castillo, I am so sorry he did this, but I can't. I'm in the middle of work and I'll lose my job if I don't deliver. This is the busiest time of year for me. Can I speak with Blaise?"

"Ms. Brown, this is the fifth incident this year," she says, barely containing her anger. "He needs to learn consequences to his actions. I've already given him a one-day suspension and that didn't seem to teach him very much. Right now, I'm filling out the appropriate paperwork to have him suspended from attending our school for one week, following the winter break."

"I'll be there as soon as I can. He may just have to sit in your office until I arrive. It could be a few hours though. And Dr. Castillo?"

"Yes?"

"If you suspend him for a week, I'm afraid he'll just take it as an extended holiday."

"That will be up to you to make sure that it's not perceived that way. This will be going on his permanent record. He'll be waiting here for you." Dr. Castillo hangs up.

Within a minute my phone rings again.

"Mom, it's Blaise." Then there's silence.

"Blaise, tell me you weren't the one who set off that alarm."

"But I was."

"Why did you do something like that? You know better," I urge.

"I wanted to hear what it sounded like," he says without a hint of emotion.

"Yeah? Well, you heard. Are you happy? Now you're going to get suspended and they want me to come down there and pick you up. But I can't, I have to work. And chances are it's going to be a few hours, so you'll have time to think about that fire alarm for a good while. Wait there and I'll get you when I can."

I don't know what's gotten into that boy lately. His counselor warned me that he has reached the age where a boy *really* needs his father, but what am I to do? I've made sure to give him as many positive male role models as possible. His teacher, swim coaches, piano teacher—all men.

Blaise used to be so well behaved, loving and a joy. He actually used to *want* to bring his teachers apples so he could be their "pet."

I would buy all the apples in the world if we could return to those times.

I cautiously wind my way up to Jock Straupman's putty-colored hillside home, high above the Chateau Marmont Hotel, where John Belushi spent his last moments indulging. The road is a long series of hairpin curves and blind spots that seem to spin wildly even though I'm creeping along at seven miles per hour.

Only yards away from the Sunset Strip, the main artery pulsing through West Hollywood, is a residential neighborhood where mange-infested coyotes walk casually down the street in midday. Homeless folks make campsites behind bushes that cascade down steep canyons full of five-million-dollar homes. Within earshot of "the Strip," where horns blare and sirens scream, wild deer ravage residents' gardens, leaving only the lilies, oleander, garlic and mondo grasses alive. Even with this, the streets are lush and green all year around. Mediterranean-style abodes hug the hillside next to Frank Lloyd Wright homes. Directors live next to producers who live within spitting distance of someone who is, was, or will be famous.

For my clients, the price of living in the Hollywood Hills, one of L.A.'s most coveted neighborhoods, doesn't stop with the $40,000-per-month mortgage payment. They cope with frequent power outages, mud slides, rattlesnakes in the garage, rats invading the house, tarantulas in the potting sheds, scorpions behind the pool equipment and bears drinking from their pools.

Friday and Saturday nights, they have the added pleasure of dealing with the Sunset Strip nightclubs' valet parking companies who use the hills' narrow streets for their additional spaces. The bar hoppers who party past the time the valets pack up and go home are left on their own to find their cars. Inevitably, the drunken partygoers, having hiked the hills in search of their vehicles, feel free to quench their thirst and express their lust. The next morning, the streets are littered with beer bottles, condom wrappers and the occasional spent syringe or wayward brassiere.

Jock's neighbors pay an additional price for living here. It's an all too familiar spectacle witnessed by the gardeners, the florist, the *National Enquirer* and many an unsuspecting driver happening by— Jock Straupman, out on the street in broad daylight, locked in a lusty embrace, fondling the ass and kissing the neck of yet another blond-haired, blue-eyed, eighteen-year-old girl.

The neighbors shake their heads in disapproval and go back inside their houses. The gardeners' $1,500-a-month paycheck helps them avert their eyes and keep trimming the bougainvillea. The national rag magazines have photographed this scene so many times it has become routine. When other stars aren't living up to their quota of bad behavior, the rags fill their pages with Jock's sexploits.

Unsuspecting drivers invariably snap their heads back to see Jock, a very recognizable movie star, typically postcoital, dressed in only a skimpy pair of nylon shorts, the kind that were all the rage for runners back in the 1980s. This results in the same car doing a drive-by three or four times to get a peek at an actor's love scene without having to pay the ten-dollar price tag for a movie.

Ever since Lucy Bennett broke up their four-year romance, Jock hasn't had a relationship that has lasted longer than three days. Not one to let moss gather, this rolling stone was already getting busy on his couch with a young blonde as I was directing the Chipman United Van Lines moving crew around him to gather Lucy's possessions and load up the moving truck.

I say a quick prayer to the parking gods that my favorite spot, across the street from Jock's house, is empty. With parking at a premium in the hills, I covet that space. On his side of the street, there are NO PARKING AT ANY TIME signs, and on the other side of the narrow lane, there are mostly red zones with an occasional spot that can fit two subcompact cars.

I maneuver my Toyota 4Runner, fondly named Black Betty, around the tight bends. As I lumber through the final blind curve, the driver of a spicy-red Porsche behind me decides he just can't wait. He passes on the left, in the path of oncoming traffic, and careens around the corner.

I hear the collision before I see it. Pulling around the corner, I see that the Porsche convertible, bent in all the promised "crumple zones," and a once-white, older Ford F550 pickup truck, unscathed, have been brought together in a union that was never meant to be consummated.

A Latino gardening crew tumbles from the cab of the huge truck, its bed filled to the top with trimmed branches, leaves and foliage. Before the accident, a dead deer had been perched on the truck's load like a cherry on top of an ice-cream sundae. They drop dead frequently in the hills and gardening crews are usually called to rid the yards of their carcasses.

The impact of the crash shot the buck's body over the truck's cab, thus stabbing its generous set of antlers cleanly through the Porsche's windshield. The driver narrowly escaped being pinned to the back of his seat. The deer's body is spread-eagle across the recently polished, buckled hood. The gardening crew walks around the sports car, scratching their heads and whispering amongst themselves.

As the convertible driver punches numbers into his cell phone, he rants to no one in particular about drivers who don't live here and don't belong here. Head-on crashes in this neck of the hood are almost always between an overly confident tax-paying resident of the Hollywood Hills and a foreigner, i.e., someone who doesn't pay for a *prime* piece of Los Angeles real estate. The driver blows hot breath about uninsured motorists and illegal immigrants. He glares at me as I try to squeeze Betty by the mess and get the groceries to Jock.

"Just how the hell am I supposed to know who to call, Donna?" he screams into his cell phone. "You're my assistant, you fix it!" Silence. His lips purse tightly, readying for Scud missile strike number two. "No, Donna, they don't know who to call. If they can't figure out how to tie dinner onto the back of their truck properly, what makes you think they'd know who to call? Call Triple A or the police. Call the fucking Wildlife Waystation, I don't care, but figure it out and make it snappy. Then get your ass over here and get me to Universal by three, you hear?"

I should have known . . . a Hollywood high roller and his miserable assistant. For Donna's sake, I stop and call out to Mr. Happy. "Hey, guy, you want me to call the proper authorities?"

He opens his door and approaches me, looking desperate.

"Thank you, would you mind?"

I get out my trusty cell phone and a computerized voice speaks to me. "Name, please!"

"Dead animal pickup."

In my daily travels I report so many dead animals on the side of the road that I had to preprogram it.

My phone repeats, "Calling 'Dead animal pickup.'" I describe the incident and the location to the dispatcher and tell Mr. Hollywood help is on the way. For a moment I feel like Superwoman in that I helped a fellow assistant from potentially getting canned or, more likely, being screamed at and berated for the rest of the day.

Moving on down the road, I see that my treasured parking place is taken by Tito's truck—another Ford F550, the preferred choice of transportation for landscaping crews. Tito and his gang of gardeners, who descend upon Jock's house every Monday, Wednesday and Friday, always get the prime spot. I marvel at Tito's consistency. He has four orange cones—two in the back, two in the front—warning other drivers to give him a wide berth.

There's not another "legal" space to be found. I sit for a moment in the middle of the road, wondering whether to chance parking in the red zone across from Jock's house and get a whopping big ticket or in front of his garage and risk having the garage door open and dent my Betty's body.

Suddenly, I'm blasted with a horn. The driver behind me doesn't appreciate my current dilemma. I start to park in the red zone and glance back to see my client, actress Daisy Colette, behind the wheel of her BMW, trying to maneuver around me. She pounds on the horn and motions for me to get the hell out of her way. She obviously doesn't realize it's me—her assistant. As she passes, I call, "Slow down, Daisy. Cool off!"

"Fuck you!" she screams, roaring past me, around the corner and down the hill.

Betty's dashboard clock reads 2:06 P.M. I'm six minutes late. I pull four very heavy bags of groceries from the backseat, trot across the street and set them down in front of the gate.

Jock's abode is more a fortress than a home. Years ago a drunk threw an unopened champagne bottle through his front window. The next week a wall was constructed. A week later a fence was added along with landscaping filled with thorny, prickly bushes. Then came the "cage," an impenetrable, unclimbable metal security enclosure with a magnetized lock surrounding the original entrance to Jock's home. Now security cameras record every move. Anyone coming to the house either has their own access code or they have to announce themselves through the intercom to be admitted.

I punch my access code into the "Door King." Once past the security door, the true adventure begins. Beyond the metal gate is a thick, worm-eaten wood door with another magna-lock and chunky, rusted-metal hardware. It guards the ascent to Jock's house, a mossy and often wet brick staircase perched at a forty-five-degree angle. Even with the handrail in place, I had eleven years' worth of scraped hands and knees from occasionally falling up or down these stairs.

Then, four years ago, Jock requested the safety handrail be removed . . . for aesthetic reasons. I fantasize about asking for
hazardous-condition pay. Combat pay. I'm sure the gardeners have
had more than their fair share of laughs at me grabbing the vines on
the walls in order to regain my balance rather than making a free fall
to the bottom.

The last time I had the intercom replaced and the communication system updated, I decided to give individual codes to the gardener and florist. The pool guy, the water delivery guy and the gas
meter reader received another code. Jock and I would share one.
Jock's housekeeper, Concepcion, and her triplets, Hubert, Rupert
and Wilbert, age twenty-two, would share one. After school, Concepcion's sons visit their mom and help out around the place. They
move the furniture for her to vacuum under, rearrange rooms per
Jock's request, and now and again move the piano from one room to
another.

As I cautiously ascend the staircase, I pass Tito flying down the
slippery stairs with such incredible balance I'm convinced he has
suction cups imbedded in the bottoms of his work boots.

"Hi, Miss Corki."

"Hey, Tito."

Tito, the quintessential gentleman, sweeps the four bags from
my hands and carries them the rest of the way.

"Did you see the accident?" I ask.

"No. One of my *compadres* told me about it. I wanted to go down
there 'cause it sounded like something I would want to see, but I
have too much work. I wouldn't want Mr. Jock to think I was slacking off."

Tito can't stand still. As we speak, he starts picking dead flowers
off bushes. I dig around in my purse for the door keys.

"No one's going to think you're slacking off. The garden looks fantastic and I appreciate you helping me. Is Jock home?" I whisper.

Tito nods toward the living room window. I peer through it and see the back of Jock's brown curly-haired head resting against the leather couch. Suddenly, a blond ponytail rises up from what I assume is Jock's lap. His company.

"He's consistent," I say to myself.

I ring the front doorbell, announcing my arrival, then glance down to the grocery bags at my feet.

For a man with such variety in his sex life, Jock's choice in food is downright boring. Week in and week out I shop for the same foods. I don't even need a grocery list anymore. Jock eats four tubs of cottage cheese per week and three gallons of Silk brand soymilk. Only "Original" flavor, because that has the lowest fat and the lowest sugar content of any soymilk on the planet unless he personally squeezes the edamame beans.

Then there is his tuna. He bases the entire balance of his diet around his consumption of hermetically sealed foil pouches of tuna. When I hit the grocery stores for a "Jock run" and clean out the entire tuna supply, other shoppers stare.

I ring the doorbell again just to make sure he knows I'm here. No one answers. He is, after all, busy. I slowly count to ten and then open the door. He's on the living room couch with a young Icelandic-looking woman draped across his lap. I keep an expressionless face as I remember my grandmother putting me across her lap and giving me a hard spanking for not minding her.

"Hi, Corki!" Jock smiles.

"Oh, hi!" I say without blinking.

I pass by his living room "art" collection, consisting of children's stuffed animals with all their limbs and tails severed and resewn on in improper places. Donald Duck has a monkey's mouth sewn on his crotch. Woody Woodpecker has a huge pecker indeed, with Pluto's tail sewn in place of his private parts. A matching pair, Tom and Jerry, have cloth penises so long they twist and turn, are intertwined, plaited, then go up the back and end up as toupees on their heads.

I quietly put the groceries away. As I place them in Jock's stainless steel side-by-side Sub-Zero, I can't help hearing what's happening in the living room: slurping.

Jock calls out, "Oh, by the way, Cork?"

"Yes?" I say as I enter the living room. He strokes Icy's ass and she turns her face toward the couch cushion, running her hand over his six-pack abs.

"There's some stuff in the out basket for you. And what's going on with Concepcion? She didn't do all the laundry in the hamper. I need some clothes laundered before she comes back on Monday. I gave her tomorrow and Friday off and look what she does. This is terrible."

"I'll drop them off to be done tonight and pick them up tomorrow. Is that okay?" I ask.

"Mmmmmm, yes, that would be perfect," he moans. "There is one other thing in the out basket I'll be needing today. Probably sooner than later."

I slip into the office. Concepcion's list awaits me: green kitchen sponges, Windex, a new mop, vacuum bags and laundry detergent. Under her list is an unopened condom. No note. I don't need one, I know what I have to do. Find this particular brand and find it quickly. He has apparently changed brands while my back was turned. This rubber with its "pleasure-enhancing pouch" offers "oodles of sexual pleasure." It certainly doesn't look like typical grocery store or pharmacy fare.

The clock reads 2:16 P.M.

I dodge into Jock's bedroom closet and throw open the lid to the hamper to get the laundry, but it's empty. I search the floors of both of his walk-in closets, places he might have piled the shirts. None to be seen. As I start back down the hallway, I hear Jock calling me from the living room.

"Corki, the clothes are in here."

I walk back into the living room and he points to a pile of thongs, panties, bras and other assorted Iceland wear.

Bile rises up into my throat. This isn't "laundering." Laundering is for button-down men's shirts. This pile is fluff and fold, and not even *his* fluff and fold.

"There's a bag to put it in at the bottom of the pile," he says.

Miss Icy turns to watch me put her dirty underwear in the bag. My anger makes my head swim. I can't find a way to pick up someone else's used panties discreetly. I want to find some rubber gloves, but Jock has perked up to watch me separate the pile and put the panties in the bag and the jeans and blouses over my arm. I lower my head so they won't see my face. Why can't this low-rent heifer wash her own dirty underwear? There's a washing machine in the laundry room. I try to find a clean place to pick up the thongs, but with thongs, there is no clean place.

Hurrying out the front door with a barely audible "Bye," I race across the walkway, slowing down to descend the "Stairway to Heaven" so as not to plunge to my death. I wave goodbye to Tito's workers, who are carefully returning escaped gravel to the lined pathways leading around the house.

Pressing the appropriate buzzers that release the doors and gates of Jock's citadel, I dash across the street. My cell phone rings as I throw Icy's clothes on the floor behind my seat.

"Hello."

"Ms. Brown, this is Dr. Castillo again. I'm sorry to bother you, but school has ended and someone *must* come pick up Blaise. He's been sitting here for over an hour while the other children are playing out on the yard in the after-school program. He's miserable watching the other children and he's making everyone in the office miserable. The office is closing early today. What time will you be here?"

I exhale deeply.

"I'll come now. But I promised Shelly Ford that I'd pick up her daughter, Star, and her niece, Eden. Is it possible to have them called to the office and waiting for me so I can get them all in one fell swoop?"

"Yes, I suppose we can accommodate you," she says.

"Dr. Castillo, I know you can hear the frustration in my voice, but it's not at you. I'm annoyed with Blaise that he's done this. I know you're just doing your job."

"Thank you, Ms. Brown. We'll see you when you get here."

I get into my SUV when a silver BMW pulls up beside me and stops in the middle of the road. Daisy Colette leans out the driver's-side window. She pushes her auburn-colored bangs from her face and hikes her sunglasses up on top of her head.

"Corki, after I rounded the corner I realized it was you I'd told to fuck off. Can you ever forgive me?" she asks.

Daisy gets out of her car, leaving it in the middle of the road just as I had mine a few minutes before. She comes to my window and leans inside.

"Daisy, I'm fine," I say, "I know you can't control your potty mouth. But wait just a second." I get the box of perfume off the passenger seat. "I'm glad I ran into you, it saves me one stop. Voilà!" I say in a French accent. "Your *parfum* has arrived!"

"Oh, you're brilliant, Corki. Thank you so much. I knew you'd do it."

She opens the box, takes out a sample of the perfume and gives it to me. "Merry Christmas."

I thank her and open the bottle. A scent of gardenias and something else floats in the air. I can't name the other flower, but it's beautiful.

"I'm so glad I could apologize and make amends. You know me, I fly off the handle a little too quickly."

I flash on all the times she's nearly mowed down motorists, flipped birds and turned red in the face with anger.

"Why were you in such a hurry?" I ask.

"I'm editing my film and I get a frantic call from Odalis saying that the police are at my door with an arrest warrant for some guy who lived there before I bought the place. So, I had to get home."

"Did you get it all straightened out?"

"Yeah." Daisy pauses and looks pensively at me. "I'm going to miss you, Corki," she says.

"What?" I ask, thinking I misheard. "I'm not going anywhere."

"Look, I've been meaning to talk to you about something. Well, this film . . . you know I'm basically funding it. It's a huge undertaking, financially, one of the biggest things I've ever done. And like all films, it's costing a lot more than I thought it would. And since Peter left me, well, you know, he's not helping out with Smith's child support. I guess what I'm trying to say is that I'm really going to have to tighten the purse strings and cut out all the extraneous expenses. Between Odalis and the nanny, the pool guy and the gardener, I'm paying out almost eight thousand a month. Add on the film, the mortgage and everything else and I have my accountant screaming at me that I'll run dry in two years at the rate I'm going. I mean, I'm sure he's exaggerating slightly, but still. . . ."

"I understand," I say softly. My voice doesn't give away the panic I feel.

"Do you really understand? I still want you and Blaise to drop by. Smith loves playing with him. Come over anytime you want, promise?"

"Of course."

We hug our goodbyes and I watch her get back into her new BMW.

To override the panic fighting to spring to life, I turn on my internal calculator to tabulate how much less we'll have to live on. We'll forgo Blaise's swimming lessons, piano lessons, the weekly lunches out, my occasional pedicures, those cute shoes I saw on Rodeo Drive. Getting back to the work at hand, rather than letting my emotions overcome me, I drive toward Blaise's school and call Concepcion on her cell. She picks up after the first ring.

"Allo!"

"Concepcion, it's Corki. Jock wants to know why you didn't do all the laundry in the hamper."

"I did all *his* clothes."

"No. He wanted you to do all the clothes. Even hers."

"I don't do whore's underwear," she states flatly. "I did his ex-wife's underwear, I did Miss Lucy's, but I don't do the underwear of prostitutes *y putas!*"

"Yeah, well, Con, she may be a hussy, but I don't think she's a prostitute. There are plenty of girls givin' it up for free—he doesn't have to pay. Besides, you could have used rubber gloves—I had to pick the nasty-ass things up with my bare hands . . . with Jock standing over me! Thanks a lot."

I hang up with a "humph" and scan the glove compartment for some antibacterial hand sanitizer. I wonder if the steering wheel would peel if I rubbed it down with alcohol.

I pull into the parking lot of Crown Cleaners on Fairfax Avenue and grab the panty bag and other clothes from Betty's floor. I plop them down on the counter and wait for my turn. Watching a young girl next to me place some neatly folded clothes on the counter, I notice that she clutches a white envelope in her hand with a return address of a local business accounting office. I know instantly that she is a new celebrity assistant.

She's dressed nicely because she hasn't had to scrub dog shit off the bottom of her client's shoes yet. She's innocent—who else would carry five hundred dollars in petty cash around in a flimsy envelope tearing under the weight of the coins rattling at the bottom? She's careful, spineless and enthralled. She tries to be charming, thinking she needs the job more than her new star needs her. She's just graduated with a degree in Theatrical Arts, one of the least-useful degrees in the history of universities, and thinks her celebrity will help her get an acting job. She treats her client's pants like gold because they still have the eight-hundred-dollar price tag attached. What she doesn't know is her client will no doubt donate them to charity without ever wearing them because Meg was wearing a pair just like them. This fresh-faced assistant is in awe because eight hundred dollars is three times the amount she's paid per week. God bless her innocence. In a few years she'll have a full portfolio of dignity-robbing moments.

Susan, the owner of the cleaners, approaches me with her usual smile and nod of the head. I try to stop her from dumping out the contents of the bag, but she is already diligently at work, upending it. She isn't ready for just how much I have stuffed in there. Thongs shoot across the counter and onto the floor near the new assistant's Prada-knockoff shoes. New assistant steps back, away from the roving panties, innocent and embarrassed. I pick them up.

"What name should I put? Colette? LeMay?" Susan asks.

"No, no, not this time. Straupman. First initial, J."

I find myself saying this a bit louder than I had intended, as if to make sure the new assistant knows the kind of details her future will most certainly hold. I note her head turning, curiously, when I say Jock's last name. I ask Susan if I can use her restroom. Before I maneuver around sewing machines and ironing boards to get there, I nod my head to the new assistant, the assistant I used to be, and mouth the words "Good luck."

Pushing through the bathroom door, I spy two things so beautiful tears practically spring to my eyes—antibacterial soap and a hot water spigot.

Blaise and his two friends, Eden and Star, wait in the school's office. The girls look nonplussed by their situation. Blaise surreptitiously shoves spitballs into the lock of the door next to him. I gather the kids up, take Blaise by the collar and lead them to the truck.

"Mom! Let go of me, you're bugging me!"

"Boy, you'd better be happy that's all I'm doing!"

Blaise wriggles free and runs ahead to the truck.

"Mama Corki, are we in trouble?" asks Eden.

The girls' mothers, Shelly and her sister, Dani, insist the girls use "Mama" in front of my name as a show of respect. Sweet and old-fashioned.

"No, you girls aren't. I just had you taken to the office so I wouldn't have to spend time looking for you on the schoolyard," I explain. "I would have let you play after school but Blaise messed that up!" I say loud enough for him to hear. "So now you guys have to go to work with me."

I stick my hand in my jeans pocket and feel the condom slipping around in its package. How am I going to pull this off?

"Mama Corki, what will we be doing?" asks Star.

"Nothing special."

As I unlock the 4Runner, the kids poke at each other, titter and giggle incessantly. Blaise acts nonchalant. I'm more worried about him not having a conscience than I am about the naughty behavior. I hadn't planned on raising a sociopath.

The kids pour into Betty's backseat and put on their seatbelts. Eden has dark brown skin, a perky nose and twisty braids in a rainbow of colored barrettes. Star, with her shoulder-length dreads and wide-set brown eyes, fumbles with her pink backpack. Blaise puts his seatbelt around himself, pulls Star's hair and gives me a guiltless smirk. This is an unlikely trio with whom to shop for condoms.

I drive toward a well-known porn shop. To lessen the chances of having to go to more than one place, I pick up the cell phone and whisper, "The Pleasure Chest," into the microphone. When the salesman answers, I try to speak in code.

"Uh, hello, do you carry prophylactics . . ."

The salesman yells into the phone, "Speak up! You're whispering. I can't hear you."

"Mister, I'm at work, I can't yell."

The kids quiet considerably, all ears.

"I want to know if you carry some prophylactics that, uh, offer an 'enhancing pouch.'"

I hold the line while the salesman checks his supply.

"We have them in micro-thin and plus sizes only. Which ones do you need?"

Faltering, I dig the specimen out of my pocket as I negotiate a turn back onto Fairfax Avenue.

"I'm not sure."

"You don't know the size of condoms you wear, sir?"

"I'm a ma'am, not a sir, and I don't wear them, but I think I need a plus size." I look at the single condom as the kids try to crane their necks to see what I'm doing. I shove it under my leg. "I have an unwrapped one. I'll bring it in."

"Well, we don't usually let people bring in unwrapped ones . . . because of health codes, you understand."

"For Pete's sake! I mean I have one out of the box . . . unused, sealed, but not in the box."

"Yes, ma'am, you do that . . . just bring in the sealed one you have. I'm sure we have what you're looking for."

I pound the "end" button and toss the phone onto the passenger seat.

Blaise leans forward. "Couldn't you have left us at school rather than subject us to this?"

"Blaise, mum's the word. Cooperate so life as you know it will continue. *Comprends?*"

"*Oui, oui,* Mom-mee!"

"Where are we going?" asks Star.

I slide the condom out from under my leg and shove it in my front pocket.

" '*We*' aren't going anywhere, but I have an errand to run," I say as I make a right turn onto Santa Monica Boulevard and cruise slowly into the seedier section of West Hollywood. A sudden proliferation of gay bars and Russian pharmacies crowd the streets. I see the gay porno theater, The Tomkat, across the way.

"Okay, kids, I know a fun game we can play."

"Yeah!" the girls scream out in excitement. Blaise rolls his eyes.

"Listen up! When I count to three, I want you to take off your seatbelts and jump into the back of the 4Runner. When you get there, you guys need to hide your eyes and cover yourselves with the flannel blanket I have back there."

"What's in it for me?" Blaise asks.

"A one-way ticket to Juvenile Hall if you don't comply!"

"The green blanket?" Eden asks.

"Yes. You guys will all win and I'll give you ice cream when we get home if you hold perfectly still. I should be able to walk by the truck and not be able to tell that there are three kids in the back. Can you do that?"

"Yeah!" the girls say in unison, laughing.

"Now, I'm going to have to leave you guys under the blanket, but I'll only be a minute or two. I'm going to alarm Betty, so you can't move around or you'll set off the alarm. Can you handle that?"

"Of course we can!" Blaise says.

The kids sit in anticipation as I ease into the left lane in front of the Pleasure Chest, the only porn store I know that has an entire wall devoted to condoms. I pull into their parking lot.

"One, two, three!"

The kids jump into the back of the SUV and nestle down under the comfort of the warm flannel cover. They laugh and I warn them again about moving around. I alarm Betty and walk as fast as I can into the shop.

I open the glass door and rush past the wall of greeting cards with pictures of men confidently holding their schlongs and women licking their own nipples in mock spasms of pleasure. Darting around the penis enhancement counter and arriving at the wall of condoms, I see rubbers for admittedly underblessed men, rubbers for the Cro-Magnon man, studded condoms, thin rubbers and ones formulated to stimulate the G-spot. The first fifteen times I shopped here for my clients I was embarrassed and flushed in the face. Now I consider myself a "frequent flyer" at the Pleasure Chest—I know the entire sales team by name. I call out to the bald man behind the counter.

"Hey Hairy, where can I find the ones with a 'pleasure enhancing pouch'?"

"Corki, *you* were the lady on the phone?"

"Yes, and I'm really in a rush."

Hairy pulls out two boxes from behind the counter of the proper condoms, each containing a count of three.

"This is all I could find. One is the plus size and the other is the micro-thin."

I fish the condom out of my pocket and slap it down on the glass counter. Hairy looks at me with disdain.

"Careful, these can break, you know."

I look at him incredulously.

"The countertop," he says, "it's glass."

Oh.

"Sorry. All you have is this one box of plus size?"

"Yep! Make good use of each one, they're like gold. Anything else for you today?"

"No, that's it."

As Hairy gives me my change and the receipt, he throws in, "Enjoy!"

"Uh, I'll be sure to do that. Thank you . . . Hairy."

I hustle out past the blow-up sheep and spike-laden black leather masks, through the glass doors to fresh air.

I peer through Betty's blackened window and see that the kids are absolutely still. I disarm the car and warn them that the game isn't over until I say so.

As I pull into the alley leading away from the store, I announce that the game's done. The kids pile into the backseat and laugh hysterically at how good they were. As I pull up in front of Jock's house, I let them hide one more time while I deliver the goods.

Thankfully, he has moved Miss Icy into his inner sanctum. His bedroom door is closed; I have no intention of bugging him to see if, perhaps, he needs my most recent purchase. I leave the condoms in his office out basket and notice a huge manila envelope that has been messengered to his house from his talent management firm, Film Industry Entertainment. I snatch it and rush down to the truck.

Tumbling from the back of the SUV, Blaise inquires, "Mom, what's in the envelope?"

"Just fan mail."

"Like the kind you send to a movie star?" Eden asks.

"Yeah!" Blaise says. "This is Jock Straupman's house. The star of *Insectoids*."

"When did you see *Insectoids*?" Eden asks.

"Well, maybe I haven't seen it, but I've seen the fan mail pictures that people send for him to sign. One has Jock buck-naked!"

The girls let out high-pitched screams at the sheer naughtiness. As they talk about *Insectoids*, I thumb through the fan mail.

Whoever separates the fan mail at Film Industry Entertainment does a sucky job. Mixed in with Jock's mail is fan mail for Mia Farrow, Whoopi Goldberg, Leonardo DiCaprio and Cameron Diaz.

Starting the engine, I look up to see the exact place where Daisy and I stood an hour ago. The panicked thought of living with less money returns and lodges in my gullet. I know I'm going to need every tidbit of work that can possibly be thrown my way.

"All right, kids, there's one more place I've got to go. I have to return some mail Jock got accidentally."

We drive straight down Crescent Heights Boulevard, past Wilshire Boulevard and onto a tiny section of the street that changes names for two blocks, then goes back to being called Crescent

Heights. Film Industry Entertainment sits on a corner that I suspect was an urban-planning snafu.

We all ride the monitored elevator up to the third floor and I let the kids sit on the floor of the outdoor breezeway next to Suite 350.

"Kids, wait right here. I'll be back in a minute."

The busty young woman sitting at the reception desk consistently provides Film Industry Entertainment. Young and perky, she always wears low-cut blouses with copious amounts of cleavage pouring forth. She sits with perfect, erect posture, as do the men in the waiting room. She's a shining reminder as to what good posture can do for you. I stand up straighter as she looks up from her computer.

"Hi! Can I help you?"

"Uh, yeah, I just want to return some mail that was sent to Jock Straupman by mistake."

She reaches out for the small bundle of envelopes in my hand. She takes Mia's, Cameron's and Whoopi's mail and sets Leo's aside.

"Your name is Cookie, right?"

"Corki."

"Sorry. Corki, I can get Cameron and Mia's mail to them, and forward Whoopi's, but we don't represent Leonardo anymore and I don't have a forwarding address."

I look at the handwriting on the letters—all prepubescent girls—covered in stickers and glitter glue and, God bless 'em, perfume. I remember my eleven-year-old crushes on Donny Osmond and Michael Jackson.

"But while you're here," she continues, "let me get Squid on the line and see if he needs you for anything."

While the receptionist calls Squid, Jock's business manager's assistant, I peek outside and see the kids lined up along the wall like peas in a pod, giggling.

"Corki, if you'll wait just a second, Squid wants to see you."

I wait by the front door so I can watch the children. I entertain the fantasy of having eyes that move independently of one another—the perfect tool for mothers who need to have one eye on the kids and the other on work. I wander over to the receptionist's desk.

"What will your office do with Leo's letters? Toss them?"

The receptionist gives a short I-don't-know-but-it-probably-won't-be-good shrug.

"You know what," I say, "I'm gonna send these letters back. I'll just put 'no longer at this address,' then they can hunt Leo down through *Tiger Beat* or whatever magazine it is these days."

I sense that the receptionist has had a few heartthrob crushes in her day. We smile, shake our heads in mutual silent agreement, and I take Leo's fan mail. I'll consider my time forwarding the mail as a charitable contribution.

"Corki, good to see you!"

Squid. He looks nothing like a sea creature or a Greek food staple and I exercise great restraint in not asking for further details on how he obtained such a name. Squid is standard assistant-on-the-way-up-the-food-chain fare. His mousy brown hair is conservatively cut short with skimpy, weak sideburns. His freshly shaved face has a slight nick where his razor got a bit close, and his pale green eyes blink rapidly behind almost nonexistent eyelashes. All in all, he is absolutely unremarkable. He approaches and grabs my hand, shaking it exuberantly.

"Would you like something to drink? Coffee, soda, Evian?"

"No, thank you."

"I'll be quick, then, so you can get on with your day. I'm sure you know that Jock is leaving for Paris in a couple of weeks. Since he'll be gone six months, he said to contact you to determine a way to get his mail to him on a consistent basis."

"Paris? Are you serious?"

"He didn't tell you?"

"No, he never tells me until the last moment. I can't believe it. Six months?"

"Is there a problem?" he asks.

"Well, yeah, I'm not on salary. I only get paid for the work I do. If he's gone . . ." I say, helplessly.

Squid squirms. His discomfort trumps mine.

"Not your concern," I say, perking up. "I can pick up the mail weekly and FedEx it to him."

When I turn to go, Blaise has his face pressed against the glass door, sticking his bubble gum to the glass. I open it, snatch his arm and pull him down the walkway.

"Where'd you get that gum?" I ask.

"Under that ledge. It was still soft."

"Blaise, you're ten! We've been having the 'germs talk' since you were two and trying to eat Mr. Fu's dog food."

The kids and I leave the building discussing the leper who left the gum there.

$As\ I\ wait$ for Shelly to pick up the kids, I put the teakettle on the stove then plop down in my 1950s Herman Miller desk chair I got at a garage sale. The kids get washed and settle down to eat their ice cream and I jot a note to myself to pick up Jock's thongs tomorrow.

I press my blinking answering machine.

Call number one is from über–film producer Liam Schwartz's wife. She sounds hostile and annoyed. It's nothing new; her voice always drips with stinging sarcasm. "Corki, it's Esther. Somehow, one of the construction workers who was working at the house walked off with the master bedroom French doors that up until today were firmly attached to the walls. And to top that, he took an antique porcelain toilet lid from my office bathroom. Asshole prick. I need you to get hold of Dwayne immediately and get him up here to board up the gaping wound in the bedroom wall. And I need you to find me a new toilet lid! I don't want to have to replace the whole fucking commode over this. You know, when shit like this happens, Zoloft just isn't enough. . . .

"Oh, and I'm sure you'll hear from Shelly, I'm hosting a sit-down dinner for fifty for the Environmental Media Association on Saturday, and I sure as hell don't want to have to explain to Al Gore why the back of my toilet has no lid." Esther's tone softens a bit. "Whoever walked off with the doors must have thought we weren't using them, for some reason. Otherwise why would they bother?"

She hangs up.

Nineteen-hundred-dollar doors installed not two days before by the same crew working there every day, and one of the guys walks off with them. I'd fire the whole crew. Not Esther, though. She makes up excuses for them. I'm stumped. I suspect this is part of her guru's training exercises where she must try to forgive all and accept that people can't truly be bad to the bone.

Call number two is from Shelly: my friend, Star's mom and Esther's housekeeper. "Corki, I'm not sure if you heard, but Esther's having another one of her dinner parties at the house. Only fifty people this time, but Al Gore's supposed to come as well as some dude who wrote a controversial book on the Amazon rainforest. Also, guess what? Some brother, and I use that word loosely, was caught selling crack, of all things, a half block from the kids' school. I told Esther and she's really pissed off that the kids can't even go to school without being pursued like future customers. Anyway, we'll discuss it when I get there to pick up the kids. I'll be there about four-thirty. Peace."

Crack? Some knucklehead was selling crack near the kids' playground? In an Orthodox Jewish neighborhood surrounded by million-dollar homes and a few nice apartment complexes, someone's doing that? I remember the bucolic farm town nestled in the heart of California's San Joaquin Valley where I was raised. I wonder if it's true that you can't go home again.

Call number three is from Daisy Colette. "Corki, I just wanted to thank you for all the work you've done and I'm sorry about having to let you go. Call Gary. He should have a severance check waiting for you. It's not much but I hope it'll help. Bye."

Call number four.

"Hi, it's Veronique."

Veronique LeMay was *the* sex symbol of the 1990s. Besides being blessed with an I.Q. of 161, she is tall and perfectly proportioned, with an illustrious shock of chestnut brown hair. From certain angles she resembles Judy Garland, with huge and seductive brown eyes so dark they seem to house a well of inaccessible pain. Born on the same day, decades later, Veronique seems at times to be Judy's identical twin.

Whether in corduroys, cashmere or Calvin Klein, Veronique attracts unwanted male attention. Men find themselves behaving poorly upon setting eyes on her. She has been followed home, flashed and sworn at for pretending not to notice. She has perfected the art of being a female movie star.

"Corki, I want to talk with you. I've just returned from Italy, doing the film role of a lifetime. I really think it's going to take my career to new heights. In fact, my agents are predicting I just might become the flavor of the week once again. God, that would be nice!

Besides wanting to catch up with you, I'm going to need your help on a little project. Love you. Call me so we can arrange a get-together."

The last call is from Lucy Bennett. Lucy giggles with giddiness. "Hey, it's Lucy. Sweetheart, I know I'm going to see you tonight, but I also want to see you tomorrow, in private. How about four o'clock—no, five—no! Four would be better. Shit, you know I struggle with decisions. Meet me at the Four Seasons on Doheny. We'll have tea . . . or maybe at Paddington's, oh shit, there I go again. Four Seasons. Four o'clock. Just call me and confirm. Bye, honey!"

I listen to Lucy's message again. I've never heard this particular affectation before. Usually Lucy's clothes or her musical tastes or the type of car she drives changes. This time, however, Lucy's speech has taken on a small, almost imperceptible Southern cadence. I wonder who he is . . . her new man.

I sit back and breathe deeply for the first time today. As the messages conclude, the news of the day converges in my mind. First Daisy, then Jock. I think about homeless shelters, bus benches and drained bank accounts.

I go to the bathroom and throw up.

Chapter Two

Shelly comes up the front walkway to my apartment in her military camouflage pants and olive green cashmere sweater. Her waist-length dreadlocks are swept into an elegant chignon, pinned up with a set of knitting needles.

When Shelly's career as a recording-studio mixer started to interfere with her ability to be there to tuck in her daughter at night, she quit and took on a less fulfilling job—cleaning houses. At first, her ego was so bruised she couldn't even talk about her change of employment. But after a few months of watching her daughter, Star, develop a new sense of security and assurance, Shelly was at peace with her decision. On the rare days she has to work late, I pick up Star and her cousin, Eden.

While Shelly eventually adjusted to the fact that she was working as a housekeeper, Esther, her boss, did not. She hired Shelly partially because she didn't want to be accused of *not* hiring a black woman. For the first couple of months, Esther called me complaining that she felt guilty for hiring a black woman to clean her house, of all things—too many historical implications, what with slavery and all. "Too much 'white liberal guilt,' " I told her.

I liked to taunt Esther and ask her whether she would rather pay a hardworking American black woman, historical implications and all, $750 per week to clean or a Latina woman who didn't speak the same language and would be sending her money home to Mexico. Esther could never stomach answering the question. She tried to mask her guilt by complaining that since Shelly was a fellow follower of Gurumayi, it was too much like having your own sister scrub your toilet.

Shelly climbs my front steps with vigor. After a full day of cleaning a six-thousand-square-foot home, I wouldn't be able to muster a smile. Shelly looks up at me standing in the doorway.

"Hey, mama!"

"Hey, Shell. You sure you worked a full day? You have a little too much spring in that step."

She walks through the door, brushes past me and flops down on the Shabby Chic lounge chair I inherited from Lucy when she last changed her style. Shelly smells like a mixture of sandalwood and 409. She takes off her black-rimmed glasses and shoves them into her bag.

"I'm telling you, Corki, it's clean living. Herbs, vitamins and an organic, vegetarian diet. No meat, no dairy."

The kids come in from Blaise's room.

"You kids almost ready to go? Mama Corki has to get a move on and go cook a dinner for the stars!" Shelly prods as she gathers their backpacks and shoes together. "Real quick, Corki, you hear the latest?"

"About the doors? Yeah, Esther left me a message."

"Oh, not that!" Shelly states. "I'm talking about the little surprise she brought home."

"No. What was it?"

"A bronze statue of Lord Ganesh. A three-thousand-dollar, sixteen-hundred-pound Lord Ganesh for the front patio."

The teakettle whistles a shrill reminder that it's ready. "I'm sorry, girl, but I threw up a minute ago. I need some ginger tea." I start to get up.

"You stay right there. Let me do it," Shelly says as she gets up and goes to the kitchen. "Is that why you look so pale?"

The sounds of cupboards opening and closing, tea mugs clinking and the click of the stove's fire being turned off unexpectedly moves me. I hadn't realized how much I miss being cared for. Forty hours a week I mother my clients, and the rest of the time I mother Blaise. I haven't been taken care of in a *long* time.

"Corki?" she calls from the kitchen, "I'm putting your tea in a travel mug so you can take it with you. That okay?"

"Perfect. Thank you."

"So anyway," she continues, "I bet I'm going to be spending an hour a day bathing this statue because he's the Hindu god that requires constant attention. A special-needs god is what I call him."

"At least you have a job," I state flatly.

"Amen to that. Thank God we both do!"

"Did," I correct.

"Oh no, what happened?" Shelly inquires.

I tell her the *Reader's Digest* version with a little gore to enhance the story.

"Doesn't Jock give you some type of retainer or something to tide you over while he's gone?"

"Are you joking? It would be nice if he would at least give me a bit of notice so I could try to get another client while he's gone."

"Really!" she says indignantly.

"What am I gonna do?" I ask.

"You'll find a way," Shelly says.

"How much you think prostitutes make?" I ponder.

"Now, there's a viable option! Come on, woman, get up and let's get you on your way."

She pulls me up out of the chair and helps me gather all the food and cooking utensils I'll need to use tonight. We herd the kids out the front door. At the curb, I kiss Blaise goodbye.

"Honey, I'll pick you up as soon as I finish work, okay?"

"Sure, Mom."

"Shelly, by the way, is it possible you could watch Blaise tomorrow afternoon? I'm sorry to have to ask you but I'm supposed to meet a client at four."

"Believe it or not, I'll have the afternoon off. If you want I can watch him from noon on."

"Bless you! That would be great. It's such an inconvenience that they start winter break in the middle of the week. What kind of school district makes decisions like that?" I ask.

We get the kids in the backseat, buckle them in, and I slop them all with "mama" kisses until they cringe. I go around to the front seat and hug Shelly goodbye. She hugs me back.

"You get my message about the crack dealer?" she whispers in my ear.

I nod my head.

"I told Esther and she was properly horrified. Sent her right into rescue mode. She started ranting and raving saying that all our kids should go to Atom's school, where they'd be safe from that kind of thing. Of course, I pointed out that none of us have eighteen thousand dollars a year to spend on private school."

"Yeah, hello!"

"So she got on the horn with some bigwig at Envision Prep and told him that they don't have enough 'color' there and if she wanted her son, Atom Chase-Schwartz, to think that only blond-haired, blue-eyed kids deserve a good education, she would have had him schooled in Germany! She asked them just what they planned on doing about it. But before he could answer she interjected her own solution. They should admit three 'African-American' kids and she happens to have the perfect candidates."

"Oh no, let me guess. Might they be named Eden, Star and Blaise?"

"Oh, you're a smart one! You're definitely gonna find your way!"

Lucy's dinner party is a success. Most of the food on my menu is considered "legal" by Atkins, Zone and South Beach: salmon and lobster with a sautéed tangerine reduction, a leek gratin with goat cheese and prosciutto, a grated raw zucchini salad with fresh mint, and edamame beans with olive oil, scallions and cilantro. Since Ben Harper is the only one who wholeheartedly indulges in dessert, my favorite course, I spoil him. Dessert is moist chocolate cake topped with espresso mocha frosting accompanied by homemade violet ice cream.

I try to spend as much time in the kitchen as I can. I don't want to look into Lucy's dining room and see John wiping tangerine juice off his chin or Meg with lobster stuck in her teeth. Or even worse, I don't want to see someone politely saying "No thank you" to a dish that I slaved over.

As the dinner chatter gets louder, I start to feel the tension in my neck. An acute muscle spasm is starting above my shoulder blades. I rub and squeeze my neck and the pain seems to only worsen. Alejandra, Lucy's housekeeper, a tiny, beautiful woman who was a television reporter in Guatemala, plays waitress tonight in the dinner drama. She brushes past me in the kitchen as she takes drinks out to the party.

I hear Courteney laughing generously in the other room, followed by a hearty chuckle of Melissa's. What was Lucy possibly thinking, asking me to cook for movie stars who have dined in the finest restaurants in the world? I can't concentrate with all the butterflies fluttering in my stomach.

I grab a red plastic cup and make a dash down to the small, personal-size wine cellar in the basement.

Lucy doesn't drink wine or spirits. Every bottle in here was a gift. I move the bottles around and all are unopened. I finally find a bottle of cognac that is open. It was a gift from Kevin Kline. I hope he doesn't mind.

Remy Martin Louis XIII.

I pour a full cup, take a gulp and pour some more. I trot carefully up the stairs, and before I hit the last step, I feel a comforting warmth spread through my stomach. I know this would be a no-no on Dr. Trabulus's list of ways to feel better after throwing up, but . . . I sip some more cognac and am ready to finish cooking.

Dinner slips by in a bit of a blur. As they eat, I stand behind the dining room door, unseen, watching the guests through a crack. Seeing John smile lovingly at Kelly, Courteney laugh at David's jokes and Laura rub Ben's back makes me suddenly melancholy. I take another generous drink of the Rémy Martin.

It's almost Christmas, I'm tired and alone, quickly on my way to becoming tipsy, and I still have to pick up Blaise. I tiptoe to the sink and dump the rest of the cognac down the drain.

At ten P.M. I finish washing my pots, pans and dishes and start hauling them back to my truck. After being on the go for eighteen hours, I'm ready to go home and climb into bed. Alejandra helps me. I wrap up the remaining cake for her to take home.

"Before you leave, Corki, Lucy wants me to show you some stuff she'll need for tomorrow night."

Alejandra and I quietly make our way past the dwindling party and into the guest bedroom. When she turns on the light, I am assaulted with the vision of a mountain of shopping bags. There are twenty-six visible—more hidden behind the bed. Each one contains a number of gifts with nametags. This is the trouble with actors who are out of work during Christmas—they like to shop. There must be 150 to 200 gifts that will need to be wrapped in twenty-four hours—not possible.

"She wants to have them for her road trip," Alejandra says apologetically.

"What road trip is this?" I ask, appalled by the sight.

She raises her shoulders. "I don't know. All Lucy said was that she was going away for Christmas."

"This is the first I've heard," I say with exasperation. "I'm sorry to ask you this, Alejandra, 'cause I know you're as tired as I am, but will you help me load this into my truck?"

"Of course."

We load the bags into Betty's trunk space. I hit the twenty-four-hour store for wrapping supplies before I pick up Blaise.

After five hours of sleep, I spend ten hours wrapping gifts with $528 worth of holiday paper, ribbon, boxes and tape and deliver them to Lucy's house. I go directly from there to the Four Seasons Hotel to meet Lucy for tea and pray I can stay alert enough to write detailed notes.

I pull my SUV, which hasn't been cleaned in a good month, into the stone-paved driveway. The lineup of Rolls-Royces, BMWs and

Maseratis, all shining clean, is intimidating. I don't see infant car seats protruding from the backseats or spent milk cartons in the cup holders. I see a plethora of brand new ghastly expensive cars that get replaced every two years with new models. Maybe I should park my eight-year-old Betty a block or so away.

I know when I pull up to the valet (who will look down his nose at me, but who will almost certainly have a car very similar to mine in age and dirt level parked beneath the hotel), he will search frantically for a place to put Betty where no one else will see her. I suppose if my job depended on it, I, too, would scramble to hide Betty in order to preserve the image of a perfectly manicured hotel.

I roll down my window and a young man approaches. His hair is trimmed and clean, his uniform is pressed with perfect creases, and his nametag reads "Homer." Homer smiles widely, showing a set of dazzling teeth he probably got whitened in an hour and paid for with a Visa card he can't pay off.

"Hello, ma'am. May I ask how long you'll be staying?"

"Just an hour or so."

"Okay, ma'am, if you'll pull your truck over there"—he points to some tall bushes—"I'll take care of it for you."

I park Betty and quietly slip into the lobby of the hotel, where people are milling around waiting to be checked in. I veer to the right and enter the crowded tearoom.

As I scan the drinkers for Lucy, the room goes silent for an instant as the "tea-totalers" look up from their steaming brews and stare just long enough to dismiss me as no one of importance. Lucy hasn't shown up yet. Besides being incredibly indecisive, she is always late.

I look for a host or hostess to seat me, but none is present. I go to a table in the corner and pull out a seat. It's the only table left without a reserved sign on it. Waiting for Lucy, I stare out the window at the sky starting to open up and sprinkle water droplets everywhere.

A clean-cut, blond-haired host breaks into my reverie.

"Ma'am, I'm sorry, but you can't sit here. It's reserved," he informs me.

"It doesn't have a 'reserved' sign on it."

"That may be so," he says curtly, "but it is still reserved."

"What's your name?" I ask.

"Michael."

"Michael. There was no sign on it, so I sat down. There are other seats with 'reserved' signs."

He clears his throat.

"Yes, ma'am, I know, I put those signs on there and was on my way to put a sign on this one when you came in and sat down. So, this one *is* reserved."

"Well, Michael, I'm not a psychic, how would I have known?"

I gather my purse and sweater, get out of the seat and walk toward the door, wondering where Lucy and I are going to sit. Everyone in the tearoom watches as Michael sweeps the table off. I brush by Denzel Washington sitting with a few executive-looking, Creative Artist–agent types. Angelica Huston sits in a far corner enjoying crumpets with two other women.

I wait in the hotel's foyer and recall walking shyly into the third-grade classroom of my new elementary school in Visalia, late for my first day. As I slid into my assigned seat, the boy sitting behind me leaned forward and whispered into my ear, "Niggers don't belong here."

A high-pitched shriek comes from behind me.

"Miss Corki Brown!" Lucy sweeps all seventy-two inches of her fat-free body through the crowded hotel entrance. She throws her arms around me and we hug each other tightly.

"Hi, darlin'! It's been forever!"

There it is again, the slight twang. I didn't notice it so much last night, but it has returned with a vengeance.

"Hi, Lucy. I have some bad news. I tried to get a table and was told the last one was reserved. I was kicked out by that guy over there."

I point to Michael.

Lucy drags me, lovingly, by the arm back into the tearoom. "Don't be silly, Corki. I'm sure they can do something for us."

Lucy walks in, commanding as much attention as a slim, pretty, six-foot-tall, blonde, double Academy Award–winning actress can. She waves the scarf in her hand at Michael, who suddenly smiles graciously. Lucy rolls on, full steam ahead.

"Hi, my friend here says she tried to get a table and there wasn't one. That can't possibly be true, can it? What's your name?"

"Michael," I pipe in with disdain.

Lucy continues with her twinge of Tennessee coming in a bit stronger. "That can't be right, can it, Michael?"

"No, Miss Bennett, I'm sure there was a huge misunderstanding," he backpedals ferociously.

Lucy pours it on as thick and sweetly as Memphis-style barbeque sauce. "Michael, I know we don't have a reservation, but I've never had a problem here before."

Michael guides us back to the same table where I had sat before. "And Miss Bennett," he oozes, matching her syrupy tone, "you certainly won't have any problems here today."

He pulls out Lucy's chair for her. I pull out my own. As Lucy turns to say hello to a studio exec at the next table, I give Michael a cold stare and mouth the words "Ass kisser!"

Slightly embarrassed, he smirks, then says to Lucy, "I'll send your waiter over immediately."

The moment he turns away, Lucy announces, "What an asshole!"

The people around us erupt in nervous laughter and Michael shoots them a look that could carve pumpkins. I wonder if he's going to spit in our teapot.

I wait quietly for ten minutes as Lucy makes her rounds to each table. While she's doing her kissy-kissy routine with all her "film friends," I order food and tea for both of us. My watch reads 4:41 P.M.

Lucy comes back to our table and scoots her chair over until it touches mine. She lets out a huge sigh, as if all this networking exhausted her.

"So, Corki, first off, I want to tell you how much everyone enjoyed your dinner last night. Rave reviews from all."

"Thank you," I say, embarrassed but pleased.

"But that's not why I wanted to meet you here now. Let me get straight to the point. Cork, after my marriage to Roger broke up . . ."

She's not going to get straight to the point, that I can already see.

". . . well, I went out with a couple of fellas."

Fellas?

"I mean, you know, none of them were really for me. A woman knows these things. If I meet a new man, I just know whether it is meant to be or not. For instance, I knew Roger was meant to be."

Roger, whose last name I could never pronounce because it's French and complicated and laden with so many vowels that I can't wrap my tongue around it. Roger, who I truly liked in the beginning because he remembered me on his trips to Paris and always brought me back chocolate-covered truffles even though Lucy told him she didn't want him contributing to my gaining an ounce . . .

"Corki, what's that look on your face?"

"I'm sorry. I'm here."

"You weren't thinking Roger wasn't meant to be, were you?"

"Oh no, he was certainly meant to be with you. I was just re-membering the truffles."

The waiter brings tea with a silver three-tiered tray full of small, crustless sandwiches, crumpets, lemon curd, jam, a small scoop of Devonshire cream and teacakes. I serve us both. Lucy stares long-ingly out the window. It has begun to rain, hard. The windows are becoming streaked with sheets of water.

"He *was* meant to be with me. He had his demons, and even though it ended like it did, we had a marriage made in heaven."

The "heaven" only lasted six weeks. When Roger lost it one night after drinking an entire bottle of Lafite Rothschild '82, he pushed Lucy so hard that her head snapped back and caused her to be bound in a neck brace for a month with acute muscle spasms. Roger refilled the wine bottle with his own urine that he said was "almost as good as the original contents" and proceeded to drink some and pour the rest on Lucy as she huddled in the corner holding her neck, crying hyster-ically. It wasn't heavenly when I was jarred from a deep sleep at three o'clock in the morning by Lucy, who called and begged me to come help her. I carried my crying child out into the cold night, packed him into Betty's backseat and drove to Beverly Hills to rescue her. I calmed Roger, calmed Blaise and simultaneously washed the urine out of Lucy's hair. Their relationship ended after I caught Lucy writing in bloodred lipstick on Roger's garage door, "Make Love, Not War." Roger's gardeners tried scrubbing it off, but the waxy, oily lipstick had already sunken into the paint job. When I drive by his house today, I still see the faded note that no one bothered to paint over.

"So, Lucy, who's the new honey?"

She leans closer. "How could you tell there's a new man?"

I scrunch my nose and giggle. "Oh, an assistant just knows these things!"

"Corki, I'm going to tell you, but you need to take this to the grave," she says, suddenly serious.

"Lucy, unless I'm hit by a car as I leave here, the news is going to leak out way before I make it to the grave."

"Granted, but I want to keep it private and special as long as I can. I don't want the rags getting hold of it and making it out to be just a fling for front-page fodder. I'm convinced he's my soul mate. You know how long I've been waiting for him. He's arrived."

I look around the room pretending he's walked in. Lucy pinches my arm.

"Not here, silly."

"Lucy, how long have you known this guy?"

She has a reputation for "falling in love" within a week and for knowing he's "the one" within two.

Lucy stares at dark thunderclouds out the window. "Oh, five, ten thousand years."

Oh God, here we go.

"We did a past-life regression with this guy Laura Dern knew of and we identified at least three lifetimes we shared before. The strongest one was in Atlantis, where I was a slave and he was the master. God, it was so tragic and so romantic."

My watch reads 5:10 P.M. "How long ago did you meet him in the present life?"

"About two weeks. We did *Live with Regis and Kelly* together . . . as separate guests but on the same show."

Two weeks. One week longer than she knew Roger before they tied the knot in Vegas. And about one year less than I knew my husband, Basil, before he was gone.

I suddenly remember Daisy Colette suggesting that Lucy wait a year before she and Roger got married. After that, Daisy's calls went unreturned and she lost her confidante-of-the-week status. Only recently has Lucy begun speaking to her again. I should keep my mouth shut since I need the income she provides, but I can't help worrying about her.

"Lucy, you're gonna take this slowly, right? I mean, you went straight from Jock to Roger and never took time to heal in between. I don't want to see you get hurt again. You want to bounce back slowly."

Lucy looks at me incredulously.

"Cornelia Wren Brown, how can you say that? It's been the most intense two weeks of my entire life. I'm trusting that the Universe has brought me my soul mate and I really need you to trust me and the Universe, too. You can do that, can't you? I need you to believe in me. My mama's worried, my dad has practically given up on me, and my friends are beside themselves. Please help me with this one, 'cause I'm telling you, Cork, this one is special. He's brilliant and beautiful and sexy all in one package."

I look down, almost wanting to believe that he will be Lucy's knight in shining armor, but I've read Dr. Laura's books about all the stupid things women do to mess up their lives and I know it takes more than two weeks to tell if he's "the one."

"So, Corki," she says, "do I have your blessing?"

"Come on, does it really matter if I give my blessing or not?"

"Yes, it does. It does because I'm going to need your help."

"I'll help you. I need the work. Daisy let me go and Jock's off to France for six months. I'll definitely help you. Just tell me who he is."

"Do I have your blessing?"

I put my hand on her forehead and lightly push her head back.

"Child, you have my blessing."

"It's Tommy Ray Woods," Lucy whispers.

Oh no.

I try not to recoil too dramatically. Tommy Ray Woods has

graced more tabloid pages than I can remember for his forays into womanizing, cheating, beating and feeling up women in public, some of whom he knew, some of whom he didn't. To date, I am aware of two court cases pending against him—one for sexual harassment and the other for unlawful bigamy. I scramble to try to act happy for her, but it ain't working for me.

"*The* Tommy Ray Woods?" It's dumb, but gives me some reaction time.

"The one and only," Lucy says, placated.

"Lucy, I . . . I don't really know what to say except that his reputation precedes him."

"Listen, Corki, I need you to be fine with this and I need your help. Tommy Ray and I are going on a road trip. He wants to take me to Memphis to meet his daddy, and he wants me to see Graceland. You know, his daddy is one of the last men in Tennessee who still uses a divining rod to find water on his property. How cool is that? And Cork, you'll be happy to know, Tommy wants to take it slow. He doesn't want to rush into marriage. He's a bit more traditional than all the Left Coast types, being from the South and all."

Is getting married five times within a ten-year period "traditional"? He has five children ranging in age from six to twenty-six with four of his five wives—what tradition is that? Then, of course, there's the charge that he got married to wife number five while he was still legally married to wife number four.

"I told Tommy Ray that I really like picnics, so we're planning to stop on the first day and have one. I also told him that I really appreciate home-style cooking. So I need you to make us lunch for six. . . ."

"Six? I thought it was just the two of you."

"Well, it was just gonna be the two of us, but Tommy Ray needs his office assistant, Dave, with him, and he promised the first assistant director from his last movie that he'd give him a ride back to Little Rock on the way home."

"Okay, that's four."

"Well, there are only four of us going, but Bubba, that's his first assistant director, eats for three. He'll take up the entire third row of the SUV we're going to rent."

"Bubba? That's not his real name, is it? Bubba?"

"Well, if it isn't his real name, he's been called it for so many years he's not telling anybody anything different. So, I'd like a menu of fried chicken, potato salad, black-eyed peas, coleslaw and a buttermilk icebox pie. Also, get some other food to snack on. You know, road trip food. And maybe for me, on the side, a braised tofu with sesame seed kale . . . but don't pack that in the main cooler. I can just eat mine in private."

I try to envision where she's going to have enough privacy to pee, let alone eat her tofu and kale. She'll be road tripping with three men, one of whom takes up the entire backseat.

"Do I have to make this by hand or can I order it and pack it as if you slaved in the kitchen making it yourself?"

"Oh no, I want *you* to make it. I bet you can whip up some good Southern-style food. I know you aren't from the South, but you can cook anything, Corki."

"Maybe I could throw in some chitlins and home-fried pork rinds," I joke.

"You know Bubba and Tommy Ray would probably love that, but I'm trying to steer him clear of pork right now," Lucy says seriously. "I'm trying to clean up his diet."

Two weeks and she's already trying to convert him. Good luck.

"We're leaving tomorrow night, so if you could just whip this up in the morning, we'll be out of your hair for the holidays. Oh, and buy some Bud Light for Bubba, Diet Coke for Tommy and Dave and mineral water for me."

I quickly jot down these notes and get ready to leave.

"Lucy, I have to pick up Blaise. Anything else?"

"I know you've heard a lot about Tommy Ray, but most of it's not true. He's the love of my life and I really want you to feel good about him."

"I'll try," I say.

We hug goodbye.

The windshield wipers beat frantically back and forth in rhythm with the Gypsy Kings coming from Betty's stereo speakers. I sing loudly, off key, making up Spanish lyrics as I go along. I pull up in front of the Baldwin Hills house Shelly inherited from her grandmother.

I dash from my truck and knock on the front door.

Shelly opens it looking frayed. Before I can say hello, she pulls me in and guides me to the front bedroom, then pushes the door closed behind us.

"Shell, what's wrong?"

"Corki, you know I love Blaise to death. Like one of my own."

"Oh God, what's he done?" I ask, my heart sinking.

"I was cooking lunch, the kids were playing, and I started smelling the most horrific burning stench coming from the backyard."

"Oh, no!" I gasp.

"Girl, he was back there burning shit up."

"Like what? The wood behind your shed?" I ask.

"No. Shit. Dried-up dog shit."

"Did anything catch on fire?"

"Thank God, no. It started to rain just in time. But living in the hills with all the brush and old wood roofs, we're a brush fire waiting to happen."

"Shelly, I am so sorry. I beg you to forgive him."

"Corki, you know I love that rogue, but this is all I have. I just can't risk it. If I lost this house I wouldn't know what to do."

"I understand. I really feel terrible."

"I know, girl. Look, it's all over, don't worry."

I take a deep breath and walk from the room behind Shelly. Under the scent of Jamaican Love incense, I can smell the odor of burned feces. Every window we pass is open, letting the rain and fresh air blow in.

I turn the stereo off as soon as I twist the key and the engine turns over. I start driving down the road, fuming silently until I can't hold it anymore.

"Blaise! Just what the heck did you think you were doing?"

"I was just playing," he says calmly.

"No, honey, 'playing' is throwing a ball. Lighting fires is seriously bad news. Do you realize the damage you could have done?"

"But I didn't *do* any damage."

"Thank God!"

We drive home in silence. I pull up into the driveway and start to get out to unlock my gate.

"Sorry I'm such an 'inconvenience,'" Blaise mutters.

"What's that supposed to mean?" I ask, still perturbed.

"That's what you said to Mama Shelly—that it was an 'inconvenience' having me around."

"Honey, I said no such thing," I say, heartbroken. "Is that what you thought? Because it's not true. I said that school getting out midweek is an inconvenience."

"Same difference, Mom."

I pause before getting out to open the gate.

"Are you hating your school?"

"No, school's fine. Why?"

"Well, there may be this other opportunity—"

Just then, my cell rings.

"Hello. This is Corki."

"Hey, it's Dwayne, handyman extraordinaire! I just called to let you know I'm done with boarding up Liam and Esther's master bedroom. In fact, I finished just before the rain started. What's going on up there, anyway? The doors ripped from the frame, the toilet tank's lid has gone a-missin'. That place is becoming a wreck and they're a good ways from finishing the remodel."

I unlock the gate and pull Betty into my backyard.

"I need to replace that toilet lid before her party this weekend. That means I have tomorrow to find a lid and get it up there. And I just got a request to cook for six tomorrow. Where can I find a lid like that?"

"Well, Corki," he says in his Louisiana drawl, "you're in a bit of a pinch, huh? I reckon the best thing you can do is get yourself a piece of cardboard and draw an outline of the toilet tank that the lid sits on. Then take it over to that plumbing place over on Pico and Bundy and go through their spare porcelain lids out back."

"Dwayne, that sounds awfully complicated. Can't I just get the brand and model and go pick it up at Home Depot?"

Dwayne sucks in air. He's obviously dealing with an incompetent in the toilet department of life. Without even seeing him, I can tell he's lighting his pipe. Dwayne, thirty-two, with sandy blond hair and green eyes, looks a whole heap like Brad Pitt. Dwayne smacks his lips, and inhales to get the tobacco lit.

"Listen to me. That there toilet is a good fifty years old. They don't even make that brand anymore, so it ain't gonna help you none to have the brand or model number. Toilet lids come in different shapes, colors and sizes, so you're just gonna have to go down to that plumbing place. I'm not even sure how the house passed inspection with those big old toilets that take ten gallons to flush."

I know how those big old toilets passed inspection. Esther took them out and had them replaced, then put them right back in after escrow closed. Esther likes those big old toilets and her goal was to keep them even if they were environmentally un-sound. I thank Dwayne, get out of the truck and close the gate to my backyard.

"Pick up, Mom, it's me," I say into her answering machine. "I know we're supposed to come there on Christmas Eve, but I have to bring Blaise up tonight."

She picks up her phone. "What did he do?"

"Hi, Mom."

"What did he do, Cornelia?"

I give her a sanitized G-rated version of the day. "If I don't get my work done, Mom, we won't even be there on the twenty-fourth. Please, I need your help."

I hang up the phone and exhale. Blaise sits at our piano and bangs out the beginning notes to Beethoven's Fifth Symphony.

"Grandma says you can spend the next week up there with the understanding that for your punishment there will be no television, no computer and no Game Boy. You're going to help her clean out the garage, clean up the yard and put up the decorations. And if you so much as get close to a match, she'll kill you and me. Under-stand?"

Blaise nods.

"All right, go pack some books and I'll get your clothes. I'm taking you now."

"Now? Mom, it's Thursday night! You said you desperately need sleep and that you've got to work in the morning."

"I do, but I can sleep and work a lot better knowing you're safe with Grandma rather than lighting someone's house on fire."

"God, Mom, it's like you're desperate to get rid of me," Blaise says, sulking.

"Blaise, I *have* to work. I don't want to live at a bus stop. We need a roof over our heads—"

"Blah, blah, blah," Blaise interrupts. "That's always your excuse. I don't care where we live."

"Well, there's a nice covered bus stop down on the corner. Want to try it out for the night?" I bite my lip and regret saying it as soon as it comes out of my mouth. "Blaise, I'm sorry. I know I've been very busy, but if I don't work, we don't have money. And living here or anywhere costs."

"Whatever." He goes to his room and plops some books on his desk. "I'm ready."

I drive the 179 miles north to Visalia, in the heart of California's San Joaquin Valley, drop Blaise off, then turn around and head back to Los Angeles. I usually can't drive late at night, but being fueled with guilt and worry keeps me awake. Home at two o'clock in the morning, I fall asleep in my clothes.

. . .

Six hours later, barely able to keep my eyes open, I break at least thirty traffic laws to get the twenty miles down Sunset Boulevard, toward the beach, before nine A.M. As the higher-paid working stiffs are driving toward their offices in Century City and Hollywood, I fly past them going in the opposite direction, clutching my Starbucks double espresso.

I pull past Shelly's old Mercedes parked on the street, into Liam and Esther's driveway, grab my cardboard and pencil and disgorge from Betty unsteadily as I try to dance over thick lines of black ants covering the driveway.

Esther can't see why I would suggest an exterminator visit when ants are just a part of nature. She calls me a "human supremacist" who thinks ants have no souls. Since she won't let there be any bug spray in her home, I get out the countertop cleaner and spray them all I want when she's not looking. It does the same job. Shelly, who believes the same way as Esther, looks the other way when I destroy my karma by spraying or stepping on bugs. However, Liam, who thinks like I do, has me call the exterminator to eradicate the swarms of ants the moment Esther goes out of town.

I push open the two-inch-thick outer door to the huge hacienda-style covered patio, and there, staring me in the face, thirty feet away, is Lord Ganesh. I can tell Shelly has been bathing him because the stone patio flooring is wet. Terra-cotta pots, filled with orchids, surround Lord Ganesh's feet, and all the bamboo patio furniture has been rearranged to face him. I give him a wide berth and push open the door to the house.

"It's Corki!" I call out.

Shelly comes out of the kitchen. "Girl, how did you make it here so fast? It's only a quarter to nine. You have a helicopter or something?"

"Parked out on the helipad right now. How about you?"

"My sister has the girls 'cause I knew I was gonna need more than a full day to have this place looking good for tomorrow's party. I've been here since seven-thirty." We both shake our heads and roll our eyes.

"Where's Blaise?" she asks.

"I took him to my mom's house last night."

"And you're back already? I thought you don't drive so well at night."

"I don't. But thinking about his recent attempt at being an arsonist kept me up. Is Esther here?"

"No, but Liam's here. Esther's walking the dogs. I'm surprised you didn't see her on the way up."

"I wasn't exactly looking for her. . . ."

I pick up my cardboard and pencil and head out of the foyer. "I have to go measure the loo. If you need me, you know where I'll be."

Liam and Esther's home was originally two very big 1950s ranch-style houses. The present huge living room is where both backyards butted up against each other. Ebony polished hardwood floors are topped by "Gauguin sunset" orange walls with "wainscoting" of imported Tahitian woven fibers. The entire place has been converted into a Balinese work of art. All four fireplaces have been covered with thousands of seashells.

The bathroom with the missing tank lid is approximately the size of my living room. The shower/bathtub combination is lined with massive boulders shipped in from Hawaii. Water comes out of a hidden showerhead and simultaneously tumbles down a waterfall of rocks. It always reminds me of a television commercial that shows a woman shampooing her hair in a waterfall.

Esther had the former bathroom completely demolished to create this tropical island paradise, but insisted on keeping her high-volume, old-fashioned toilets. I thought perhaps she'd have a real bush hidden behind a wall where you could squat and do your business as you would in nature. But no!

I set to work balancing the cardboard on the toilet tank and trying to sketch it from underneath to achieve the most accurate shape. I'm suddenly aware that the room has darkened slightly. Looking up, I see Liam resting casually against the doorframe. He is clad in the plush terry-cloth robe he acquired from the Phoenician Spa and Resort in Arizona.

I have worked for Liam for nineteen years, ever since he was voted one of Hollywood's most eligible bachelors by *Premiere* magazine. When he hired me, Liam was a young, handsome, white-hot producer for Columbia TriStar Pictures. He had a success record as long as the line of women queuing up to be the one he chose to marry. He dated frequently, had his heart broken a time or two and kept up the search into his early forties.

One time I tried to fix him up with a movie producer at Twentieth Century Fox who later went on to produce knockout plays on the West End in London. He was crazy about her, but she was too powerful in a field he considered his territory. Then I tried to set him up with Veronique LeMay. They never dated because Liam was intimidated out of his skin after he spoke with her one time. Not only was Veronique the hottest sex symbol of the day, but she spoke three languages fluently and was interested in producing . . . another territorial problem. I wonder if Liam goes around his office building peeing on the foundation to mark what's his.

Liam runs his hands through dark curly hair that is quickly becoming streaked by gray.

"Should I even ask what you're doing to my toilet?"

"Sketching it."

"Sketching it? It *was* rumored that Rauschenberg stayed here at one point, but I didn't realize his artistic vibes were here. Is there a particular point to sketching the toilet tank?"

I struggle to keep my lines contiguous.

"Well, the goal is to have you a replacement lid by the time the party starts tomorrow so Al Gore won't have to wonder why water's splashing out the back."

Liam shakes his head in bewilderment. "Another one of Esther's projects, right? This and the bedroom doors? Are those getting replaced before the party? I think those are more important than a toilet tank lid."

Esther pushes past Liam and bolts into the bathroom.

"Honey, don't bother her, she's doing exactly what I asked her to do. A little late, but she is getting it done," she says in a harsh, scolding tone.

She stands over me, then helps by holding down the cardboard as I finish. I jot down her reproach in my mental notebook to play over again when I feel like berating myself. If I find a lid, I'll be a hero. If I don't, Esther will work this one for a few months. I can hear it now.

"How much is the lid going to cost to replace?"

Liam is my only client who is as cost-conscious as I am. Before I can answer, Esther jumps down his throat and practically pulls his testicles out via his windpipe.

"What do you care how much it costs, Liam? It's a toilet lid. A porcelain toilet lid. Not gold-plated. Not lined with rubies. Jesus, Liam, you're getting on my nerves about this money issue. It's a necessity. Don't try to worry Corki about the cost. You two are disgusting the way you play into each other's issues about money. Leave it alone. It's not healthy."

As Esther pushes her way out of the bathroom, I quietly gather my stuff, wondering if emasculating a man in front of his assistant is "healthy."

"It shouldn't be more than ten dollars," I whisper to Liam. He nods his head without looking at me.

Liam and I both remember a childhood of suffering from having less than we needed. Our clothes were hand-me-downs. He ate way too many meals that starred Top Ramen and Kraft Macaroni & Cheese. My mom made more soup by adding more water.

Esther was raised with unimaginable riches. Each child in her family had her own governess and rarely saw Mother, because she was out spreading herself thin hosting charity events (much as Esther does now). They even more rarely saw Father, because he was in Mexico running his three toy factories. He was ahead of his time in realizing where the cheap labor force was found, so he basically relocated there, leaving his family in Beverly Hills to lead a money-laden but parentless life.

When Esther grew up, she went through her entire trust fund in two years by traveling the world, first-class. She lived by day with the poorest in Nepal, India and Thailand so she could feel as if she were poor and surviving off the land just like them. However, at night, she returned to her posh, four-star hotel room, where she bathed, and slept in fine linens. When her money ran dry, she came home and was able to hit up Mother and Father. Esther's Republican-to-the-bone parents financially subsidized her in a three-bedroom, one-million-dollar home near the beach as she eked out a "modest" living working on Bill Clinton's campaign for the presidency. With spasms of pain, her parents supplied her with a Volvo rather than the BMWs her sisters received.

When Liam met Esther at a political fundraiser, they fell instantly in love. They were married within a year. While he pulled himself up and over the top, earning millions per year, Esther worked very hard at spending each and every dollar to secure the lifestyle with which she was familiar.

. . .

I pause in the foyer and peek into the kitchen, where Shelly is cleaning the dogs' feet. Esther stands at the kitchen counter with a bottle of Xanax in one hand and a Diet Coke in the other. I watch her knock a couple of pills to the back of her throat followed by a huge gulp of soda.

I clear my throat so they know I'm there.

"Okay, I'm done and am on my way to the toilet graveyard . . . actually, it's a mass grave for toilets that couldn't afford a proper burial."

"Whatever it is, just make sure you find a lid exactly like the one that was there. It shouldn't be *that* hard," Esther says.

Liam walks in and solemnly pats my shoulder as I open the front door. "Good luck, little soldier."

From the gray, peeling exterior of the plumbing supply house, and the buzzing emanating from the faded neon sign hanging above the door, I assess it as being a downscale version of the super-expensive La Brea Avenue store Liz's Antique Hardware. At Liz's, everything interior-hardware-related, from the 1960s or earlier, has been cleaned, sorted and catalogued.

I enter and push my way through the throngs of butt cracks belonging to plumbers leaning over pipes and elbows on display. I get in line behind a burly, unshaven man, suspecting I'm the only novice in this store. Impatiently, I check my watch. It's a quarter to ten.

Finally, it's my turn. I put my cardboard sketch up on the counter and explain my toilet dilemma. Without so much as a word, the man points to a dirt-encrusted, oily door that I'm afraid he intends for me to touch and go through. I use a Kleenex to push it open.

I had no idea how close my joking with Esther was to the truth. This is indeed a mass burial ground for toilet lids. An entire wall, from dirt floor to three feet above my head, is piled with precariously stacked toilet lids. Shorter stacks are in front. I have no idea where to start except to rule out the black ones. I need white, the most plentiful color. Only trouble is, the lids are so deeply covered in filth and the lighting is so bad, I have no clue what is pink, tan, yellow or white. I am the sole human occupant in the dim toilet crypt. I see rat paw prints and hear some type of vermin movement when the door slams shut.

I use my Kleenex to dust off a place to set my purse. I stupidly wore light-colored jeans and a yellow, long-sleeved turtleneck. What was I thinking?

A store clerk opens the door. "You finding everything okay out here?"

I try not to whimper.

"No, I don't even know where to start."

"Well, if we weren't shorthanded, I'd help you, but I can't. I suggest you start right there at your feet and pull each toilet lid out and measure it. I see you brought an outline of your lid, so you're way ahead of the game." He shuts the door and leaves me.

I don't feel ahead of the game, I feel overwhelmed. I pull the first impossibly heavy lid off the pile and measure it against my sketch. No match. As I pull the next one off, I set it down too hard and it cracks.

An hour and a half later, I've gone through six 3-foot piles, a total of fifty-two lids, and have made exactly zero matches. My clothes are black, my hands are filthy, my hair has spiderwebs and undoubtedly a few spiders in it, my back hurts, and I've killed so many bugs *I'm* starting to question my own karma. I see a mouse run behind the pile and have to stop digging. This was never in my job description. I'm sure of it. I get out my cell phone and open it.

"Esther home, line two."

Shelly answers. "Schwartz residence."

My voice quivers.

"Shelly, I am buried knee-deep in other people's crappers and I'm filthy from head to toe. If there were an earthquake right now, I'd be killed instantly by falling toilets. Is Esther there?"

"Yeah, hold on."

Esther comes on the line.

"Hello," she says nasally.

I explain where I've been for the past hour and a half and Esther laughs. I'm up to my waist in toilet lids and filth with a good chance of getting hantavirus from breathing in mouse feces and she laughs.

"Esther, can we just use the toilet lid from the guesthouse for the party since I suspect no one is going to be hiking up the hill to use that bathroom?"

"God, Corki, had you thought about that to begin with, you wouldn't be in this mess, would you? Good idea. I'll have Shelly bring it down."

Esther hangs up without saying goodbye. I punch my telephone's "end" button, shove it in my purse and throw my purse over my shoulder. I angrily push the door, not bothering with my stupid Kleenex, and march past the plumbers, who fall silent upon looking at my disarray. I stare down an employee.

"Sir, do you have a restroom I can use to clean up?"

He points to another door, equally greasy, equally grimy and equally gross. I push it open, take one look and instantly figure out that even in my present state, I am cleaner than the room. The sink is so foul that I decide to disinfect everything from now on when I have a plumber come to the house. I walk out, disgusted.

It's eleven-thirty and I haven't even gone grocery shopping or started cooking for Lucy's picnic. Out on the street, I pour my bottle of drinking water over my hands. I rub them together, climb into the backseat of Betty and close the door. Betty's back windows are tinted limo black, so I'm able to change in privacy.

Right on Pico Boulevard, a main thoroughfare running from downtown Los Angeles to the beach in Santa Monica, I pull off my sweater. Hunching down in my bra, hoping to hide myself from prying eyes looking through the windshield, I scrub myself with Blaise's emergency wet wipes for backseat food disasters. Then, turning my sweater inside out, I put it back on.

With no time to waste, I hit the road. The Whole Foods market on Crescent Drive in Beverly Hills seems to await my arrival with a parking space open. I throw my bag over my shoulder and rush in, trying to look confident while inside I'm crumbling with embarrassment. People pass me, stand back and stare as other shoppers grimace and then smile politely.

Quickly gathering all the food I'll need for Lucy's picnic, I get in line. Stepping in behind me is actress Rae Dawn Chong, Tommy Chong's daughter. I smile at her and hope she doesn't recognize me as Veronique LeMay's assistant. We met a few years back at Veronique's hillside home.

In spite of my funky appearance, Rae Dawn sweetly says "Hello," and I say "Hello" back. She looks at me, trying to figure out where I might possibly fit into her memory banks. Am I the one who stands at the exit of the bank drive-through with a cup in my hand? Am I the one curled up, covered with newspaper, who sleeps in the doorway over by the Chinese restaurant, Chin Chin's on Sunset?

The grocery clerk, who has helped me at least three hundred thousand times, smiles blankly as if she has absolutely no idea who I am. Just as well because I don't want to chat, I just want to hurry and get out of here.

The cashier clears her throat. "Ma'am. Your total is $183.33. Will that be cash or charge?"

"Cash."

I put my purse on the counter and pull out a lime-green Hermès wallet, a Christmas gift from Lucy. The women in line stir as they strain to see how much cash the derelict with the Hermès wallet has. I try to select two one-hundred-dollar bills and accidentally bring out nine hundred dollars in petty cash along with it.

Oops!

The young clerk bagging my groceries screams and backs away. Dang, girl, it's not that dramatic. Everyone in line inches away from me, including Rae Dawn. As I awkwardly move to gather up the bills, my line disperses and I am given lots of room. I just want to leave. I put my hand out for my change, and the grocery store clerk freezes, her eyes pinned on my purse.

Now I'm getting upset.

"What is wrong with you people?"

I follow the clerk's line of vision, scream and jump back. A family of giant, toilet-dwelling beetles are crawling from my purse. They look like wide-bodied cousins of the Malaysian Three-Horned Scarab beetles I saw in Blaise's book on insects. I scream again. With horror and embarrassment, I snatch my change and receipt and run from the store with my purse, the portable bug bus, and groceries in tow.

At Lucy's home, I gingerly step into her bathroom and see what a true wreck I am. I'm a little hesitant about using any bathroom in her rented house because all four have walls decorated with padded, pure white silk fabric. For this plush luxury, the owners insisted she leave a huge deposit for cleaning. I consider washing up in the laundry room.

As I peer into the mirror, I better understand the reaction of the people at the market. In addition to spiderwebs in my hair, I pick out a couple of twigs and leaves. I don't recall being in the vicinity of a tree, so it's anyone's guess how they got tangled there. Not only do I look off-kilter with my sweater turned inside out, my nails are also neatly edged with filth.

After a birdbath in the sink, I put a towel around my torso and go to Lucy's room to see if perhaps she has some old shirts of Jock's folded away in a drawer. Lord knows I won't fit into any of Lucy's size-two clothes.

Opening her bedroom door, I see her entire nine-foot-long window covered in a huge Confederate flag. Chills go down my spine as I wonder just what the heck Lucy and Tommy Ray have been up to. Have they been playing out that past life as slave and master with a location switch from Atlantis to Alabama? I'm prepared to see a lynched Negro and some slave costumes in the closet. I open the closet door tentatively and find some fancy cowboy boots I know do not belong to Lucy. It doesn't seem to me like Tommy Ray is moving slowly.

I pull out the bottom drawer of the bureau and rifle through the clothes. There on the bottom I find an extra-large shirt that will do the job. Unfortunately it has the word INSECTOIDS splashed across the chest.

As I slip it over my head, I remember how Concepcion almost got fired when Lucy moved into Jock's house. Concepcion, who thoroughly loved Jock's previous wife (movie star Teri Tulane), kept wearing T-shirts from Teri's amazing array of movies in front of Lucy. Lucy, who was obviously threatened by this, put her foot down and said, "If Concepcion continues to wear Teri's shirts, she can find somewhere else to work." Apparently, Concepcion's paycheck won out over her loyalty to Teri. Suddenly, her tees were pure white or, not surprisingly, shirts from one of Lucy's films.

I started prepping at twelve forty-five P.M. and have been cooking, chopping, stirring and cleaning up my Southern cuisine for over four hours. I have scrubbed splattered oil off the walls so Alejandra won't have to clean up after me, but I can't get the odor of fried chicken out of the house.

I had every intention of being true to the South, but the black-eyed peas end up laced with coconut, my Jamaican grandmother's influence too strong to resist. For the buttermilk icebox pie, I obtained the recipe from the Satsuma Tea Room in Memphis. That should make Tommy Ray happy. The potato salad has cornichons instead of sweet pickle relish, and the road snacks are rounds of chèvre rolled in rosemary, young Manchego sheep cheese from Spain and loaves of rustic bread. I put cut-up pineapple and peaches imported from South America into the cooler. Perhaps Martha Stewart has inspired my Southern cooking as well.

The adage that it never rains in Southern California has sprung a leak. The clouds are full again and it's pouring. As I drive through the wet streets, I picture Lucy, Tommy Ray, Dave and Bubba sitting in the SUV, windows closed, trying to hold back their flatulence from the black-eyed peas. I can almost guarantee Lucy won't ask for black-eyed peas ever again.

Chapter Three

"Mom, you there?" I shout into her answering machine.

"I was outside," Mom says, breathlessly. "You have to give me a minute to get to the phone."

"Is Blaise behaving himself or driving you nuts?"

"Cornelia, I have no idea what the problem is. He's been a delight. Today we went to the Quaker Christmas Tree Farm and he picked out the tree. He even helped cut it down. He mowed the lawn earlier. . . ."

"Mom, you let him near a gas mower? He could have blown your house to bits!" I say, thinking I'd better go get my boy.

"Cornelia, I wasn't born yesterday. I let him use the old push mower. Remember, I raised you? I think I know how to do it. Anyway, he's out raking the yard now."

"Okay."

"I really don't know what all the hullabaloo is about. He's been an absolute gem. Very willing to work and help out. Wants to please. Maybe *he's* not the problem, Cornelia! Maybe it's you."

I gulp.

"I'm not the one lighting feces on fire, Mom. I have to go now. I just wanted to make sure he was all right."

After I hang up, the phone rings immediately. I know my mom. She's calling back to have the last word.

"Hello, Mom," I say, annoyed that I'm about to receive a lecture.

"It's Veronique!"

"Oh! I thought you were my mom calling back. Welcome home from Italy! We've been trading messages—"

"Listen, Corki, I'm sorry for interrupting, but I'm walking into my hair appointment at the John Frieda Salon. I know this is a bit of a last-minute request on a Saturday morning, but I'm going to New York tomorrow for Christmas and I need a few gifts."

"Okay. Give me the list," I say confidently.

"Bob and Harvey Weinstein over at Miramax in New York. And Julia Roberts, Woody Harrelson and Demi Moore. I'll need you to deliver the last three; they're in town for the holidays. The others I'll take with me or we can FedEx them—it's up to you."

"Price limit?" I ask as I jot ideas on a notepad.

"Well, a lot for the Weinstein brothers; the other three, say up to five each?" she asks.

"No problem," I say. "I think I'd rather FedEx the gifts—I'll have them wrapped appropriately and insured. Don't worry."

"I'm not worried. Do whatever you think best."

I hang up, go take a shower and put on my Beverly Hills shopping clothes.

Not only are the streets of Beverly Hills crowded with local shoppers, but the tourist buses have let off throngs of Midwesterners with bulging pocketbooks and cameras bouncing against their generous bellies. They cross Rodeo Drive illegally, stomping on the freshly planted poinsettias in the median strip, anxious to see if that was really Jennifer Lopez going into Giorgio Armani.

Parking at the post office, I pay the valet parking attendant and dash across Little Santa Monica Boulevard as I straighten out my skirt. Applying one last swipe of lipstick before entering a brick courtyard full of small shops that have sister shops in Nice and Cannes, I pass through the outside dining area of a small restaurant frequented by an odd assortment of actors, mini-mafiosos and the Secret Service.

I push open the glass door to a small, dimly lit shop and approach the man behind the counter. He has never given me his name, although I have given him mine as well as all my pertinent information. We have a dance we regularly participate in when I come here. He acts surly and suspicious and I, appreciative and thankful.

"Good morning. I'd like to—"

"I know what you want," he interrupts. "You're the one who lives on welfare, right?"

"I beg your pardon?"

He checks his computer and I look at myself in the mirror. Can he tell I've just lost two clients and am heading toward poverty? I feel my shoulders tensing.

"Yes, I have it right here, Corki Brown on *Wilshire* Boulevard!"

"Oh, yes, my mailing address *is* on Wilshire." God, I'm becoming paranoid. Welfare, Wilshire, whatever. I clear my throat. "I need a full box today."

"All right, wait right here."

He surreptitiously leaves the shop through the front door, looking both ways before he exits and locks it behind him. I wait at the counter looking at the security cameras watching me. He has a smart system here—we're both committing crimes and we can implicate each other—me by buying, him by selling.

He returns with a box wrapped in brown paper. I hand him $1,250 in cash, he counts it, and I leave with a small nod. Always nice doing business in the underworld, where I can't ask for a receipt and don't expect one. Thank God Veronique doesn't ask questions, but trusts me implicitly.

Walking down Rodeo Drive to Tiffany's with over a thousand dollars' worth of Cuban contraband bouncing against my hip, I laugh at the thought. Welfare. I'd scrub toilets again before going on government assistance.

I scurry up a cobblestone walkway that resembles the streets of Paris and pop into Tiffany's, excited by my idea for Demi and Woody. My mood immediately deflates when I see Arnold Schwarzenegger and Maria Shriver walk into the same room. I can't compete with them and it will take me forever to get a salesperson's attention if I have to wait lurking in the governor's shadow. I hate to act like this, but I have a schedule to keep and other celebrities can't get in my way.

"Arnold!" I say with so much enthusiasm that I even surprise myself.

He spins around and looks at me, his brain working overtime to figure out who I am.

"*Fröhliche Weihnachten!*" I say.

"Merry Christmas to you!" Arnold replies.

"You don't remember me? I'm Jock Straupman's assistant!"

"Of course!" he says.

I cozy in next to them, make small talk about Jock's well-being and wave to the saleswoman. I put in my order for twelve crystal champagne flutes, pay for them and leave, once more wishing Arnold and Maria a merry Christmas in German.

Mission accomplished.

Julia Roberts has the same fondness for angels that I have for antique saint figurines. I drive to West Hollywood, where my favorite antique mall is filled with both, sweep in past the guard, and within five minutes have located a sweet, small, eighteenth-century Italian angel, bare-bummed and blowing a horn. I pay the $675 and take note to tell Veronique that I had to go over the $500 limit.

One last stop at Almor Liquor for two bottles of champagne and a bottle of cognac for Bob Weinstein and it will complete the shopping portion of my Veronique "project."

"Mary! Merry, merry!" I say, rushing in the front door of Almor.

"Hi, Corki," I hear from behind a pile of wrapping paper, boxes and ribbon. She peeks her blond head out. "You look nice today, what's the occasion?"

"Every once in a while I like to shock people. Keep them off balance. Mary, I need two Cristal Rosés—they're $350 each, right? And a bottle of cognac . . . the Rémy Martin in the Baccarat decanter."

"Okay," Mary says as she gets up, takes her keys and unlocks a glass-enclosed case. "The Cristal *is* $350 but you know this Rémy Martin is from Louis the Thirteenth's private reserve. It's hundreds of years old."

I think guiltily of the Rémy Martin I threw down Lucy's kitchen sink when I got too tipsy to drive.

"How much is it?" I ask, mentally apologizing to Kevin Kline . . . such a nice gift he gave Lucy.

"Most places sell it for fifteen hundred. I sell it for thirteen and change."

"I'll take it! You have a regular bargain basement here!"

She rings up my $2,164 purchase.

. . .

At home, I wrap the Rémy Martin in blue and white Hanukkah gift paper for Bob. My illegal Cuban cigars, though, I open and carefully dump out on my kitchen table. Removing the rice paper and then the layer of cedar with the word "Havana" burned into it, I take each cigar and cautiously remove its band. After wrapping the cigars in one carefully chosen gift box and the cigar box, cedar and bands in another, I make out separate FedEx labels and put them in their respective mailing boxes. To reduce the chance of jail time, I have to separate the cigars from their origin—Cuba.

I know why I go to the trouble for Veronique, but don't know why she goes to the trouble for Harvey Weinstein. My one and only lasting impression of him was in a client's brand spanking new home theater, where he refused to use an ashtray and let his cigar ashes build up in a pile on the carpet.

I send the Weinstein gifts to New York and wrap and deliver Woody's Cristal champagne and six Tiffany champagne flutes to his office. I wrap the same gift for Demi, drop it off to her holiday beach house in Malibu and deposit Julia's gift at the front door of her beach house a few miles up the Pacific Coast Highway. I have driven 155 miles and am finally done for the day at nine P.M.

At ten P.M. I'm eating a reheated dinner of shrimp pesto pasta when my phone rings. I let the answering machine pick it up.

"Corki, it's Jock Straupman."

After all the years I've worked for him, he still uses his full name when he calls to leave a message. His voice drips syrup and I wonder if he's going to tell me about Paris.

"How are you tonight? I need you to come over first thing tomorrow morning and gather up some things to return to Britt. Just some clothes and personal effects. Oh, and return the things you picked up at the cleaners to her, too. She should pay for the cleaning. Also take her Georgia O'Keeffe coffee table book. You know, Georgia's the artist who made everything look like a vagina."

His voice tightens around the word "vagina." Britt must have mentioned the word "commitment" or something, because obviously she's getting dumped, and I'll be the one doing the dumping.

"Also, if I'm not here, there's a letter I'd like you to deliver along with her things."

The "Dear Jane" letter, I'm sure.

"And I'll leave her address on a note for you. Thanks."

He hangs up. This is the second goodbye letter and return of personal effects I've handled in the past six months. God, I hate being the deliverer of bad news.

My phone rings again.

"Corki, it's Jock Straupman. I also need you to clean my collection. It's time, right? Hasn't it been two months? I've been going to the range a lot lately. I think it's time. Please. Sometime after the holidays would be good. Thank you."

Break up with conquest of the week and clean my guns. Fantastic.

Fifteen years ago, when I first started working for Jock, Concepcion came across firearms stashed under his bed, in certain drawers, in his car and in the gym. After she found the guns, Jock's lawyers cooked up a paper for her to sign in which she was sworn to keep her mouth shut about every aspect of his personal life. Jock didn't know she'd already told me about her findings.

Right after that, I saw Jock go into his meditation room, but when I entered the room he was gone. His meditation room is a pristine alcove off his bedroom. There are no pictures, awards, books, windows, doors or artwork. The room is wallpapered in an unusual pumpkin orange stripe pattern. It features a pillow on the floor and a huge statue of a Buddha in a recessed niche on one wall. That's it. Jock is what they call a Jew-Bu, genetically Jewish but practicing Buddhism.

I stood in the doorway, dumbfounded, searching for an explanation as to where he had gone. I called out to him. No answer. Stupidly, I picked up the pillow, as if to find him there. I leaned into the niche and looked behind the figure . . . only a renegade dust bunny and the earthquake strap securing the carved figure to the wall in case of a temblor.

The following week, Lucy and Jock left for a two-week trip to St. Tropez with Jack Nicholson and Angelica Huston. Concepcion had the two weeks off, and I was left to my own devices. Jock asked me to get the air-conditioning filters changed for the summer season and the pool's bottom paint changed from light blue to black. Before they came home, he also wanted me to drain, clean and rearrange the scenery in his wall-length fish aquarium that was home to a two-foot shark and other fishies that kept getting eaten when "Jaws" wasn't fed enough. Not willing to lose my right arm in this endeavor, I called the pros. While they cleaned the tank, I had plenty of time to snoop in the meditation room.

I went in, sat on the pillow and stared at the walls, ceiling, and floor, then examined the motion detector sensors whose invisible beams cross the middle of the room. I touched Buddha in every place

I could, even some unmentionable ones. Standing in front of the statue, I looked out across the room.

I found what I was looking for when I ran my fingers over the molding that surrounded the recess. One piece of molding was looser than the rest and slightly separated from the wall. I pulled it gently. As if it were on hydraulic hinges, the entire wall opened to reveal a steep staircase going down to complete blackness.

Silently scolding Buddha for keeping secrets from me, I went to get a flashlight from Jock's earthquake kit and returned to the meditation room. As I descended the tightly twisting spiral staircase, I entered another world. Images of hell, Italian catacombs, Parisian sewers and Cold War bomb shelters flew rapidly through my mind. I hit the last stair and it dawned on me where I was. This had to be his safe room, and here, all this time, I had thought the basement was the only room below the house.

It was explained to me by an FBI agent I once dated that criminals who break into celebrities' homes don't typically want to kill them. Thrilled by the proximity to their idols, they want to steal their stuff or perhaps even kidnap them. Celebs respond by finding a way to barricade themselves from such a threat. Safe rooms are lined in steel so no gunshot can penetrate. They have telephone lines that are buried underground so no one can cut them, or they are equipped with cellular. They usually have television monitors split into four or more screens so occupants can watch everything going on outside their home. Some have safes in the ground or wall. Some also have a wine cave, storage room, closet, bathroom and dressing room. All have a button that when pushed forces the alarm system into panic mode. And most have a loaded gun for the worst-case scenario.

I turned on the lights. Bright, fluorescent bulbs flickered on throughout a room as big as a winery's cellar.

Before me was a full-scale gun range. There were four lanes, each with a station divided by walls. At the ends hung paper figures of people riddled with bullet holes.

Lying on tables next to chairs were magazines with flashy headlines that read "Glocks Rock!" and "Make your .38 great!" I found night-scoping equipment and camouflage clothing and became very confused. Jock was on the mailing list of several Democratic organizations trying to raise funds to abolish private gun ownership. He always sent them a donation.

Paranoid, I turned off the light switch and rubbed away my fingerprints with my shirt. If he had to have his little hideaway, I sure wasn't going to rain on his parade. I ascended the staircase, closed the wall and went about the job I was paid to do.

Two weeks later, Jock and Lucy returned home. Tanned, relaxed and looking more in love than ever, they left the unpacking to me. I made piles of dry cleaning, laundry and things to return to the bathroom, kitchen and library. I figured out what to refill, restock and repack for the next time they decided to take off on a last-minute whirlwind vacation. Not many stars can plan a vacation too far ahead. After all, they may get the offer of a lifetime, that perfect part in a wonderful movie destined for box office success. They live waiting for that moment.

As I carted their dirty clothes into the huge, walk-in closet for Concepcion to launder later, Jock came into the room. He smiled dreamily and I wished a vacation like that for me. A holiday that didn't leave me worrying for six months about how I was going to pay off the credit cards for my indulgences. Oh, to come home and walk around looking dreamy, jet-lagged and ecstatic.

Jock stood there a little too long without saying a word.

"Did you have a good time in St. Tropez?" I asked.

Jock's smile widened even more, if that was possible. He resembled the Cheshire Cat. "Oh yes, we had a very good time. How 'bout you, did you have a good time?"

Doing what? Working?

"Yeah, sure. Jaws didn't bite anyone. The pool came out nice. Good time had by all."

He shifted in the doorway. "I mean down there."

Was he getting nasty? Too much sun, French wine and sex.

"Down where, Jock?"

He pointed to the ground. "There."

Oh shit, he knew.

Jock repeated himself. "Did you have fun down there?"

"It wasn't exactly fun," I stammered, "but definitely eye-opening."

He moved into the room. "You had your eyes open for seven minutes and thirty-three seconds. Did you see everything you needed to see?"

Something timed my stay at the range? For a man who can't program his VCR, and who has me go in the basement to change the tapes in his security cameras because he can't figure it out, he sure had some sophisticated monitoring equipment.

I tried to keep it light, as if I frequently snooped in private hideaways. "More than I ever imagined."

"I do imagine then that you can keep your eyes open, but your mouth . . ." He mimicked securing a lock and tossing out the key. "Understand?"

I nodded. "I have no idea 'down there' even exists."

Jock obviously liked my immediate placatory stance.

"You ever shoot a gun?"

Time to surprise him back. "Yep! I have a Brazilian Rossi .38 at home . . . for protection. I was stalked once. In fact, I even have a CCW."

I sensed Jock, at that moment, liked me or perhaps respected me more than he did two weeks ago. Permits to carry a concealed weapon are virtually impossible to get in Los Angeles and damn hard to get anywhere else in California.

"You know how to clean a weapon?"

"Of course. That's taught in Responsible Gun Ownership 101."

"Good. Since you now know more about me than I cared to share, you have a new chore. I need my collection cleaned once every couple of months. The cleaning supplies are under the sink, down there, where you explored at two-fifteen P.M. on June 16. I'll arrange to have your fingerprints entered into the memory of the gun safe so you can open it when you need to."

Jock came into the closet and stood over me as I dumped the last pieces of laundry down the chute. I pretended to be calm as he reached out and patted my head rather hard.

"Understand?"

"Yeah, I told you I did."

As he took his hand away from my head, his ring caught on a strand of my curly hair. He yanked it out of my head, turned and walked out of the room, then paused and turned around as if he was going to say more. Then, deciding against it, he went quietly from the room.

Chapter Four

I stare out my living room window at a sunny, beautiful December morning. Days of rain have washed away the smog, and the blazing sun makes everything glisten and sparkle like diamonds. I see diamonds in the trees, in the grass and in the puddles that are quickly evaporating in the morning's heat. My outside thermometer reads seventy-two degrees. It will surely rise.

The calmness outside belies the panic I feel inside. I have work to do before I pack my SUV and drive the three hours to Mom's house in Visalia. I quickly drink my coffee, shower and dress. In thirty minutes I'm ready and on my way to Jock's.

I don't know what Britt did or said, but I can safely assume that whatever it was, Jock is pretty pissed off about it. Her clothes are dumped in a pile at the foot of his guest bathroom toilet, where whatever man last peed there missed—by about a foot. Her clothes are soaked in urine. Next to them is another pile containing two hairbrushes, several tampons, assorted makeup, a pair of pink satin slippers and one lacy brown pair of panties. On top of these items is a note neatly written to me giving Britt's address and phone number. A spit-sealed "Dear Jane" letter is clipped to the note.

Jock is nowhere to be seen. I snag the Georgia book from the coffee table, collect the fluffed and folded thongs and clothes I'd picked up from the cleaners, then go into the kitchen to gather a couple of big, heavy-duty garbage bags. Next, I go into Jock's dressing room and get a pair of surgical rubber gloves, the kind he uses when he secretly dyes the gray out of his hair with Clairol Loving Care #83 in Natural Black.

I gather all the peed-on clothes and stuff them in the double-thick bags, neatly put Britt's personal effects in her pink-satin-lined overnight makeup case, tie huge knots in the plastic bags and haul them down to Betty, who seems to groan as I approach.

On the way to Britt's house in Korea Town, I still smell urine. I roll the windows all the way down.

Standing on Britt's porch, I knock a couple of times and hear rustling behind the door. The chain slips out of its holder and the lock slips back. Miss Iceland doesn't look quite as icy today. Her mascara is smeared under her eyes and her hair is a tousled mess. It looks as if I have just awakened her.

"Jock's assistant," I say, "Corki."

"Oh," she says rubbing her eyes. She opens the door farther to reveal herself in a T-shirt and panties.

A small poodle slips past her and circles the bags, sniffing them. I give Britt her pink makeup case.

"Jock wanted me to drop off your stuff," I say awkwardly. I hand her the letter and she accepts it with a pained look in her eyes. Before she can gather up her things, her poodle looks up at me, squats on my foot and pees.

"Oh God, Corki, I'm so sorry! Fifi, what in heaven's name do you think you're doing? Oh God, hold on. Let me get a rag."

I stand there with dog pee soaking through my shoe and into my sock as Britt bolts into her house and reappears with a wad of paper towels in her hand.

I make a mental note to have my shoes and socks professionally cleaned and take it out of Jock's petty cash.

"Well, merry Christmas, Britt," I awkwardly say as I walk down her front steps.

"Yeah, to you, too, Corki."

Chapter Five

When Blaise is good, he's very good, and my mother, for the life of her, cannot figure out what *my* problem is. She doted on him and he lapped it up like a kitten finishing off the cream in a bowl. Blaise went out of his way to help her paint, clean up and lug in logs from the woodpile. She cooked his favorite meals, lost gracefully at chess and showed him off to all her friends.

Now, with a few days left in December, we're back to reality.

As soon as we return to Los Angeles from our short Christmas holiday, I need to prepare myself for the New Year's Eve onslaught. Lucy may be gone, but she'll be home soon, and Jock is always one to throw in a last-minute request.

After hauling the last of our luggage upstairs to our apartment, by myself, without the assistance from Blaise that he was credited with at Grandma's house, I sit and listen to my answering-machine messages.

"Corki, Jock Straupman. Thank you for taking care of returning those things to Britt. I hope you had a merry little Christmas."

Yes, it was little, especially with no end-of-the-year bonus.

"Ummmm, I have a project for you." Jock's voice continues on the machine. "I need you to find a teddy bear tonight to send as a gift to someone. A pink teddy bear . . . is that possible? Pink. Surely there must be pink teddy bears out there, right? I need it to be delivered tomorrow morning, from a service, not you. Maybe a courier service? I don't know, you tell me what's best. It's going to Studio City to Tree Pink."

Tree Pink? Is that an apartment building or a business?

"P-i-n-q-u-e is how her last name is spelled. The card with it should read, 'Friday night was ours, Pinky Promise.' Don't put a name or anything on it, she'll know. The address is—"

Beep.

Do other assistants get overtime for working nights? I doubt it. Maybe I should ask for it. I remember what happened the time I told Lucy I wanted to be paid time-and-a-half for working weekends. Her response was more a threat than a statement. "Well, Corki, it sounds like you don't want to work anymore . . . on the weekends."

Call number two is from none other than "Jock Straupman, again. Your machine cut me off. Just call me and I'll explain how to get the teddy to Tree."

Calls number three and four are from the *National Enquirer* and *Star* magazine, respectively. Both had reports of a Ford Excursion going down Route 66 containing Tommy Ray Woods and Lucy Bennett kissing madly and passionately, with Tommy Ray at the wheel. In the back were unidentified persons. Can I expound on this? Please call back with details or this will have to go to press as is.

How did they get my number? I'm not a publicist. I don't make three thousand a month whether I do an ounce of work or not. I jot down a note to call Moro/Castle PR first thing in the morning and ask Missy Moro to deal with this.

Call number five is from Esther. "Corki, I really need some help cleaning up. The party and the holidays were a hit, but the house is a disaster. It's a bigger project than Shelly can do by herself. Obviously bring Blaise. He and Atom can swim and jump on the trampoline and Shelly's bringing Star and Eden. There's a ton of food for the kids. I just need help taking down all the decorations and putting away the Christmas and Hanukkah stuff. Call me. Thanks. Hope you had a good Christmas . . . or do you celebrate Kwanzaa? I get mixed up about that holiday. Bye."

So do I.

At least Blaise will have a good time with Atom, Liam and Esther's kid, and Shelly will be there to share my pain.

Call number six is from the Italian Stallion Ferrari place where I get Lucy's car serviced. While Lucy's away being "serviced," I scheduled for her car to be serviced, too. They confirm my appointment. The phone rings.

"Corki Brown, please!" a man says. A rather chipper-sounding man. I spin my brain Rolodex trying to remember if there are any outstanding bills I haven't paid. This guy sounds like a collection expert.

"May I ask who this is?"

"This is Bob Caplan from the *National Enquirer*. I need to confirm some information with a Corki Brown, please."

"Yes, what do you need? This is Corki."

"Miss Brown, I did leave a message earlier—"

I interrupt him. "Yes, I know. I heard it. But you're wrong. I just left Lucy Bennett's house, where we ate braised tofu and sesame kale. I can guarantee you that she is in Beverly Hills exactly where I left her not fifteen minutes ago."

"That's not so, according to our sources," he replies.

"And your point, Bob?"

"Miss Brown, we are ready to go to press, with photographs to back up our statement that Lucy Bennett and Tommy Ray Woods were seen driving down Route 66, together, kissing and fondling each other."

"Look, Mr. Caplan, there are a million blondes in the world, and I'm sure your sources saw one of them, but it wasn't Lucy. As I said, I just left her home and she was there. Good night."

I quietly hang the receiver back on the hook.

"Well, that was an out-and-out lie!" Blaise states as he leans against the door leading to the hallway. He has a boxing glove on the end of an accordion-like arm that punches when he pulls the trigger. I don't know what to say. But he does.

"You're a stellar example, Mom. You tell me not to lie and then you do it in a big way. Hypocrite!"

Ouch!

"Blaise . . ."

"Why are you lying for her?"

I remember all the impossible situations Lucy has put me in for the past two decades. I think of the lies she's told me and the lies she's told about me . . . of how she pays me the least and expects the most . . . of the marriages she's broken up and the children whose lives she has devastated. Then I think of the generous Christmas and birthday gifts she's given me, the good times we've shared and the times we've cried together over shared pain. Dear God, if it were only black and white!

"You're right. I was being hypocritical. I'll try not to lie for my clients anymore."

"You always tell me, 'Don't try it, do it,'" he preaches.

Lord, hearing my words come back to me is humiliating.

"Fine, I'll do it. Even if I lose more work, I'll do it," I say with conviction. I don't want to hear any more lectures.

"What work did you lose?" he asks.

I tell him everything, burdening my ten-year-old as if he were my peer. I tell him we're cutting out piano and swimming lessons, neither of which seems to bother him. In fact, I get the sense that he is thrilled.

The phone rings. It's Lucy on her cell.

"Hi, Corki! Belated merry Christmas!"

"Thank you. To you, too. *And* thank you for the bonus, I really appreciate it," I say, very honestly.

"Honey, you deserve it for all the trouble I put you through! And sit down, 'cause I'm about to put you through a bit more!"

She's still using her twang *and* she's speaking with exclamation points. I sit down and brace myself.

"I know I'm only giving you three days' notice, but I was thinking a New Year's Eve party might be fun."

Please, please, don't ask me to cook, I beg silently. I want to fall into bed with a glass of champagne on New Year's with a good book, then sleep like I've never slept before.

"If you can't cook," she's reading my mind, "get it catered or make it look as if you did it."

"How many people?" I ask, feeling as if my prayers have been answered.

"Hold on!" she says.

I hear her consulting Tommy Ray in the background.

"Not many. Forty is our closest estimate. And I think it would be really cute if we did party favor bags for everyone when they leave. Wouldn't that be precious?"

It's pathetic that Lucy needs to "buy" friends through party favors when they're not required . . . according to Miss Manners.

"Oh yes, absolutely precious! What do you want the price limit to be per person?" I ask, jotting down ideas.

She consults Tommy again. Laughter. Kissing.

"About three hundred, three-fifty each. That's enough, right?

"That's more than generous."

"And obviously, you are invited. In fact, surprise me, bring a date!"

Thanks . . . it would surprise me, too, if I could find one on such short notice.

"I will! Thank you for inviting me."

Shit, why did I say that? If I haven't had a date in so long I can't remember, what makes me think I can rustle one up on New Year's?

"And Corki, you know there are always last-minute guests. Get enough food et cetera for fifty."

Before we say goodbye, we confirm that she's doing the invites by phone and I'm doing the rest.

I breathe deeply, and then start making calls.

Apparently there's a postholiday run on pink teddy bears. I have called every place listed in my Rolodex that would have such a thing and have even considered a night run to Toys "R" Us, since they refused to answer their phone. Finally, I succumb to defeat and call Jock. His phone rings three times before he answers.

"Mmmmm, hello."

"Hi, it's Corki."

"Did you get my message?"

"Yeah, that's what I'm calling about. I just can't find a pink teddy bear tonight. I have found sixteen different teddy bears ranging from brown to purple to coral orange and sea foam green, but no pink. I can order a pink one online but it will be a two-day delivery because of the New Year. I did find a pink teddy, though. In fact, I found four pink teddies. The kind you wear. Not you personally, but the kind girls wear."

"Hmmmmm. That sounds interesting. Tell me more."

"Well, all of them were pink and lacy. Some had underwires, sort of like a built-in bra; some were thongs."

"I think I like your teddy idea better than mine. Get one in small and have it gift-wrapped. I want it delivered tomorrow by courier."

He gives me her address. I wonder if Britt complained about the type of delivery service I provided.

I call Late Night Lingerie and ask them to gift-wrap one small-sized pink teddy with lace, a thong and no underwire. I am informed that I can certainly get that in a box, but they've run out of wrapping paper.

"Honey, put on your coat. We have to do a run," I call out to Blaise.

"We just got home, Mom," he complains bitterly.

"It's a quickie run. We'll be back in an hour. I need every ounce of work I can get right now and Jock gives me overtime for nights and weekends. Come on!" I say as I head toward the door.

We pull into a strip mall in the seediest section of Hollywood Boulevard. Frightening people linger in dark doorways scarcely lit by buzzing neon bulbs. Runaways that live on the streets walk in groups down the sidewalk. Their gel-spiked glow-in-the-dark hair colors and ringed noses flicker in the flashing lights. The Late Night Lingerie parking lot is empty and we get a space immediately.

"What kind of place are we going to?"

"It's scuzzy, I'm not going to lie. And frankly, I don't want you exposed to this side of life, so I'm going to have to blindfold you."

"Mom!" he complains, "I'm ten years old!"

"That's exactly right, so you're putting on the blindfold."

"Mom, what if I see somebody I know?"

"That's the second good reason—you won't be *able* to see anyone you know."

I whip out a sleep mask compliments of Virgin Atlantic Airways. After much debate, Blaise agrees to humor me by doing me this one favor.

I lead him into the store and straight to an antique cash register. The heavyset woman behind the counter has powdered white skin, bats her impossibly long eyelashes and speaks with a heavy Romanian accent.

"Can I help you?"

"Hi. I called earlier and you put a pink teddy and a gift box on hold for me."

Madame Romania pulls out a petite, beautiful piece of lingerie, but it isn't a teddy.

"I don't think that's the one. That's not a teddy, is it?" I ask.

Blaise rips off his mask. "Show me! I know a teddy when I see one!"

His blindfold has become hooked on a rack behind him, and when he turns around to loosen it, he comes face-to-face with a black brassiere saucily decorated with two fingers on each cup, pinching nipples. Blaise howls with laughter. Forgetting all the convincing it took to get him in here, he is delighted to roam around. As Madame Romania looks for the pink teddy, Blaise runs his fingers over a black thong number displayed on the bottom half of a mannequin.

"Mom, where's this string supposed to go?"

"Blaise, don't touch the mannequin, you could knock it over."

"But Mom, where does the string go? Tell me!"

"It goes in between the butt cheeks so a woman doesn't have panty lines," I state emphatically.

He snatches his hand away from the display and frowns with tons of drama.

"Ewww! This was up some lady's ass? Gross! I want to wash my hands."

He sniffs his fingers, imagining he smells something.

"Blaise!" I say, pushing his hands away from his face, "stop that and I don't like you using that kind of language."

"This is a disgusting place."

Embarrassed, I smile at Madame Romania and excuse myself. I pull Blaise to the side of the store and put my lips next to his ear.

"We'll get out of here a lot faster if you put the mask on so I don't have to lecture you every five minutes."

"What's the point?" he asks. "I've already seen what's here."

Romania calls out. "Ma'am, I found it. Would you like to see it before I put it in the box?"

I call back, "Yes, please. I'll be there in a second."

Romania hands me the teddy and looks at Blaise, who is fingering the edge of the counter.

"It's better that children stay home. They don't belong out late at night," Madame advises.

I hand her a fifty-dollar bill and wait for the change and the receipt before heading out the door.

"Mom, why were those fingers pinching the bra?" he asks.

I disarm Betty's alarm system, load Blaise into the back and try to avoid answering him.

"Why, Mom?"

"I'll tell you later."

"Why later? Tell me now."

"Put on your seatbelt."

"Are you mad at me?"

"No, I'll just have to tell you later."

"How much later?"

"In about eight years."

It's seventy-six degrees outside and I dress as if I'm going into the deepest, darkest jungles of Panama. I put on my thickest jeans, my low-heeled, calf-length boots and a long-sleeved cream-colored shirt. I get out some protective clothing for Blaise.

After breakfast, he takes one look at the clothes that I've set out for him and refuses to put them on.

"Mom, it's hot today. Why are you putting all these clothes out? I can dress myself and I'm going to wear shorts. We're going swimming!"

I insist he slather himself with bug repellant and sunscreen and recall the times Shelly has told me about coming home with mosquito bites all over her legs when she wore shorts up to Liam and Esther's. She also found ticks on the master bedroom duvet cover from when the dogs were sleeping there, and I remember a rattlesnake the house inspector killed and the scorpions that constantly invade the garage.

"Mom, this stuff stinks. You worry too much."

"No, this is the absolute minimum," I say. "I'll let you wear shorts, but I don't want you running all over the yard. Only play in the cut grass, not near any big rocks or bushes, do you hear?"

"Atom *lives* there and he's never been bitten by a snake."

"Yeah, just by everything else under the s<del>BASALT REGIONAL LIB</del>RARY stay where I said. Snakes are supposed to be hibernating in winter, but it's warm so they might come out."

I place Tree's gift-wrapped box on my front porch for the courier to pick up. Blaise brings his swim trunks, towel and goggles and we are on our way to the Schwartzes' for a day of fun and sun.

Driving down Sunset Boulevard toward the beach, I glance back in my rearview mirror to see Blaise deeply engrossed in the latest issue of *Popular Mechanics* magazine. This was his Christmas gift from my friend Noah, who says he's worried that anything less would "insult the poor boy."

I pull into the Schwartzes' driveway, noting that Shelly hasn't arrived yet. Before I get a chance to turn off the engine and gather my things, Blaise is out and rushing through the hacienda's front door.

Esther is already getting Atom and Blaise prepared for the short hike up the hill to the pool by the time I arrive.

"Corki, you go ahead and start in the garage. I threw all the decorations from the holidays in there, but never got them back in their boxes. There's an odd assortment, but all the boxes are labeled. Then, they need to be taken up the hill for storage."

Sunlight floods into the garage as the door opens to reveal a mess. Decorations from Halloween, Thanksgiving, Christmas and Hanukkah are all jumbled together. Wrapping paper and ribbon clippings lie everywhere. The concrete floor is littered in so much paper and holiday "droppings" that it reminds me of a country-and-western bar's floor covered in peanut shells and sawdust.

Snakes, rats and scorpions could be anywhere. God knows I've encountered and killed enough of them to know. I sweep the ground with my eyes and walk the perimeter of the garage looking for stinging tails and rattlers.

"What on earth are you doing?"

I look up to see Shelly, Eden and Star standing there watching me in amusement.

"Just checking the place out for any pestilence that might be lurking here."

"What's a pestilence?" Star asks.

"Technically it's an epidemic disease. But if I find any animals that might *carry* disease, I'll scare them away."

Before Eden and Star can ask any more questions, Shelly herds them to the pool.

I'm deeply into packing and cleaning when Shelly comes back into the garage.

"Esther's in a snit today!" she whispers.

"About what?"

She starts wrapping the glass Hanukkah menorah with bubble wrap and tape. "Well, she's sitting out by the pool, iced tea in one hand and the portable phone in the other, yelling that she has contributed a shitload of money. . . ."

"She said 'shitload' in front of the kids?" I ask.

"Yeah, but the kids were so busy with the water guns, they weren't paying any attention. So she says she has every right to talk to the principal on a holiday if she damn well wants to."

"What's she so upset about?"

"Hold on, hold on. Let me finish. She holds the line long enough to tell me to help you, then jumps back on the horn announcing that this is an emergency."

"An emergency?"

"Yep. I think she freaked out when she heard Atom ask me why I was putting sunscreen on the girls. He understands that you use sunscreen so you don't get dark, and since the girls are already dark . . . it was innocent enough. You know little kids. They take everything so literally."

"Esther must've been embarrassed," I say, wishing I could have been there.

"Atom didn't mean any harm by it, but Esther's so uptight, she exploded. Says she's going to save her child by saving these three 'African-American' kids. She's back there popping Xanax and demanding that the principal grant our kids immediate entry into the school, all fees waived, so Atom won't be 'indoctrinated' with a right-wing mentality!"

I can't help but gasp, then laugh out loud.

"Right-wing mentality? Because he didn't know that black kids could get sunburns?"

"Wait, wait, it gets better!" Shelly shushes me.

"She reminded them that for being a good, strong, liberally minded school, they sure as heck do lack color and she's really upset 'cause she's already made one phone call about this last week and apparently someone wasn't taking her seriously!"

"And what are you doing this whole time, just standing there, listening?"

"I'm applying sunscreen as thoroughly and slowly as possible, trying to hear every last word," she says. "Have you told Blaise about Esther wanting the kids to go to Envision Prep?"

"No," I say. "Have you told Star and Eden?"

"Yep. And they're already excited."

Chapter Six

I hold on to the trunk of a palm tree for dear life. The winds that whip up the sea's white, foamy waves are bringing in dark skies behind me. No matter which way the tree bends, I keep my eye trained on the small patch of blue sky ahead. The more I stare at the patch, the bigger it becomes. But the longer I stare, the more fiercely the wind whips, pulling me, inch by inch, loosening my grip on the tree's trunk. As I start to slip, a swirl of wind lashes out and snaps the tree away from me. With nothing to hold on to, I find myself falling, falling into . . .

Giggles.

"Mom!" Blaise calls out insistently as he shakes me by the shoulder. "Mom, I think you'd better wake up now. The clock says it's seven-thirty."

I sit up and throw the blankets off.

"I thought I set the alarm. What happened?" I ask, breathing hard.

"Your alarm clock went off at five, but you said you needed more sleep."

"Oh no! Honey, I'll say anything to get more sleep." I blink my eyes repeatedly, trying to focus. "Good for you, being dressed already, Blaise. Just change your shirt. You dripped toothpaste on it."

I push myself toward the bathroom, turn on the shower and get in. I let the water run over my face, then quickly wash my hair, dry off and get dressed. I put a cup of yesterday's coffee in the microwave and scrub the jam that missed Blaise's toast off the counter. He watches me from the doorway.

"What's on the agenda today?"

"Well, I solidified most of it yesterday. We got the band, flowers, catering, bartenders, waiters, psychic, seating, artist, outdoor heaters, tables, what else?" I ask.

"The main thing is the party favors," Blaise adds.

I sip my coffee. "Yeah, the party favors are going to drive me crazy. That and trying to figure out what to wear . . . and who's going to watch you if I go . . . and I need a date!"

"I'll be your date, Mom."

I stare at him lovingly. This is the sweetie-pie boy I remember. Maybe our new year will be better.

I set my coffee down on the French bistro table in front of my breakfast nook's huge double-hung window that gives me a view of all the red-tiled roofs in my neighborhood.

"Honey, come sit down for a minute."

"But we don't have a lot of time."

"Just sit down," I say.

Blaise sits down and sneaks a sip of my coffee.

"Stop," I say, mockingly mad. "Listen, Esther may be creating an opportunity for you to go to Atom's private school. It's supposed to be an excellent academy and I wanted to ask you what you thought about that."

"What's wrong with my school?" he asks.

"Nothing . . . okay, something. A couple of weeks ago, a drug dealer was arrested near your school. I don't want you exposed to that kind of element when you're at a young, impressionable age."

Blaise laughs. " 'Young, impressionable age'? Mom, I'm not stupid."

"I'm relieved to hear that!" I say. "Eden and Star would be going to Envision Prep, too. And apparently if you get in now, it's a school that you could stay in until your senior year. They feed into the bigger universities and their scores are top-notch. The girls are very excited about it."

"What's their science program like? Because that's the only thing I'm interested in."

"It's one of their stronger programs," I say excitedly, sensing that he's opening up to the idea.

"I'll think about it," he says nonchalantly as he gets up and goes into the living room.

First stop, the Apple Store. I'm estimating the guest list high rather than being caught short and having someone complain that Lucy Bennett is a cheapskate and didn't buy enough favors. Besides, everything is returnable. I buy twenty iPod minis at two hundred and fifty a pop. I get them in a variety of colors—all super shiny: blue, pink, silver, gold and green.

Next stop, Samy's Camera on Fairfax. For the guys, because this could only be a guy thing, I buy twenty-five binoculars equipped with infrared night vision at four hundred a piece. I first saw these hanging in Jock's closet and he's a man's man, so they'll do fine.

Next stop, a store on Beverly Boulevard—Mo' Hair—where I buy fifteen camel-and-cream-colored mohair throws for three-seventy apiece.

Last stop, the wrapping paper store for festive paper and streamers and other party decorations.

Blaise and I spend the next four hours wrapping all the gifts, then take them to Lucy's house and set them up near the front door. By the time we're done, the party planners are arriving to set up the tables, chairs, heaters and linens. The caterers, florists, bartender and the band follow them. Everyone's arriving so quickly and Lucy is nowhere to be seen. I phone her.

"Lucy, it's Corki!" I say in a panic.

"Is everything okay?" she asks, "I hear stress in your voice."

"Everything's fine, but it's getting close to curtain time and the star of the show hasn't arrived!"

"You're so cute, Corki! Don't worry. We're on the 405 just past LAX. We'll be home in twenty, thirty minutes. Just enough time to shower and change."

"Okay. I just had this vision of folks starting to arrive and me telling them you guys weren't going to make it home to your own party."

I count thirty-five people here to turn her house into a magical Parisian street scene for New Year's Eve. The cooks are buzzing in the kitchen, starting to prepare a menu chosen by none other than *moi,* featuring escargots in garlic; the bartender is searching for an electrical plug that doesn't exist; the crêpe maker is setting up his corner to become an on-demand crêperie complete with selections of fillings—crab, lobster, chèvre, chives and French Swiss cheese. The psychic, Madame Marie for the night, is setting up her booth, while Pierre the artist is setting up his easel and sketchpads. Almor Liquor's delivery guy arrives at the door with cases of chilled Dom Pérignon, and I show him to the kitchen. He pulls one chilled bottle of Dom out of a separate bag along with an envelope and hands them to me.

"Compliments of Mary! Happy New Year!"

"Wow! Thank you. Please tell her thank you, too."

He winks at me, and leaves after I tip him handsomely with my leftover petty cash. I open the envelope and count four one-hundred-dollar bills with a note clipped to them. It simply reads, "Thank you for all your business. Mary."

My mood lightens considerably. I barely notice the room as it transforms into a sidewalk café complete with bistro tables and chairs that are being set up while the workers are putting on their costumes—French striped sailor's shirts and berets.

Blaise is helping the band set up, pretending he's a roadie, I suppose, by hauling in their equipment and instruments for them.

I am so overwhelmed by how quickly the French Foreign Legion has descended upon me, I start longing for a visit to the old French king down in the wine cellar, Louis XIII and his most excellent cognac. But now, my fantasy of falling into bed with a glass of champagne, the truly fine stuff, will come true. Maybe I can go home soon. I don't have a date, I don't have a dress, but I have Dom!

Alejandra, Lucy's housekeeper, pushes into the kitchen past the caterers and waiters. "Happy New Year, Corki!"

We hug hello and survey the organized confusion.

"Sorry I'm late," she says. "Traffic!"

"Don't worry, you beat Lucy here."

Lucy and her new swain, Tommy Ray Woods, pull up to the house, literally ten minutes before the first guests arrive. Dumping their luggage with Alejandra, they sweep through the room, ohh and aah, and then head for the bathrooms to do the fastest shower and primp of their lives.

I tell Alejandra my plan, to skip out while the coast is clear, and give her the last-minute directions. I gather Blaise, wish everyone a *"nouvelle année heureuse"* and hit the pavement, just as Will and Jada Pinkett Smith's limousine pulls in.

Chapter Seven

Today, one week after school has started, is the first day back at school for Blaise. He sat out his suspension without his computer, television or entertainment of any sort. I was hoping this would teach him that being suspended was no holiday; however, I don't think it did. He spent his time at the library researching geothermal gaseous explosions and earthquakes. Rather than deeming it punishment, he enjoyed his time off immensely.

After dropping him off at school, I go directly to Jock's house, a mere six-minute drive. Since I'd told him I'd be here at eight-thirty, he'd given me permission to enter his home without buzzing first to announce my arrival.

I let myself in and tiptoe past his office, where I see the pink teddy that I bought now slung across one of the blades of the ceiling fan, which runs on low, spinning it around and around. I hear Jock moaning behind his closed bedroom door. Tree must have spent the night. His conquests usually don't enjoy that privilege.

I quietly slip down the stairs leading to the range, flip on the lights and go directly to the cabinet containing Jock's collection of guns. I place my right index finger on the scanner and let it collect the data it needs to disarm and allow me access.

As I set the guns out, I realize the room is completely void of sound. This is how I imagine it would be in outer space. There are no indicators, auditory or otherwise, of the day springing to life within and around the house. I can't hear the sprinkler system turning on in the backyard or the system activating for its morning filtering of the pool and hot tub. I can't hear the master bedroom shower turning on or the heater in the basement lurching to start pumping out heated air. It's too quiet.

I double-check each gun to make sure there is no ammunition in the chambers. Then I proceed with the monotonous details of meticulously cleaning each one. I entertain myself by musing about what's going on in Jock's bed, directly above my head. As I push a wire brush through the gun chamber, I'm suddenly gripped by an impulse. I get up from my seat and turn the television monitor to face me. This monitor continuously displays pictures of the entire house and perimeter. I watch the images as I continue to clean.

As the camera scans Jock's office, suddenly Tree is standing in the doorway. I push a button on the remote to make the TV into a single screen showing only the scene in front of me. I watch as Tree enters his office. She's alone and clad only in a pair of panties. She closes the door behind her. I push the intercom button and can hear the whirring of the fan and a creak as Tree lowers her half-naked body into the office chair.

She picks up the receiver to the dedicated-fax phone line, dials a number, and sits back watching her teddy spin around. She speaks softly and I can only hear snippets of her conversation. She opens the top drawer of Jock's desk and rifles through the contents as she speaks. I know that the drawer contains his wallet, passport, car keys and credit cards.

In the bits of sentences I catch, Tree sounds like my sixteen-year-old niece. Her conversation is peppered with "No way!" and "Oh my God, no way!" The volume of her voice carelessly increases and I hear what sounds like an announcement. "Guess who I did last night?" Pause. Then "Oh, aren't you smart!" she coos. "Don't ask me stupid questions, just know that I did him." She spins around in the chair. "I'm not sure I'm gonna make it to class today, maybe drill team, though."

I wonder if Jock knows how young this one is. I watch closely as she flips through his passport, scans his checkbook, then takes a wad of bills and his credit card out of his desk, right here in front of my eyes.

I put the gun down and rush up the stairs. Running down the hallway and bursting into his office, I scare Tree. She covers her naked chest with one hand and tries to shove the credit card and money down into the cushion of the leather chair.

I must be a fright, huffing and puffing, madder than hell, holding out my hand to indicate she'd better hand over what she's in the process of stealing. She picks up the phone receiver she dropped.

"I'm gonna have to call you later."

She hangs up without ever taking her eyes off me.

I stare down this little hussy, sitting here in Jock's office, ripping him off while he's in the shower washing off last night's sex. Between the two of them, I'm vacillating about which one is worse. It doesn't matter. I have a kid to feed, clothe and put through college. Who is Jock going to question if his money goes missing? The help. The thought of Concepcion or me getting blamed for this slut's thievery makes me fume.

"You better get your 'ho ass' out of this house."

Tree's eyes widen. "Excuse me? Who are you?"

"I'm Jock's assistant."

I'm also a mom and Jock is one of my relatively helpless "kids," led around by a brain not firmly attached in his head, but all too often tethered in southern regions.

"Now, without a fuss, missy, give me what you just shoved under the cushion, get your clothes on, and get out of here."

She looks at me incredulously.

"I don't have any way to get home. Jock picked me up. Jock has to take me home," she states with her lower lip starting to tremble.

"You can call your mama and have her pick you up at Sunfax Arco down on Sunset and Fairfax. Get it done and get walking before Jock gets out of the shower."

Tree suddenly looks genuinely frightened. She throws the cash and credit card down and rushes past me. I wait in the hallway, feeling triumphant and, might I say, a bit cocky.

Tree rushes from Jock's bedroom wearing hip-huggers and a tight pink T-shirt over her bare breasts. With a nail file in one hand and her purse in the other, she brushes past me and bolts out the front door. Watching from the office monitor as she hurries down the front brick steps, I see her fumble with the permission-to-exit buttons, then leave.

A small trickle of wetness runs down my arm where Tree pushed by, and blood stains my sweater. That witch stabbed me! Counting the years it's been since my last tetanus shot, I go back downstairs to finish the job I was summoned to do. I watch the monitor as Jock goes room to room looking for Tree. When he enters the office, he grumbles as he sees the money and credit card on the floor.

"What the hell?"

He picks them up, then heads for the phone. I punch the button to the intercom to release it, turn the monitor back around and am suddenly plunged back into peaceful silence. But only for a moment. I hear crackling, then Jock's voice over an intercom speaker.

"Corki, what happened up here?"

"I kicked her out," I say unabashedly, without any of the emotion I felt two minutes earlier.

"You did what? Come up here!"

I set down the guns and climb the stairs. Jock stands in the doorway, arms folded, with only a towel wrapped around his waist. I pray his towel doesn't fall off.

"Expound!"

I don't bother with stammering or nervousness.

"I was downstairs doing the cleaning when I looked up and saw Tree walking into your office. She started going through your desk and I saw her take your money, so I went upstairs and told her to leave. That's it. And if you don't believe me, rewind the tapes and you can see for yourself."

Jock doesn't say a word, but continues staring at me, arms still folded. I keep thinking his towel's going to unravel and the situation is going to be about fifteen times more uncomfortable than it is right now.

"So, I'm going back downstairs to finish what I came here to do," I say.

I turn around and head back down the stairs. Before I turn the corner at the bottom, Jock's emotions explode.

"Next time, mind your own fucking business."

You're welcome.

I finish my job, gather my things and walk to the front door. Hanging on the doorknob is Miss Tree's teddy with a note stuffed in it telling me to throw it in the garbage can outside.

I slowly drive down the hill from Jock's house and make sure to pass by Sunfax Arco. Like an obedient child, Tree waits by the phone, looking angry. Still reeling from my good fortune of catching her in the act, I pull into the parking lot and roll down the window.

"Did you get someone to pick you up?"

She flips me the bird. I guess that means yes.

I pull Lucy's blinding-yellow Ferrari 360 Modena out of the garage and back it up the narrow driveway toward the automated gate. The gate slides open and I go backward, up the hill and out blindly onto a relatively busy street. I don't like driving her car for this precise reason—it's impossible to see whether a car is coming around the bend.

Lucy's neighbors across the street will not allow her to put a fish-eye mirror on their property—one that would allow her to see if a car is coming. I think they *want* her Ferrari smashed to smithereens. To see someone driving a car worth the price of a three-bedroom home in West Hollywood galls some people. I just don't want to be the person behind the wheel on the day the smashing occurs.

This car is so unlike Lucy. Unfortunately, the end of the lease on her Mercedes coincided with the start of her relationship with an Italian director who had a penchant for fast cars and faster women. Lucy pleased him by leasing the car in which he envisioned her. The relationship broke up in one month. The lease, however, won't expire for another two years.

After dropping the Modena off to Giovanni at the Italian Stallion service department, I go through my wallet for taxi fare. I'm frighteningly low on petty cash. I won't even be able to pay the taxi driver to get back to Lucy's. Ever since I was robbed in broad daylight a number of years back, I try not to carry too much money on me unless it's absolutely necessary. I lock most of my clients' petty cash in my safe-deposit box to access as needed.

The taxi pulls up and I get into the backseat.

"The City National Bank on Doheny and Sunset, please."

I barely get my seatbelt on before Mustafa, the taxi driver, burns rubber and shoots down La Cienega.

My phone rings.

"Corki, tell me I'm not fucking amazing!"

"Who is this?" I demand.

"It's Esther, you idiot."

"Oh! Okay, you're amazing," I lie.

"Tuesday morning at eight-thirty your son, Eden and Star will all start at Envision Prep. You don't need an interview. You don't have to pay one red cent. You just need to go there beforehand and fill out all the paperwork. No more crackheads pandering to the kids outside school. Your son will receive the best education private school offers," she states proudly.

"Well, Esther, this *is* amazing!"

"No, not 'this,' *I* am amazing," she demands.

"Pardon me, *you* are amazing. Thank you."

"Glad you acknowledged just how fantastic I am. And you're welcome. Call Shelly and her sister and arrange a time to go take care of the paperwork. Do it this week because Envision is closed next Monday for a teacher-training day. Bye."

Mustafa's driving is getting me sick to my stomach. He rushes toward the stop signs and then abruptly crunches down on the brake pedal at the last second. The sound of metal on metal doesn't deter him whatsoever. I can't let go of the door handle to put my cell phone away. Ten minutes later, we pull up into the driveway at City National and I exit the cab, thankful to be alive. I instruct him to wait for me even though I'm not looking forward to his extreme maneuvering in the hills leading up to Lucy's home.

I wait in line for an authorized teller to sign the appropriate papers, then let me into the vault. We use her key along with mine to open my safe-deposit box.

Just as my teller leaves the vault, another teller escorts in a young blond couple with cameras hung around their necks. A strange clicking sound emits from the vault's doorway and the teller hurries out, closing a metal gate behind her, then shoving closed the foot-thick steel vault door behind her. The air suddenly fills with a bizarre, electrical burning smell. The wretched odor overcomes me and I start coughing violently. My throat burns from the acrid, pungent, gaseous smell, and my nose starts dripping blood down my face.

I pull my sweater up over my face and search my purse for my hankie. Tears are pouring out of my eyes and my nose is bleeding heavily. Choking on the gas, I huddle in a far corner, as far away from the door as I can get, cradling my safe-deposit box. Through my tears and burning eyes, I look over at the couple and can barely make out their shapes, seemingly bathed in purple, crouched in the far corner. I try to speak but can't without coughing so hard my lungs feel ready to explode. I wonder what Mustafa is going to charge me for making him wait.

What seems like forever passes, and the vault door is unlocked. The bolts slide back, the door opens and a German shepherd police dog, in a bulletproof vest, bursts in, barking and snarling. His vicious stance holds me and the other couple at bay, as if we're in any position to take him on.

Four members of the Beverly Hills Police Department enter, shouting orders, guns drawn. The police drag the couple off the floor, handcuff them and drag them out of the vault. One officer looks at me, radios an ambulance, then approaches and kneels down next to me. Even though my eyes are blurry, I can see that he happens to be a very fine-looking man.

Why is it when you look like you've been beaten up, someone appears who looks like a knight in shining armor?

"Ma'am, can you get up with my help?" he asks, gently.

"Yeah, I think so," I cough.

I struggle to stand up and find myself a little woozy and unbalanced. He walks me to the vault door and I promptly throw up.

"Ma'am, there's an ambulance right outside. Come this way with me."

I feel too sick to be as embarrassed as I should be. The ambulance attendant helps me take off my sweater and seats me in the back of the ambulance. He's a gentle man with a warm glow to his olive skin.

"My name's Angelo. What's yours?"

"Cornelia, but I go by Corki," I cough.

"Okay, Corki, I'm going to be putting plugs in your nose to stop the bleeding. Are you hurt anywhere else?"

I shake my head.

"What about this on your arm?" he asks as he pulls up my shirt-sleeve.

"Oh yeah," I whisper, "someone stabbed me with a nail file earlier today."

Angelo raises his eyebrows. "Must be your lucky day. How long has it been since your last tetanus shot?"

"I was afraid you were going to ask that. I'm not sure, but it's been a long time. Eight, nine years."

"Close enough for me. You need one every ten years," he says as he inserts two plugs that look curiously like a couple of slender tampons up my nostrils. He then puts drops in my eyes and gives me a tetanus shot. With the tampon nose plugs and strings draping down tickling my upper lip, my shining knight comes back to take my account of the incident for the police report. I have no hopes of flirting with this man when I'm sitting here looking like a five-year-old who got into her mama's medicine chest.

Mustafa is long gone.

"Tell me more, Mom. Did the robbers have guns?"

Blaise sits in the hallway outside the bathroom, pressing for more details. He has visions of Wild West robberies complete with horses, covered wagons and Indians with bows and arrows.

I can only whisper. My windpipe burns and every breath stings like it will be my last. I try to turn over in my bubble bath, but can barely move. I whisper hoarsely to Blaise the story that was told to me.

"A young couple in their twenties robbed a bank in Arizona and were given a pack of money filled with purple dye. That's what tellers are supposed to do when they're robbed. If everything goes well, the dye pack explodes when triggered by the bank's detection system. But it didn't. The robbers got away, and thought they'd be smart and come to Los Angeles and put it in a safe-deposit box to use at their discretion. Only problem was that *my* bank's detection system *did* work and it exploded, flooding the whole place with tear gas. Unfortunately, I got caught in the bank vault with the robbers."

"But did they have guns?" Blaise asks.

"No guns. It wasn't *that* exciting. The police kept calling it a freak accident."

"Wow! I can't wait to tell my friends about this," he continues. "It's so cool."

"Cool, huh?" I squeak.

"Yeah, really cool!"

I tuck Blaise into bed, then fall into bed myself. For once, I don't bother with the answering machine. All night I wheeze, suck in burning air, cough violently, spit up phlegm that tastes like tear gas, and cry. I slurp teaspoons full of cough medicine with codeine that sedates me for short intervals, but my coughing continues, unabated.

At seven-thirty the next morning, Shelly picks up Blaise and takes him to school with the girls. They leave, chatting happily about Envision Prep, bank robberies and Mama Corki's bravery, as if I took down the robbers myself.

I sit down at my desk to make a series of painful phone calls. Some people take my whispering voice as that of a crank caller. Half of them hang up and I need to redial and try again. The other half say I sound as if I've been smoking three packs a day since I turned ten.

I schedule a slew of doctor's appointments and cancel other appointments I had set for today and tomorrow. Finally, I brave listening to my phone messages.

Call number one is from Veronique.

"Corki, it's Veronique. I'm back in town. I hope your Christmas and New Year's Eve were good. Let's meet at Joan's on Third. Love to you and Blaise." Beep.

Call number two.

"Corki, Jock Straupman."

He sounds cold and distant, still angry.

"I'm leaving for Paris tomorrow night. I'm going to need enough vitamins for six months. I don't want to have to go through the fiasco we went through last time I was in Spain. While I'm gone, I'll need for you to take care of the cars, have the piano tuned right before I come home and at some point change the felt on the pool table, maybe an aqua color this time. Use your judgment. Have the pool heater turned down, or actually off, and cancel the florist. Most importantly, I want to have my room painted red. I left the colors for the walls and bookcases in the office. I've moved some stuff, but I want *you* to move the remaining six boxes down to the range and leave them there until I come back. I spoke with the painters and they'll be starting early in February. Please take care of all this as soon as you can. Call Squid and he'll give you an address where you can send my mail. I think twice a month should be sufficient. Thank you."

The next call is from Lucy, sounding higher than a balloon filled with helium.

"Sweetheart, hello! We haven't spoken since the party. Where were you? It was fabulous. I personally think you missed one of my best yet. Everyone loved the favors. Listen, we popped over to Maui for the week and should be home day after tomorrow. I need you to do me a couple of favors."

Her Southern accent is full and lively.

"I want you to go and get a bunch of CDs. In fact, I'm going to be totally anal-retentive and just fax you a list from the hotel. Love you, bye."

I look behind the desk and see four pages curled up on the floor. The list consists of forty-three compact discs, mostly country-and-western: Buck Owens, Johnny Cash, Dwight Yoakum, ZZ Top, Elvis, John Prine and Duane Diamond. She wants them to be opened and mixed in with everything else in her CD case in order to give the appearance that she gave a shit about Buck Owens's music before she met Tommy Ray. I wonder if she'll want me to get a set of bull's horns for the front of the Ferrari.

She also instructs me to rid the house of "ANYTHING and EVERYTHING pre-1940s" and "ANYTHING and EVERY-THING that looks too classy." I am to pack the antique silverware and put it in my garage. Put the rococo-style table that is in the foyer in the garage as well. Wrap it in blankets. And for God's sake hide the old English china her grandmother gave her. Use my judgment and clear the house of anything sentimental from old boyfriends or from men who happen to be friends or, come to think of it, *anything* from *any* man unless it is from her own father. In addition, she wants me to collect all her old diaries, love letters, former wedding rings and personal mementos from past movies, love interests and co-stars. All these items should be packed in boxes and stored at *my* apartment. "And by the way, as soon as we get home we're going to be looking into buying a house together. Be happy for us."

I think about the limited space in my place and the equally limited space in Lucy's brain. What on earth is this woman thinking? My garage seems to be a favorite spot for movie stars to hide all their belongings that they don't want their new mates to discover. I have no room to even park my car, let alone another six or seven boxes filled with Lucy's love-life paraphernalia. The last remaining room in my garage was taken up by the four-hundred-pound gun cabinet that Esther insisted leave their home when she married Liam. Liam swore that after the L.A. riots, he was not going to be caught defenseless. He bought a heavy metal pump shotgun and a .357 Magnum—now sitting in my garage. Liam bought the cabinet because someday he said he'd sign up to take lessons on how to the shoot the darn things and until that day, the arsenal must be safely tucked away behind lock and key. That was years ago and Liam has never found the time to learn. I, however, have enough guns and ammo in my quiet little home to fight a small revolution.

The last call is from Officer Gregory Holt from the Beverly Hills Police Department, stating that I should call the department if I want to press charges against the couple foiled in the bank incident.

Going through with pressing charges will be awfully time-consuming. I return his call and leave a message for him that I will press charges if they need me to because it is my civic duty, but I get paid by the hour and every hour spent doing something other than work is money gone.

Chapter Eight

Packing as many chores into one stop as possible, I tell Veronique that we can meet at Joan's on Third, our favorite small, casual restaurant. Since it's Lucy's favorite, too, I call ahead and order food to pick up for her and Tommy Ray's arrival home.

The place is packed. Joan's is one of the spots celebrities go to *not* be seen. The celebrities I "haven't" seen there range from Shari Belafonte with a cap pulled down over her eyes to Cameron Diaz in a corner playing footsie with Justin Timberlake.

When my sixteen-year-old niece, Stephanie, came into town from the San Francisco Bay area, she requested to be taken "somewhere, anywhere" where she might see a celebrity. I took her to Joan's, and Matthew Perry walked in. Stephanie spotted him and morphed into what looked strangely like my old cat who used to sit on the windowsill watching hummingbirds. Her mouth opened and her chin quivered ever so slightly, and it was as if at any moment she might pounce and move in for the kill. For days afterward all she could talk about was how she wished she'd had the presence of mind to speak to him or at least whip out her camera and take his picture.

I push past the throngs of diners waiting in line to order or pay their bills and find Veronique at a corner table in the back. In true movie star form, she's wearing sunglasses.

After hugs and kisses, we sit down to turkey meatloaf, chili aioli and Szechuan green beans. I recount my being fired by Daisy, abandoned for six months by Jock and my bank robbery to explain why my voice is so hoarse.

"Don't take offense, Veronique, because I love working for you, but I can only take so many hits. I need a new job, like soon!"

"You're right. You do! But not until you finish helping me."

"Tell me what you need."

"I'm presenting Best Supporting Actor this year. And that won't take too much time, but I've been offered a part in a movie filming for three weeks in New Mexico right in the midst of it all. I only shoot for ten days and I'll be back and forth in between then. It's going to be hectic and I have a new boyfriend. He's coming from Italy to stay with me for a while. I really need you to cook for him, Corki."

"Hmmm. I thought you were looking a bit rosy in the cheeks. Who is he?"

"Roberto Tratelli. Dependable. Independent. Loving. Affectionate. Dreamy. A count."

"Account? He's an accountant?"

Veronique leans forward.

"No. He's a count."

"Get out. Like Dracula?"

"Yeah. Count Roberto."

"Sounds sexy."

"It is sexy," she purrs saucily as she rubs the diamond cross hanging around her neck.

"And?" I urge.

"I met him on the set when we were filming in Rome. He's *not* in the film industry," she says emphatically. "His brother is."

"Thank God for small favors. Continue."

"He's a commercial real-estate developer. A magnate. He's very well established, well mannered and well bred."

"Well, well, well!"

"I don't think he's your stereotypical Italian fare. He's quite reserved, a widower—his wife of fifteen years died in a car accident. He's a staunch Catholic and, well, you know, I've always flirted with Catholicism."

"And no doubt you're flirting much harder now," I add.

"No doubt."

"Back to the count part," I prod.

"That's his title. His money comes from his business," she says matter-of-factly.

"It may be just a title, but I confess, I'm impressed. It's not a title anyone I know has. You?" I ask.

"No. I mean I met Prince Charles once at a film premiere in London, but I don't *know* him," Veronique says.

"Would you move to Italy if you marry him?" I ask.

"Corki, you're jumping too far ahead. But he is going to take me on his yacht for a tour of the Med."

"Oh, impressive. *Molto impressionante!*"

"*Grazie!* For the here and now, though, I need you to cook for him while he's here. I would attempt to, but you know my cooking—less than impressive."

"I would be happy to do it. What does he like?"

"I don't know!" she confesses. "Surprise him!"

. . .

Surprise him. Surprise him. What meals would surprise a count? I try to think of all the small corners of the world whose cuisine might be fresh and exciting to Roberto Tratelli and can't come up with one. This is going to haunt me all night until I can come up with something new and fresh.

Balancing Lucy's bags of take-out food carefully while waiting for a break in the stream of cars, I run across the street and pass the place where I used to be able to afford manicures. I nod and mouth "Hello" to the ladies working there behind the large glass window painted with delicate, long hands showing the different colors of nail polish and French manicures they perform.

They wave to me as I disarm Betty and roll down the back window to place the bags of food in the trunk space.

"Uhhhh!" I hear.

I look around.

"Mmmmm."

There it is again. I look under the SUV. Nothing.

"Uhhhh!"

I roll Betty's back window up, realarm her and go to investigate, slowly walking around to the passenger side. I hear what sounds distinctly like a baby's wail.

Phlit!

A wad of something hits my leg. White viscous fluid is dripping on the cuff of my jeans. I look up and see a pasty-faced, unshaven guy dressed in sweats shoving his penis back in his pants. He runs away.

I can't even muster a scream. My vocal cords have been burned by the tear gas and the doctor told me my windpipe and lungs now resemble those of a man on the front lines in war. I look back toward the manicurists' shop to see if anyone else noticed what happened.

A young woman getting a pedicure sits close to the window, her short skirt revealing her thigh and crotch as she holds up her leg for a heel scrub.

Disgusted, but trying to force my mind not to dwell on what just transpired, I dig through Betty and find four old napkins from the last fast-food run Blaise and I made a few days ago. I wad them up and attempt to wipe the semen off my pants. Where are the cops when you need them? They'll probably arrive the one time in my life when I litter by throwing the napkins down on the curb. I'll end up with a three-figure citation.

"Dang, girl, you have a good old selection here! We should have taken these to Maui with us, Lucy." Tommy Ray continues to scan the rows and rows of Lucy's music. "How can you say the CDs you have might not be to my taste? I see Buck Owens, Duane Diamond, Johnny Cash, Dwight Yoakum, ZZ Top, John Prine. I've never seen a better collection. You even have some of Elvis's best stuff."

I smile politely at Lucy, who stands over Tommy Ray, acting as if her newly fortified collection of CDs is old hat. Lucy mouths the words "thank you" to me as she strokes the back of Tommy's neck.

I smile and nod my head slightly to acknowledge her.

"Lucy, let's bring along some of these for the road," Tommy suggests. "You almost ready?"

"Honey, now that Corki's here, we don't have to go. We can stay right here," Lucy says seductively. "Corki can go pick up the car."

Tommy swings around and playfully nips Lucy on the thigh. "Meow!" he purrs. They tumble on the floor and start kissing and fondling each other.

I clear my throat.

"Corki, don't be so uptight," Tommy Ray manages as he gets on top of Lucy and straddles her. "You ain't never seen live sex shows before?"

"Tommy Ray, shut up," Lucy says playfully. "Get off me!" she says, pushing him off of her.

Tommy uses a wrestling move and negotiates her into a half nelson. She squeals with joy.

"Corki, ignore us," Lucy whispers.

"Lord, girl, can't you tell when two people need to be alone? Get the girls and all of you go pick up Lucy's car together," he demands.

Before I can ask what girls he's talking about, two come out of *Lucy's* bedroom. They *are* mere girls, maybe nineteen or twenty. Both of them rub sleep from their eyes and both wear men's, probably Tommy's, pajamas.

The taller of the two is very pretty with long, blondish hair and a cattish grin plastered across her face. As she passes by, I can smell the scent of old cigarette smoke clinging to her hair.

The shorter one has a decidedly round face reminiscent of a ball of rolled pie dough. Her already big, wide-set brown eyes appear larger than normal behind Coke-bottle-thick magnifying lenses set in tortoiseshell frames.

The "girls" giggle between themselves, then, without warning, the prettier one pounces on top of Tommy Ray and Lucy and they all start wrestling around together, hugging, kissing and saying good morning.

I look at my watch. It's 2:15 P.M.

Pie Dough looks on affectionately, then wanders down the hall toward the kitchen.

"Corki, I want you to meet Jolene McGraw; Jolene, this is my friend, Corki Brown," Lucy says in a winded, exasperated rush.

"Nice to meet you," I say.

I don't mean it.

"Real nice to meet you, too," Jolene says with as hard a drawl as Tommy's.

"And the other girl . . ." Lucy stops, then calls out to the kitchen. "Bobby Sue Hunsucker, get in here and meet Corki. Don't be antisocial."

Bobby Sue peeks her pie-dough face around the corner.

"Nice to meet you, Corki," she says in a flat tone.

I return the coolness.

"Likewise."

I fidget, not quite wanting to say "Could you two get off your asses and get dressed so we can get going to pick up Lucy's car."

"Lucy, why don't I just catch a taxi. The service department closes at four on the dot and it takes a good thirty minutes to get there at this time of day," I plead, wanting to vacate the premises immediately.

"Slow down, woman. Give the girls a moment to shower and they'll get you over there. Jolene here was my driver on my last movie, she'll get you there soon enough," Tommy protests. "Besides, I want you to show them the ropes."

What's that supposed to mean? My Spider-Man "spidey senses" are tingling. I sense a hostile takeover on the brink of invasion.

The girls go back into Lucy's bedroom to get dressed, and I go to the kitchen, make myself a cup of tea and wait. I'm still waiting one hour later. It's now three-thirty, rush hour, Los Angeles time. The repair place closes in thirty minutes.

About to give up and just go home, I walk out into the foyer just as Jolene and Bobby Sue slowly exit Lucy's bedroom. Lucy and Tommy Ray come out of the living room after them. As if they're off for a trip around the world, Jolene and Bobby Sue throw their arms around Lucy and Tommy Ray and they all exchange goodbye kisses on the mouth. I watch this display and notice that when Jolene kisses Tommy goodbye, she slips him the tongue.

I get into the back of Tommy's rented Mercedes while Jolene gets behind the wheel and Bobby Sue, with her freshly powdered face, gets in the front passenger seat. I give them directions on how to get down the hill and into L.A.

Jolene can't drive to save her life. Her foot keeps tapping on the accelerator, then takes turns tapping on the brakes. She drives only a little bit slower than Mustafa. She also carries on an elaborate conversation with Bobby Sue without so much as glancing at the road. We fly down Coldwater Canyon where sharp turns and big, thick pine trees line the road. Under many trees are flowers, crosses and ribbons memorializing the people killed there. I don't want to die sharing a car with these two.

"You might want to slow down up here!" I offer. "It's a tricky curve."

"Don't worry, I drive for the union back in Tennessee."

She keeps up the same pace and the same conversation. I sit back, close my eyes and pray that it's not going to end like this.

"So, Corki! Tommy Ray says you're gonna teach us the ropes," Bobby Sue says brightly.

"What ropes are those?"

"You know, like what you do for them. Where you shop, what you get, what they like," Bobby Sue says.

"Well, we already know what Tommy likes," Jolene interjects, nastily.

They laugh to each other, confirming my suspicions.

Lucy's mama, Beryl, will blow a gasket when she takes one look at Jolene. I can already hear her lecturing Lucy to make Tommy Ray get that "blatant hussy" out of his life or else. Lucy's not brave enough to give a man an ultimatum though. The cost of losing him is too high.

"Are you two working for them?" I probe.

"Oh yeah," says Bobby Sue. "Tommy Ray says he needs folks from back home so he can be comfortable here. He doesn't work too well with you Hollywood types."

You Hollywood types.

"Mostly it's just stuff you'll be too busy to do. Like Lucy says you have a little boy, so you can't really travel with her as much as you used to. And she said you work with other people, too, so you're not available as much as she'll be needing you," Jolene adds.

"I've never not been available for Lucy," I say, defensively.

"Oh no, she never said you weren't, but what with Tommy Ray and all. He has a lot of needs. He's sort of a high-maintenance hick." Bobby Sue titters at Jolene's remark.

"He always says he can call himself white trash, but he don't want no one else to say that," Bobby Sue adds.

I let them keep talking, resolving not to give any of my information away for free.

We pull into the Stallion repair place and I tell them I can take it from here. Then, as if I'm graciously teaching them "the ropes," I offer, "This is where I get Lucy's car repaired. I'd let you two drive it back, but I'm the only additionally insured driver."

They drop me off and leave at 3:59. As I pay for the repairs with Lucy's credit card, I call her on my cell phone.

"Hey, it's me. Listen, the girls took so long, I'm going to have to pick up Blaise from school before I return your car. I hope that's okay."

"Take all the time you need. We're not going anywhere," Lucy purrs.

In the background, I can hear Tommy Ray laughing as Lucy hangs up without a goodbye.

Ever since the 1994 Northridge earthquake knocked down a part of the freeway that affected all north- and southbound traffic, Angelenos's driving patterns have changed. What used to be a quick bypass for me on Crescent Heights Boulevard is now the clogged normal route for drivers trying to make it south to Inglewood or north to Hollywood. Even after the freeway overpass was reconstructed, commuters stuck to their newly learned patterns.

I creep along Crescent Heights in Lucy's yellow Ferrari just like all the other creatures of habit heading home after a long day of work. My cell phone rings.

"Hello," I say, on autopilot.

"Corki, this is Drew Cheriff from Three Arts Entertainment."

The name sounds familiar, but I can't place her immediately.

"Yes?" I say.

"Your name and number were given to me by a member of the team at Brillstein Grey. I'm calling because you were highly recommended as a reliable personal assistant. Our client Jennifer Aniston needs a full-time assistant to help her."

Drew continues explaining what will be needed, what the pay is and the extent of benefits, time off, vacation pay, sick days, etc.

"Drew, I am very interested in this position and I think I could be of great assistance to Jennifer," I say in my best professional manner.

We make an appointment for the next afternoon at three o'clock to meet in their offices on Wilshire Boulevard in Beverly Hills. With Daisy gone, Jock absent for six months, Lucy handing out my work to her lover's assistants, Liam and Esther only needing me occasionally and Veronique potentially running off to Italy with her new man, Corki Brown has been left high and dry.

I've always avoided working for just one person, because celebrities often "clean house," leaving their personal assistants to fend for themselves. But here is an opportunity to work for someone at the top who has a reputation as being an honest, fair woman. And she is willing to pay handsomely, with medical and a 401(k) to boot!

As I pull up in front of Blaise's school, I feel like a weight is off my shoulders. Maybe my career's future won't be as grave as I thought.

I walk quickly through the schoolyard and see Blaise playing handball with his friends. Quietly, I sit on a bench and wait for him to finish the game. Afterward, he and his playmates run up and a young Russian boy named Boris plops down next to me.

"Mrs. Brown? Blaise called me Stalin."

"Blaise! What an ugly name to call him!" I say, embarrassed.

"Mom, I said he was stalling."

"No, you said I was Stalin," Boris says, indignantly.

"You were!" Blaise exclaims.

"Enough," I say. "Just apologize to Boris for the misunderstanding."

They exchange apologies, shake hands, and we walk toward the parking lot.

"Guess what? I have Lucy's car instead of ours."

"Very cool. Can we drive through the parking lot one time so my friends can see me in it?"

"Sure."

My phone rings. It's Shelly.

"Oh my God, Corki, I'm so glad I got you. Slight emergency. My sister and I went to Arcadia to buy some Indian fabric and now we're stuck in traffic. There is no way we're going to get home in time to pick up the girls. Are you available for a rescue?"

"How much money do you have?" I joke.

"However much you need. We'll be back in L.A. probably right around six to six-thirty. You're a lifesaver."

I hustle up Eden and Star from various places on the playground. While they admire the car, I come to grips with the fact that Ferraris only have two seats. I have four people. Ferraris don't come with a minivan option or small bucket seats in the back. With the children's hips squeezed harder than they've ever been squeezed before, and the seatbelt stretched around all three, I start the engine and head for Lucy's.

As I cross into the Beverly Hills city limits, lights behind me twirl red and blue and a short blip of a siren tells me to pull over. I do so and wait for the sunglasses-and-bulletproof-vest-clad officer to approach. I keep my hands on the top of the steering wheel and stare straight ahead as every black person, no matter what sex or how light of skin, is taught to do by their elders upon the day of receiving their driver's license.

"Driver's license and proof of registration please, ma'am."

I pull the registration from the leather owner's manual in the glove compartment and slowly wrestle my purse from under the kids' legs. Knowing good and well that I'm breaking the law by having so many people stuffed in a two-seater, along with my license and insurance papers, I hand him my CCW, my license to carry a concealed weapon. It's gotten me out of trouble before. CCWs, when presented, let the officer know that the owner has been cleared with the Department of Justice and perhaps the officer should cut this person some slack. I also know the reputation of the Beverly Hills Police Department, hard-ass and unforgiving. I've never had to deal with them before.

"Ma'am, is there a weapon in the vehicle?"

"No, I don't think so, but it's not my car so I'm not sure. However, I do have permission to drive it. In fact, you'll notice that my name is listed as an insured driver."

The officer doesn't say anything. I sit quietly. My three charges don't utter a peep. He takes my information back to his cruiser and gets inside. We all wait in silence. I see through the rearview mirror that he is returning.

"Miss Brown, will you please step out of the vehicle."

Son of a bitch. I know I'm in trouble now. My legs are trembling as I exit the car. I wonder what he's going to do with the children while he's hauling me off to jail for endangering kids' lives by piling them in the car as if I'm trying to break a world record in a 1960s Volkswagen cramming session. I step up onto the curb and finally look directly at the officer. He looks severe and tough, with his police-issue sunglasses that penetrate me like laser beams.

"Cornelia Wren Brown?" he says, seriously.

"Yes, sir."

"You clean up pretty nicely."

"Sir?"

Mr. Police Officer cracks a slight smile followed by removal of his laser beams, and I realize that this SOB was my knight in shining armor a few days ago at the bank.

"Officer Holt, right?" I ask, relieved.

"Gregory Holt, yes," he says as he extends his hand. "Nice to remake your acquaintance under better circumstances."

I take his hand and unabashedly hold it for too long. Shelly always says that I am *way* too flirtatious, but I notice he doesn't mind.

"I don't know if getting pulled over on Sunset Boulevard with all of L.A. driving by is a 'better circumstance,'" I say, sweetly.

"Well," he ponders, "all things considered, I'd rather be pulled over than pulled out of a tear-gas-filled vault."

"Come to think of it, me too." Embarrassed, I clear my throat, cough a few times for good measure and go on to explain how I stuffed four people into a two-seater and more importantly, *why* I stuffed four people into a two-seater. Gregory, as he asks me to call him, lets me go without a ticket. I can't wait to call Shelly. For the first time in what feels like forever, a guy has asked me out. I have a date!

After hustling the kids into Betty, I back Lucy's Ferrari down the hill into the garage the way Lucy likes because she always skims the bushes trying to back out uphill. I look around, but don't see the Mercedes that Jolene and Bobby Sue were driving, anywhere.

Knocking on the door lightly, I let myself in and put the car keys on the kitchen counter—the usual spot Lucy and I leave things for each other. A note for me is there under a fancy vase with a pointed, decorative lid. It reads: "Corki, Please see me before you go. Love, L."

I walk through the house. The place is dead quiet.

"Lucy!" I call out in a whisper. "Luuuu-cyyyy," I try a bit louder. No answer.

Suddenly, her bedroom door opens and she comes out in a light pink thong and nothing else. She doesn't bother to cover her bare breasts except to hunch her back and put her index finger up to her mouth to shush me. She motions for me to follow her to the kitchen. I follow her, tiptoeing across the wood floors.

Without a hint of reservation or modesty, she gathers up a few rolls of film setting on the counter, puts her hand in mine and deposits the film.

"Corki, these rolls have some extremely private pictures on them. I want you to get them developed, but when you do, I expect you to stand behind the man doing it and watch to make sure he gives you one copy of every picture and *all* the negatives. Understand?"

"Of course. But Lucy, everything is computerized these days. These pictures can be regenerated without the negatives! Maybe you should have used a Polaroid or, better yet, a digital camera."

"Well, these are already done and the moments can't be re-created, so I need them developed. But you have to promise to stand right over him. I don't want any copies getting out," she restates emphatically.

We stand there for a moment in silence. I know I need to ask her if I'm about to lose my job to Jolene and Bobby Sue. Looking down, I stare at the film she's entrusted me with.

"Lucy, I need to talk to you about—"

"Oh, I'm sorry, I do have one more thing to talk to you about. As I said, Tommy and I are going to buy a house together and I don't want to hear one complaint. Just be happy for us," she says as she playfully holds her hand over my mouth.

I try to concentrate on what she's saying instead of where her hand has been.

"Tommy Ray's in a weird position living in a hotel and all, and the girls are just moving here so they're sort of in transition, too. And here we are planning on moving and getting rid of stuff. We need to just clean everything out. You know I have so much stuff I can never find anything I need. I think you're the only one who knows where everything is in my life."

"Yes," I reply, "it's all in my apartment and garage . . . a very full garage, I might add. In fact, every year when I do my taxes and the IRS insists that I can't write off eighty percent of my place as workspace, I invite them over."

Lucy smiles as she places her hand on the beautiful vase under which my note lay earlier. She hesitates a moment.

"You know I'm a little phobic about certain things, Corki. Well, Tommy wants me to keep this in a safe place, but I just can't do it. You know me. I really need you to keep this in your house, in a safe place, not in your garage."

She hands me the vase, which is surprisingly heavy.

"This is his most prized possession and he wants to know where it is at all times. He needs to know it's safe, and with all the packing and everything, I could see it getting lost really easily here."

"Lucy, how much is this worth?" I ask.

"It's irreplaceable," she says.

"Does he have adequate insurance on it that will cover it staying at my house? Some policies—"

"Corki, it's *irreplaceable*. It can't be insured. It's his mother."

I almost drop the vase as I put it back on the counter with a thud. "Lucy, I've got Blaise waiting in the car. I think I better go and maybe we can discuss this later."

Lucy picks it up, puts it in a Whole Foods double paper bag and hands it to me with a look that means I can't say no.

"Corki, don't be squeamish. This is the woman who gave birth to the man I love, and we need you to watch over her. Oh, and Tommy's so sweet, he offered to take over your weekly paycheck *and* give you that three-dollar-an-hour raise you were asking for so I won't have to worry about it since I'm between films."

I pull the bag close to my chest and hold the rolls of film, forgetting everything else that needed to be said.

Chapter Nine

Envision Preparatory Academy looks like a California Jesuit mission, with red-tiled roofs and white stucco walls divided by walkways with wide arches and coved ceilings. I remember my elementary school of boxlike buildings and feel a tinge of jealousy. With architecture like this, I would have been thrilled to go to school every day. I weave Betty through Bentleys and Land Rovers in the parking lot and find a space. A minute later, Shelly pulls her car in next to mine.

Eden, Star and Blaise don't look nervous at all, but Shelly and I throw anxious glances at one another as we escort them to their new classroom.

"Thank goodness they're all in one room together," Shelly says with a nervous smile.

I take the school registration slip out of my purse and notice its strap is about to break. Great. One more expense I can't afford right now.

"Room 303. Mrs. Blessing," I read.

With a rock the size of a marble on her perfectly manicured hand, it seems she certainly has been blessed. Her white linen suit looks like something the children had better not touch.

On the way out, we pass by Bruce Willis dropping off his daughters and Billy Bob Thornton dropping off his boys.

"You think this is the right environment for them?" I ask.

"I don't know," Shelly says. "I hope they won't feel out of place. I've never seen kids with Hermès backpacks and Coach hats before."

"Aside from Bruce and Billy over there, I see mostly nannies dropping off."

"Is Blaise excited?"

"He seemed really happy about the science lab, but not much else. What about the girls?"

"Eden's excited about learning Japanese and Star's thrilled with their ballet program . . . oh, and they both can't wait for the field trip to Washington, D.C."

"And here my sister Drusilla and I were ecstatic about taking a tour of the Wonder Bread factory when we were their age."

A redheaded woman with a tightly pulled face and high ears waves at us from a Jaguar.

"You know her?" Shelly asks as she waves back, smiling.

"No," I say, smiling and waving as if I do. "She doesn't look familiar."

The crimson red Jag pulls up and the passenger window rolls down. The woman leans over to talk to us.

"Hello there! I've seen you in my neighborhood," she says, pointing to Shelly, "and noticed how pretty you are."

"Wow, thanks," Shelly says, slightly embarrassed.

"My name's Eileen and I wonder if perhaps you have a few days free?"

"To do what?" Shelly asks.

"Clean my house . . . I assume you're a housekeeper."

Shelly stiffens. "You assume wrong."

Mortified, Eileen drives off.

We walk quietly to our cars.

"Maybe this isn't the right place for the kids."

"Yeah," I say, "I was thinking the same thing."

Shelly and I pull two huge rolling landscaper's wagons with industrial-sized wheels up the hill behind Esther's guesthouse. Mine has a large shovel in the back.

"I just couldn't let that Eileen woman think that I'm nothing but a housekeeper. I have a bachelor's degree, I was a recording studio mixer, and I'm a very good mom."

"And you were voted queen at your cotillion ball."

"That's right!" Shelly says indignantly. "Esther even calls me her 'friend.' She never lets the word 'housekeeper' or, God forbid, 'maid' pass her lips."

We struggle to pull the wagons up the hill while I pant and cough. "This is a man's job. The gardener should be doing this."

Finally, we rest at the top of the paved road with Shelly struggling to catch her breath and me wheezing.

"Now, tell me exactly why we're doing this," I cough.

Shelly waves her arm to sweep across the whole side of the dense-brush-covered hill.

"Esther saw Tom Selleck's place in Hawaii and she wants to imitate the paths on his property. But instead of conch shells lining them, she wants to use rocks, three to four inches wide."

"But there are tons of rattlesnakes up here," I say.

"Yeah, but it's still winter, if you call eighty-two degrees winter, and they should be hibernating. Esther had an expert come out a few weeks ago to teach me how to catch and rerelease them into the wild."

"With all due respect, if I see a snake, I'm killing it."

I put a bandanna around my nose so I won't breathe in dust, and Shelly does the same. We climb through the brush and collect rocks for an hour. When the wagons are full, we start down the hill.

"Corki, you must have a constitution of granite. If my lungs were in the condition yours are in, I'd be in a coffin."

"Rent's due and my work is running out. I have an interview this afternoon though. Jennifer Aniston. Wish me luck."

"Don't worry, you'll nail it."

Two hours later, standing under a flow of very hot water and letting the shower carry all the dirt and tension down the drain, I wash my hair and get ready for the interview that just may change the direction of my life.

I perfect my makeup, lightly spray on perfume that smells like freshly cut grass, slip on some pointy shoes, then stare into the mirror. Dear God, I actually look good. As Officer Gregory Holt said, I clean up pretty nicely. I'll be forty in a few days, but I think I could still pass for twenty-seven—in my deepest fantasies. Hiking my breasts up to look perfectly even and fluffy, the way they were before Blaise was born, I walk out the door.

The interview goes well. I'm professional, charming and witty. They are thorough and inquisitive. They ask all the questions for which I have prepared answers.

Back in my truck, I take off my shoes, which have become devices of torture, and replace them with sneakers. I drive toward my favorite quickie film-development center on Sunset Boulevard, across the street from a grocery store the locals have nicknamed "Rock 'n' Roll Ralph's." Twenty-four hours a day the place is filled with spiked hair, black leather and piercings of every variety.

I walk into the empty photo place and ask to speak to the owner. He scoots out from the back and rushes to meet me, pumping my hand with enthusiasm.

"Good to see you, Mrs. Brown. So nice of you to bring me your business. How can I help you today?"

"Well, Mr. Kim, I'm sorry to ask you this, but my client wants me to watch over your worker as he develops these," I say, slightly embarrassed.

"I see. Nasty pictures. Pornography," he says, flatly.

"Mr. Kim, all I know is what I was told to do," I say defensively. "I'm an innocent bystander."

"No, no, you good customer. I do 'em."

And with that, Mr. Kim raises his voice and yells to the guy who processes the film. They have what seems to be a heated exchange in Korean as I watch, waiting to hear the translated outcome. At last, Mr. Kim pulls a chair out from behind the counter next to the film-processing machine.

"Mrs. Brown, you sit here. This is Seung Jae. He will help you."

Seung Jae bows his head respectfully and I bow mine back, not sure if that's the proper thing to do. He takes the rolls of film and puts them in a dark baglike container. Twenty minutes and two *Us* magazines later, he threads the rolls of film through the machine and pictures pop up on a screen.

What on God's green earth was Lucy thinking? Tommy Ray on a bed with his back arched up holding his erect penis . . . Lucy photographing Tommy going down on her . . . Tommy sticking a dildo in Jolene and himself in Lucy. Jolene and Bobby Sue and Lucy going in a round with mouths and crotches all connected.

How could they record these acts on film that someone else would develop? If these three rolls of film fell into the wrong hands, some opportunist could make a ton of money. I can't blink and I sure don't want to look at Seung Jae. He doesn't flinch except to move some dials that change the light in the pictures. He adjusts the color on each print, then asks me how many copies of each I want.

I hesitate for a moment. A moment in which I recall that my living expenses exceed the amount that I am earning. A moment in which I am all too aware of the fact that I have very little savings. A split second where I remember I am almost forty years old and my job security is now being sucked down the tubes by the girls in the pictures with their mouths on Lucy's breasts. A moment of desperation in which I see that my twenty years of solid loyalty to Lucy means absolutely nothing.

I feel sick inside.

"Two, please," I say.

Chapter Ten

"Corki, I'm in a bit of a pinch," Veronique says on my answering machine before I can pick up.

"Hey! Just dropped Blaise off at school."

"Oh, thank God you're there. Roberto's in town now and it turns out I have to leave for New Mexico sooner than I thought. He has to stay here on business and I wanted to find out if there is any way you can cook for him *and* take care of my dog, too?"

"Well, yeah. My workload is featherweight right now. I'd be happy to."

"We've already discussed Roberto and Mr. Fu just needs to be fed, walked, his daily insulin shot and sunblock application. If it's cold, he needs his coat."

"That's fine. I can do that."

We arrange meal times and when to pick up more insulin and needles.

I sit and begin to plan some sample menus for Roberto. Homemade pumpkin seed granola with Greek yoghurt and berries or homemade flaxseed muffins with whipped honey butter and a fruit salad of mango, pineapple, blueberries and cherries for breakfasts. Lunches could be a choice of plantain-pear soup with lentils or shrimp corn chowder and a variety of organic grained breads with butter and salads—edamame and sautéed red cabbage or baby greens with chèvre and pistachios. Tamarind-glazed swordfish with a mango/pineapple relish, lobster and asparagus risotto and, the next day, lime and black-pepper chicken with roasted garlic potatoes for his dinner selections. I'll fix a variety of food for him to have on hand in case of a midnight snack attack. The only cuisine I hope might be a surprise is Caribbean—I've thrown in a little taste of Puerto Rico, Martinique and the Mexican Riviera as well.

For Mr. Fu, I'll prepare a sautéed lamb liver one day and organic boneless chicken breasts the next. I fax over the menu and Veronique approves immediately. I then call the pharmacy for a refill of insulin and hypodermic syringes for Veronique's eleven-year-old near-toothless, hairless, Chinese Crested dog who likes to follow me, growl and gum my heels.

I head toward my favorite West Hollywood pharmacy counting my blessings. With this new bit of work I may just make the rent this month and have enough to clear my car payment, too. My cell phone—which has been quiet as of late—rings. I don't recognize the number.

"Hello, this is Corki."

"Mrs. Brown, this is Mr. Davidson. I'm the principal here at Envision Prep."

God, not in the first week! He was so good when he was with me over Christmas. What is it now?

"I have your son, Blaise, in the office with me."

I breathe deeply and exhale completely.

"Yes. May I ask why?"

"I would like to have him explain it. Hold the line just one moment please."

Blaise gets on the phone.

"Mom, I . . . um, I didn't mean to . . . well, maybe I sort of did."

"Blaise, just tell me what happened."

"We had a science project and Atom and I made a volcano."

"And?"

"And we made it blow up . . . with real fire and lava made from mud and rocks."

"Did anything catch fire?" I ask, exhausted already.

"Just a bulletin board and the periodic table."

"All right, give me Mr. Davidson."

The principal comes back on the phone.

"Mrs. Brown—"

"Mr. Davidson, was anything else destroyed? I'll replace what he ruined."

"There's mud everywhere. It will mostly take elbow grease to restore the room to its original cleanliness."

"Well, by all means, get Atom and Blaise to do it . . . let them clean it up."

"Mrs. Brown, Atom is not on a reduced tuition program and he won't be required to—"

"Wait a minute! Are you saying," I interrupt, "that Atom won't have any accountability because he pays more?"

"Yes, ma'am. That is exactly what I'm saying."

"I see," I say, wanting to slap Mr. Davidson good and hard. "Well, I want my son to learn to take responsibility for his actions, so please have him clean up the mess that he has made and I'll be sure to tell him that when he grows up, money can pay off irresponsibility. I'd like to speak to my son, please."

"Hi, Mom," Blaise says dejectedly.

"I have to go to work right now, but I'm going to come get you as soon as possible. I want you to clean up exactly one half of the mess. No more, no less, do you hear me?"

"Yes."

"Good. Do it."

Chapter Eleven

After dinner, while Blaise writes a report, I finish my grocery-shopping list for Roberto. I then go into my bedroom and shut the door. In my closet, I open the fireproof safe I bought after my disastrous trip to the bank and take out all the contents: the duplicate pictures I had made of Lucy and her sex gang, my .38 Rossi revolver, my wedding ring, our passports, my last five hundred dollars in savings, checkbooks, petty cash for all my clients, my credit cards and, finally, Tommy Ray's mama. Here I have his mother in my closet and I don't even know her name.

I sit on the floor unexpectedly overwhelmed. I can't believe that I took a copy of the pictures just in case. Just in case of what? I feel ashamed of myself. Lucy trusted me to do this job. Slamming the safe door shut and spinning the dial on the lock, I get up.

The phone rings and I run into the living room to answer it.

"Hello."

"Corki, it's Lucy. I just wanted to make sure everything went okay with the pictures," she says with thinly veiled fear in her voice.

"Yeah, but it was really late by the time he got through printing them. I'll drop them off first thing in the morning. Eight-thirty okay?"

"Yeah, that's fine. But you know what? Put them on the top shelf of the foyer closet. I wouldn't want Alejandra to accidentally see them. She comes really early tomorrow," she says.

"Lucy, I have a question."

"Sure, honey, what is it?"

I *want* to ask her if I'm about to lose my job to a couple of flavor-of-the-week sex birds, but I choke.

"What is Tommy Ray's mama's name? Since she's here, I'd like to know."

"Of course you would, honey. Hold on," she says. She yells out, "Tommy, what was your mama's name?"

"Who the hell wants to know?" I hear him yell back.

"Just Corki, honey. She's keeping your mama safe and sound, and she wants to know her name," Lucy says in her newly adopted Southern accent.

There are muffled sounds on the other side of the phone line. Tommy Ray picks up. His words are slurred.

"Sorry about that. I think it's real kindly of you to be lookin' after my mama the way you are. Her name is . . . shit, *was* Luella May Woods," he says.

"Did she like to be called Luella or Luella May?" I ask.

"Why the fuck you wanna know, girl? You talk to dead people?" he asks hazily.

"Yeah! Especially if they're sitting in my closet. Sometimes they talk back to me," I joke, but in a serious tone.

Tommy Ray drops the phone and starts screaming at Lucy.

"That Corki is one weird-ass chick. She's some kinda voodoo queen or something. I don't like no voodoo. That kind of shit freaks me out."

Lucy comes back on the line.

"Corki, just ignore him," she whispers. "When you come here tomorrow morning, I want you to clean out the wine cellar. I want all of it out of this house and I never want to see it again. Clean it out, everything!"

"What do you want me to do with it?"

"Consider it an early birthday present. Happy birthday! Crack open a Dom and celebrate your fortieth in style. Tommy Ray doesn't know it, but we have an intervention planned for him tomorrow night. So make sure you don't need to come by here after three o'clock," Lucy whispers.

First she wants to get him off pork and now liquor. I can hear my mom's sage advice, "Don't go into a relationship thinking you're going to change a man."

Amen, Mama.

Chapter Twelve

Before Tommy Ray and Lucy wake up, I deposit the photographs in the foyer closet and quietly haul away all the liquid in the house stronger than NyQuil: seven bottles of Dom Pérignon champagne, thirty-three bottles of various wines, six after-dinner liqueurs, one unopened bottle of Remy Martin Louis XIII and the half-empty one from a couple of weeks back, as well as nineteen bottles of various hard liquors—tequilas, rums, vodkas, etc. I drive directly home, haul the boxes upstairs and shove them in the corner.

Driving to Jock's house to start the work he assigned me in his last message, I have just enough time to fit it all in before the painters arrive and I go do my grocery shop for Count Roberto. Shelly promised to take all the kids to a five o'clock movie so I can prepare for my early dinner date with Officer Holt.

I let myself into Jock's house, go to the kitchen and turn off the pool and hot tub heater. Next, I go to move the boxes from his bedroom to the range. I walk to the back of the house and into his dim, secluded bedroom. I can't believe what I see.

The boxes are ripped to shreds and their contents dumped and thrown all over his room. Stacks of CDs, cassette tapes, videos and scripts are torn apart and strewn everywhere. The tops of the boxes are so violently ripped open that half the cardboard still sticks to the tape. Jock's clothes are scattered on the floor along with a few photos of his sisters and brothers. The sheets have been torn off the bed and the pillows taken out of their cases. Everything in the room is covered with a thick layer of goose down that resembles snow.

I walk cautiously through the rest of the house. Nothing else has been disturbed. I go to Jock's walk-in closet and go through his bureau. I look in his sock drawer where he keeps wads of hundred-dollar bills rolled in pairs of socks. All eighteen Ben Franklins are exactly where he left them. He even has one Grover Cleveland one-thousand-dollar bill he keeps inside the lining of a ski hat, and it's still there. I reroll his socks in the particular way he likes them and put them back in the exact order.

I go back to his bedroom, sit down on the mattress that is now half the bed frame and dial Squid's number. The secretary at Film Industry Entertainment puts me on hold, despite my telling her that it's an emergency. Eventually, I get Squid on the line.

"Hey, this is Corki—"

"What's wrong?" he interrupts. "What's the emergency? I was in the middle of an interview," he says, not quite as agreeable as the last time we spoke.

"Well, if you'd let me finish my sentence, I'll tell you! I need Jock's world cell phone number immediately. Something terrible has happened at his house, and I need to speak to him."

"Aren't you his assistant?" he says, irritated. "Isn't that what you're paid to do? Take care of disasters without having to bother your client?" he asks, getting testier and nastier as he speaks.

"Well, I guess you would know, Squid, since you're a peon assistant just like me. When I do eventually speak with Jock, I'll make sure to tell him that the reason I couldn't reach him sooner was you and your pissy attitude. For your information, not that it's any of your business, someone has ransacked his house. Now, give me his goddamned world cell number!"

The line is silent. While I try to decide whether he's hung up or not, I say a prayer to ask forgiveness for taking God's name in vain.

After what seems like an eternity, Squid gets back on the line. He rattles off the number sans the 011 for international and the 33 country code for France. I try to recover a little dignity and say "Thank you," but he has already hung up.

I call Jock immediately. Thankfully he answers.

"Jock, it's me, Corki. I came to your house to take the boxes down to the range and someone has ransacked your bedroom."

"What the hell's that supposed to mean?" he asks.

"Every box is torn apart, your bed is ripped apart, your pillows have been shredded, there are feathers everywhere. There are CDs, DVDs and videos thrown helter-skelter. Your books even have pages torn from them. Pictures of your family are thrown around, with the glass smashed in the frames," I say in a rushed panic.

"Oh God. Oh God," he says.

"Should I call the police or what? What do you want me to do?"

"Hell no, don't call the police. Listen to me, Corki. I'm going to guide you through what to do and *you* need to take care of this, not the police, not a detective, no one else. Take the phone with you and go into my bathroom and open the cabinet. The one next to the fireplace," he demands.

He waits for me.

"Okay, I'm here," I say.

"Now remove all the lotions and everything. When all that stuff is gone, you'll find a safe. Do you see it?" he asks.

"Yeah, it looks like the one I just bought," I say.

"Good, then you'll know what to do. Now, go to my dressing room, the walk-in closet off the bathroom, turn left, and open the top drawer on the right side. In there you should see my yarmulke and tallis bag."

I dig through some other stuff, his tefillin, his siddur prayer book, the Zohar, a book on the teachings of the Kabbalah and his Bible.

"It's a little bag with embroidery on it," he says. "It's purple velvet and has a zipper and it's where I keep my prayer shawl," he adds.

"I know what a tallis bag is, I just don't see it. Wait a minute, yes I do. I got it," I say.

"Okay, open it and unfold the shawl and inside you'll find a key that will open the first part of the safe," he tells me, calming.

I return to the safe, insert the key and a button pops out.

"I got it open, now all I need is the code."

"Here it is. Point the dial to zero. Then turn the dial to the left passing zero at *least* three times. I do it four. Then stop at number twenty-four. Then turn the dial to the right and stop the *second* time you get to the number thirteen. Finally, turn the dial to the left and the *first* time you get to the number seventy-nine, stop. It should open," he says.

I can tell he is holding his breath.

"Voilà! It's open." I see a recording device.

"Now, Corki, listen! Flip down the black panel, push the rewind button and when you see who did this on the screen, push play."

I do as he says and see myself discovering the mess in his bedroom in reverse order. Dear God, who knew he was recording my every move?

"God, Jock, do you record what goes on in every room?" I ask.

"That's none of your business, but yes, I do. I know when you look through my drawers, but I also know that nothing has ever been taken. You just like to snoop," he says.

"I snoop with good reason. You lost your passport three hours before you were to go . . . Oh, wait, here it is. Hold on. Let me just rewind a little more," I say.

"Oh shit, Jock!"

"Don't 'oh shit' me. Who is it?" he demands.

"Who are *they*? Oh no. I can't believe it. It's all three of Concepcion's boys. Hubert's the one tearing stuff up, though." I watch the playback video of him stabbing the pillows and ripping the custom-made French mattress to shreds with a butcher knife.

"Jock, they're going through all your stuff very carefully, especially the DVDs and CDs. One at a time. And that's what they leave with, either a bunch of CDs or DVDs, I can't tell," I confess. "That's it. The next person coming in is me. What do you want me to do? I mean, we have it on tape, why don't we call the police?" I ask.

"Corki, stop being so fucking naive. The first thing I want you to do is change the locks to the house, the guesthouse and the gates. Change the entry codes and delete all abort codes except for yours and mine. Alarm the house every moment—even when you're there. I want you to cancel any and everybody who is due to come to the house—the painters, everyone. Call Jerald Crest and tell him not to pay Concepcion one fucking red penny. I want her ass fired and then I want *you* to call those son-of-a-bitch kids of hers and get my stuff back," he demands.

"Me? Are you crazy? People end up buried in concrete for less than this. Concepcion's 'kids' are eighteen years old—they're men, Jock. I have a little boy. I'm not going to risk my life for a couple of CDs. Aren't there professional henchmen that do this kind of thing?" I feel panic rise in my chest.

"My entire career is on the line, Corki. I don't need a god-damned 'henchman,' I need you to make one call. Politely ask for the DVDs back. Ask what they want and tell me," his voice is firm, but tense with concern.

"Jock, I want to know what's on the DVDs."

"You snoop so much I'm surprised you don't already know," he retorts.

"Well, pardon me, but I don't. And if your entire career is on the line, if it's something that big, then it is my business. You're asking me to put my *life* on the line!"

He's silent, so I continue.

"You hired me to be your personal assistant—to do your grocery shopping and take your clothes to be cleaned. I don't need to get in-volved with stuff like this. Concepcion's boys know where I live. You don't pay me enough to get caught up in some weird shit like this. This whole thing scares me."

"I'll give you a raise. Is that what you want? A bullshit raise?" Jock asks.

"Well, now that you mention it, I certainly am due one. And not like the last one where you gave me a two-dollar-an-hour raise and then took half my work away and gave it to your sister. I don't need that kind of raise," I say, indignant.

"So, that's what this is all about? Money? Now you're into extor-tion, are you?" he asks, accusingly.

I try to calm myself by breathing deeply.

It's not working.

"Extortion? Jock, I've lied for you, pirated copies of movies for you, even signed passport papers for you—thus committing a federal crime. I've been nothing but loyal and you have the audacity to suggest I'm extorting you? I've blown right past every moral I hold dear to make sure your life runs smoothly. Well, I'll tell you what. I quit!"

I slam down the phone and burst out crying, which really pisses me off because I'm ruining my mascara. After I use thirteen of Jock's bedside tissues and calm down enough to stop, I go to his bathroom, get out some cotton swabs and try to do a quick face repair. In the middle of reapplying my makeup and fixing my hair, my cell phone rings. It's Shelly.

"Hey, sistah, have you heard about the job yet?"

"What job?" I ask, trying not to snivel.

"Hello! The Jennifer job!"

"No, but they said they were going to be interviewing throughout the week," I say weakly.

"Girl, you been crying?" she asks softly.

"Yeah. I just quit my job with Jock."

"Well, why aren't you jumping with joy? He's never treated you as you deserve to be treated."

"I know, but I've never been accused of what he just accused me of," I say, still wiping my eyes. "I've got my date at five-thirty and it's going to take me at least that long to get this room back in order before I leave to grocery shop for Roberto."

"Forever the loyal assistant. You quit the job but have to get stuff in order before you go. Let the housekeeper do it."

"Yeah, well, that's a problem all by itself. I'll fill you in later," I say.

"That's cool. You know where we'll be. I'm going to take the kids to the theater at the Grove. We should be out by eight. Should we meet at your place at eight-thirty?"

"Yeah, that'd be perfect. I really appreciate you watching Blaise after what he did at your house. At least at the movies he's contained."

I'm too old for dating if the date goes past eight P.M. Shelly and I sit out on my apartment balcony with Blaise's telescope scanning the night sky. It's eleven o'clock on a Friday night and I'm starting to fade rapidly. Shelly's running out of fuel, too, but the kids seem to be getting their second wind. Eden, Star and Blaise sit on the living room floor creating a four-foot-by-six-foot scene of an underwater coral reef for their group project on the environment. They have encyclopedias and oceanography books around them to help them identify sea life and what function each form plays in the undersea ecosystem. All this is preparatory work for their upcoming trip to the Long Beach Aquarium.

Shelly and I star search and drink caramel tea from Mariage Frères, my favorite *maison de thé à Paris*. I brought back so many canisters of tea from Paris, I was stopped in customs. They thought no one could love tea *that* much.

"So, why was your date so bad?" she asks.

"Well, you know, maybe my values are from a different era, but I was under the impression that a man invites a lady on a date so they can both to get to know each other. Officer Holt was under the impression that after dinner he would enjoy me as dessert. I told him that wasn't going to happen. Then, when the bill came, he made sure he only paid his half."

"He *is* only sworn to uphold the law. I don't think there's anything in there about being a gentleman," she says while blowing on her tea.

"Where are the gentlemen?" I ask. "I just want to have a partner in life, be a family."

"Yeah, me too," Shelly says.

"Well, you're still a spring chicken," I tease. "Thirty-four's young. You have time. I must be having a midlife crisis. In one day, I quit my job and told the first date I've had in ages to shove off," I say, shaking my head.

"Now, tell me about quitting your job."

"That son of a bitch," I whisper, "accused me of trying to extort money out of him!" I say. "Can you even begin to believe that?"

"How much?" she asks.

"How much? Shelly! I can barely ask for a raise. How the hell could I extort money out of someone?"

"I'm sorry, I was just thinking about your future."

"I could never do something like that."

The images of Lucy's lewd pictures in my safe race through my mind. I quickly close the door on them.

"Even after I quit, I still called Grover Lock and Key. I got his locks changed, canceled the painters, called the alarm company and did everything that jerk told me to do."

"Is he going to pay you for it?" she asks.

"He'll pay," I say confidently. "I just wonder when he's going to call back," I say, more to myself than Shelly.

"You don't really think he's going to call back after that conversation, do you?"

"Shell, that's the pathetic part of it. He doesn't have anyone else he can trust. Even if every other word out of his mouth is to tell me off, he can't trust anyone else," I say, truly feeling empathy for Jock.

"Then why didn't he treat you better to begin with?" Shelly asks solemnly.

"Maybe no one ever treated *him* better."

Chapter Thirteen

On Monday morning, I drop the kids off at Envision Prep. Once they've gone into their classroom, I head back to my car. Mr. Davidson, the principal, passes in between cars to catch up with me. I pretend I don't see him.

"Mrs. Brown?" he calls out.

I turn around, feigning surprise. "Good morning, Mr. Davidson."

"I was hoping I would get to see you this morning. I want to speak with you regarding your son."

It's only eight-thirty in the morning, so I know it can't be a complaint about something new.

"Yes, what would you like to say?" I say with a formal air.

"We tested Blaise last week and his scores were excellent. He's testing at the eleventh-grade level in science and math. I know he's ten years old, but I think it would behoove him *and* challenge him if he were placed in a higher grade for those two classes. It would certainly improve his chances of going directly to a University of California campus as a freshman. That's virtually impossible to do these days, but I feel with his scores and him being a minority, he would almost be a shoo-in."

"Well, Mr. Davidson, I wasn't expecting *this*. I'll have to talk to Blaise about it and see what he thinks."

We part and I have my doubts. What if Blaise is blazing through chemistry and trigonometry, but he gets stuck with a problem and I can't help him? I'm terrible at higher math and I'll look like a total loser when my ten-year-old asks me about some complicated problem and I give him a blank stare.

My cell phone rings. "Drew Cheriff here from Three Arts," she says.

"Hey, how are you?" I ask exuberantly.

"Outstanding, thank you. I'm calling to inform you that we are through with the interviewing process. Jennifer was very impressed with your qualifications."

"Well, thank you," I say with adrenaline suddenly pumping through my body.

"Corki, what we'd like to do now is have you come in to talk with Jennifer. It's ultimately up to her, but you were the only applicant we felt comfortable recommending," she says. "Let's see, Jennifer can be here tomorrow at ten A.M. How is that for you?"

"Outstanding!" I say, mimicking her.

I call Lucy as soon as we hang up.

"Lucy, this is Corki."

"Corki, you think I don't know your voice after all these years?" she asks, laughing.

"I need to meet with you *today,* in person. This is a true emergency, but it can't be done over the phone," I state.

"Well, my goodness, Corki, I have a shoot all day. I'm over here in Culver City at Smashbox. I'm doing the cover of *Cosmo*, can you believe it?" she asks.

"Of course I can believe it," I say, propping her up as usual. "Then I'll have to come there. I need five minutes tops and I want you to be one hundred percent honest with me. Can you do that, Lucy?"

"Well, of course I can. Come on down and as soon as I can take a break, I'll meet you in my dressing room," she says, sounding puzzled.

I drive over to Smashbox Studios and am led to the area where a makeup artist and wardrobe stylist are doting over Lucy. She's drinking up the attention. The photographer's lights and props are being given the once-over in preparation for the shoot. On a couch in the corner Bobby Sue sits talking on a cell phone, Lucy's bright orange Hermès appointment book open on her lap. She's obviously scheduling appointments. I think of all my jobs Lucy's given to "the girls" while I've been without work and here is Miss Bobby Sue apparently doing my job again. It takes all I can muster to wait patiently for Lucy to have a free moment.

I know good and well that the reason Lucy's going to be on the cover of a sexy national women's magazine is because of the last film she did in Hawaii, where she was willing to bare her breasts and a hint of her bottom. It was big news that she stated to the press she didn't need a stand-in, that she was more than hot enough to do it herself. The film, as of yet untitled, is scheduled to be prescreened by industry insiders at Paramount on Thursday evening. In the past, Lucy has always had me at her side during these events. This time, Lucy hasn't said a word. I only learned about it from her publicist, who tells me everything.

"Hey, Bobby Sue! What's shaking?" I ask as I approach her. I notice she closes the appointment book and shoves the papers she's working on under the book.

"Oh, you know! Just returning calls for Tommy and Lucy. Personal calls," she stutters, averting her eyes sideways.

Bless her heart, she's a shitty liar.

"I thought for sure you'd be planning Thursday's screening at Paramount."

"I don't really know anything about that," she lies.

"Okay, well, I just thought I'd check in. Get back to your work," I say with a friendliness that could kill.

"Corki, is there something I can help you with? I know Lucy doesn't want to be bothered," she asks.

"I need to *bother* her, but it's nothing concerning you, so don't worry about it. She knows I'm coming."

Finally Lucy is done and ready to speak to me. She pulls me into her dressing room and closes the door.

"My God, Corki, what's going on? What's the emergency?" she asks, truly concerned.

"Lucy, we've been working together forever and a day, but tomorrow I'm going to be finding out if I have a full-time job with Jennifer Aniston."

"What!" Lucy screams out. "Oh no, you can't do this to me!"

"Lucy, you're the one doing it to me!" I say softly. "Since those girls have come here, my hours have dropped by over sixty percent. I love working for you, but I have a little boy to take care of. I already told you that I've lost Jock, actually permanently now, and I've lost Daisy completely. I've hardly worked for you at all since Tommy brought in Bobby Sue and Jolene. I'm living on what little savings I have and it's dwindling fast," I say as I try not to get emotional. "Lucy, I won't have any hard feelings if you decide to go with these other two girls, because I know they can do things for you that I won't be able to."

I wonder if she picked up my innuendo there.

Lucy bursts out crying hysterically. I can't tell if this is part of an Academy Award–winning performance or if she's really upset.

"Cor-keeee. You're my family and you're here telling me we're about to get a divorce? You know I have such terrible abandonment issues. God, don't do this to me. What about me? Who's going to take care of me? I can't afford years more of therapy if you leave." She grabs me and hugs me tightly.

"Lucy, I need something concrete. My job has been usurped by Thing One and Thing Two. They just show up one day and suddenly they're the flavors of the week."

Lucy stops sobbing and just cries big tears.

"Corki, they're not going to last. Bobby Sue has already fucked up our reservations to Sundance so badly we may have to drive there. And right now she's out there trying to repair the problems she's made for our screening on Thursday. She's plain lazy and the other one, well . . . my mama's screaming at me to get her to leave. My mom thinks she's trying to steal my Tommy away." At the thought, Lucy bursts into tears again.

"Lucy, hello! She's all over him. You all may be fucking each other, but she's obviously out for more than a screw. Open your eyes!"

"I'm begging you, begging you not to leave me. I need you so badly. You're the only one I trust to get me through this, please! I need someone strong when I feel so weak with him. I promise you from the bottom of my heart, I will pay you if he doesn't fulfill his end of it," she says as she collapses into my arms weeping uncontrollably.

I pull Lucy away from me and hold her head so she stares me directly in the eyes. I speak slowly with my voice calm and controlled.

"Lucy, I don't want any more empty promises. I have a ten-year-old boy depending on me to keep him alive with a roof over his head. This is L.A. My rent is $2,200 a month. My car payment and insurance is another $850. Medical insurance premiums are $800 and that's with a $2,500 deductible. That's almost $4,000 per month to keep my little household afloat, without luxuries like food, broken arms and birthday parties. I need you to understand that I *cannot* make it on less than $4,000 dollars a month and those are for bare necessities. You live on $32,000 a month and complain it's not enough. Can you fathom living on an eighth of what you spend? The job with Jennifer would provide a steady income plus medical and dental insurance. If I get the job, do I take it or do I stay with you?"

Lucy lets out a piercing scream and collapses to the ground, wrinkling the skimpy dress she is wearing. She wraps her long, gangly arms around her head and neck, thus ruining her perfectly coiffed hair as well.

The door bursts open and in flies the photographer, art director, hair stylist, makeup artist, wardrobe stylist and Bobby Sue Hunsucker. They all stare at me as if I threw her to the ground and made her scream. Bobby Sue rushes to Lucy's side and helps her up. When the makeup artist sees Lucy's face, she screams as loud as Lucy did. Bobby Sue looks at me with hate in her eyes.

"What the hell did you do to her?" she asks.

"Bobby Sue, don't you *ever, ever* look me in the eye and lie to me again or I'm liable to punch you in the mouth, and I'm not a violent woman," I say vehemently. "Lucy, I need an answer right now at this moment or I'm walking out and getting on with my life."

The makeup artist is screaming and the wardrobe stylist is trying to repair Lucy back to perfection.

How did I have the gall to demand an answer? All I'll have left if she says "leave" is a chance, not even a promise, with Jennifer; $500 in savings; and my measly $200-per-week paycheck, if I'm lucky, from Liam and Esther.

"Everyone leave, please," Lucy whispers. She sounds so desperate and somber, everyone backs out of the room except Bobby Sue and me. "Especially you," she says to Bobby Sue. Bobby Sue, looking crushed, leaves and closes the door behind her. In the shadows under the door, I can see all of their feet pressed close so they can listen in. Lucy pulls my face close to hers.

"Choose me, Corki. Please. I promise I'll pay you whatever you need, but I can't be abandoned again. You and my mama, my grandma and my daddy are the only consistencies in my life. I'll treat you better, I promise. We're going to be moving soon and you're the only one who can do this right. Tommy Ray wouldn't know how to do it. He lives out of a suitcase, from hotel to hotel. He's brilliant, but he needs me to show him how to be a man again. All his other women have emasculated my baby," she continues.

"Stop, Lucy. You're getting off the subject. I don't care about your relationship with him. Well, I mean I care, but right now I'm talking sheer survival. This time it's not about what you need. It's about what I need. I've been fulfilling your needs for decades."

"I'm here for you, babe. I promise that you can depend on me. Choose me and I swear on my life you won't be sorry," she whispers lovingly. "We're family. Family means more to me than anything."

There's a knock on the door and someone yells from behind it. "We really gotta get a move on here. There's another shoot coming in to set up in two hours. We gotta hustle. You ready in there?"

"I'm ready!" Lucy calls out with a sudden flash of confidence. Control has been restored. She straightens her dress and fluffs her hair as if that fixes all she's torn apart. The fix-up crew and Bobby Sue descend to repair the mess and Lucy's image.

I start to leave quietly.

"Corki, angel!" Lucy calls out, stopping me in my tracks. "Would you take the car in for a wash while I finish up here? And there's a script that needs to be picked up at CAA. Maybe you could pick it up and leave it for me in the car?" The sweetness of her voice is as refreshing as chilled mint juleps on a hot Kentucky afternoon.

"But, Lucy, I thought I was—" Bobby Sue interrupts.

"Shut up!" Lucy retorts with poison.

I sit at the Santa Palm car wash, off to the side where they do hand washes for a mere $22.95. The man sitting next to me keeps eyeing me up and down, then staring at the Ferrari. If any more sleaze dripped off him he'd need to carry a mop. As I start to punch a number into my cell phone, he approaches me.

"Hey, lady," he says in a heavy accent, "you are very pretty."

I snap my phone closed and stare him in the eye for too long. "Save it, mister. The car's not mine. It belongs to the *guy* I work for."

"Bitch," he mutters as he walks away.

I leave my seat and walk over to the fence bordering the car wash. It is covered with blooming jasmine. I close my eyes and wonder if my fierce loyalty is an ego problem or a positive characteristic. I'm not the captain of Lucy's ship. I don't have to go down with it.

I toss around that I've never really pursued another relationship because I still feel loyalty to the man I was married to for three days, Basil Brown. Though I cope with uncertainties daily, I have problems with change. I don't like it, plain and simple. I've heard Jennifer is as lovely as can be and her husband, Brad, is a good man. But what if we just don't mesh and the only thing I have for sure is gone? I open my phone again and make the call.

"Hi, this is Corki Brown for Drew Cheriff, please."

While I'm on hold I pray I'm making the right decision.

"Ms. Cheriff, this is Corki Brown. I wanted to let you know how pleased I am that I made the final cut. However, I need to let you know that I won't be able to take the job even if it is offered to me. I truly appreciate the time you gave me and I hope this hasn't inconvenienced you too terribly."

Ms. Cheriff sounds honestly disappointed. She makes it clear that she holds me in high regard, and that momentarily boosts my self-esteem, but leaves me feeling worse for having let her down. I walk back to my seat and write her a note of thanks.

"Mom, what's the point of having a dog like this?"

"Blaise, just because he has no hair, no teeth and a bad attitude doesn't mean he's worthless. He's like family to her."

Blaise sits in the backseat with Mr. Fu, Veronique's dog, curled up in his lap. He runs his hand over the thin, weak tuft of hair coming out of the top of Mr. Fu's head. All five strands are bound by a blue ribbon.

"His skin feels wet."

"I slathered him with Coppertone. SPF 40. He burns easily."

With disdain, Blaise picks Mr. Fu up and puts him on the seat next to him. The dog shakes his nonexistent coat, then curls up and goes back to sleep.

"Honey, he's not going to be any trouble. We'll just have him for a few days. It will be easier than me going up to her house two times a day to feed him and give him his shots."

. . .

For the next week, all I do is cook for Roberto, although I have yet to see him once. I deliver the food to the house daily, watch Mr. Fu, baby him, let him think he's doing damage by nipping my heels with his gums and wait for a call from Lucy.

She doesn't call, at all.

Chapter Fourteen

Weeks go by without one speck of work. Jock's gone, Daisy's finished, and Esther, in the name of saving money, has been giving all my work to Shelly. I'm living on credit cards.

Words float through my head: *desperado, hopeless, forlorn.* I dream about the Mojave Desert, drained pools and empty houses. I spend hours berating myself for quitting Jock in a moment of heated anger and days berating myself for not going with Jennifer. I volunteer at Blaise's school, hoping to pick up some of the "new math" and chemistry. I'm not sure if it's my constant presence or the more demanding academic atmosphere, but Blaise has become the teacher's pet . . . again.

I had visualized the outcome of my confrontation with Lucy very differently. I never expected her promises to go south and stay there. I thought I'd once again reign as princess of her home. I would do no wrong. She would even tell all her friends what a treasure I was and how she couldn't have lived the last twenty years without me. She'd regale them with stories, which were news to me, of adventures we'd had in the past and how in every one I saved her from herself. She would butter me up and I would feel youthful and sweet. For my fortieth birthday she would throw a surprise lunch party at Mr. Chow's in Beverly Hills, complete with my favorite three-berry cake from Sweet Lady Jane bakery and a five-hundred-dollar gift certificate from Neiman Marcus.

For the impending move to their new house, which they are still looking for, I would pack up as much of her stuff as I could without cramping her lifestyle. I would take Polaroid pictures of all the items I had carefully put in each box and labeled. The Polaroid camera would have been my gift to her. I would catalogue everything and take unwanted goodies to donation centers where I would get her huge tax write-offs for every item. I would call in Chipman United Van Lines to come give preliminary quotes on how much it would cost Lucy and Tommy Ray to move. Everything would have been done in perfect order, just as it always was. I would be happy. Lucy would be ecstatic. Bobby Sue would be miserable, which would make me even happier. Jolene would be getting some of Tommy on the side, which would upset Alejandra so much that she would threaten to quit. Tommy would increase her pay, give her extra time off and promise not to misbehave in front of her. Tommy would be very happy with his setup, too . . . in my vision.

My phone rings.

"Corki, it's Lucy!" she says happily.

I want to say "Lucy who?" but restrain myself.

"Hi!" I say, forcing happiness into my voice.

"Listen, I'm having a get-together at my house. A few of my

women friends and I are going to start meeting once a month to have women's discussions. I'd love it if you'd make lunch for us."

"I'll do that. How many people and what day?" I ask.

"Let's see, me, obviously, Winona, Meg, Minnie, Angela, Sheryl, Melissa, Lisa Marie, Courteney, Lisa and Jennifer. That's eleven, right? Yeah, eleven for Friday afternoon at one."

I swallow hard. Jennifer's going to be there. Talk about your past coming back to haunt you. I wonder if Lucy's doing this on purpose. I'm not sure whether to be happy or hate her.

"Fine. I'll do it."

I feel my two pints of Italian blood stirring within me. I decide a lunch of Italian fare, inspired by cooking for Roberto Tratelli, will be in order for Lucy's get-together. An antipasto of warm bean salad with tuna and radicchio will start the meal, accompanied by a grilled polenta with wild mushrooms and sage breadsticks. For the *primi,* I will cook a risotto with crab and shrimp followed by a *secondi* of *coniglio* in *vino rossi* (rabbit in red wine) or the alternative for the less brave souls of swordfish stuffed with breadcrumbs, tomatoes and capers. For the *contorni* to accompany the *secondi,* I will serve Swiss chard with raisins and pine nuts and mushrooms in a tomato sauce. I will serve just one *dolci,* a *torta di mele al burro* (buttery apple cake). As far as I'm concerned, this will be a feast for a king, or a count, or a bunch of movie stars, one of whom I am trying to make sure remembers me and another whom I'm sorry I didn't choose.

The morning of the party, I chop and dice and sauté while I pour my whole story out to Alejandra. She is appalled by how poorly I've been treated. By the time I'm done cooking and kvetching, I feel much better. A sympathetic ear is what I needed.

I leave after giving thorough instructions to Alejandra on how to serve the meal. As I close the front door, I hear Tommy Ray fiddling around in the garage looking for something he can't find. He's getting agitated. Apparently, Lucy didn't plan for a grumbling Tommy Ray Woods to be hanging around, not quite knowing what to do with himself.

My cell phone rings.

"Hello, this is Corki!"

"This is Jock."

And that's when I make my mistake. A biggie.

"Jock?" I say, somewhat in shock.

Tommy Ray appears suddenly out of the darkness of the garage. His eyes flash rage and he's wielding a metal baseball bat. He raises it as if he's ready to beat the tar out of me. He swings it wildly and smashes the passenger side of Lucy's Ferrari windshield. Glass fragments and pellet-shaped chips fly everywhere.

I stand transfixed for a second, then throw my phone in my bag and run up the hill toward Betty parked at the top. Tommy screams violently after me.

"Corki, you goddamned money-hungry bitch, you better never mention another one of that cunt's men in front of me again. You hear me?" He pauses. "Do you hear me? I'll take this bat to you next time if either one of you fat-ass cows ever mentions another man's name around me. You hear me?"

I burn rubber leaving the house. The image of his huge Confederate flag in the bedroom had already made me uncomfortable, and with this volatile performance, I never want to come back here again. Lucy might come home someday and find me hanging from the front oak tree.

By the time I get down the hill, I'm shaking so badly I can't drive. I pull Betty over. Tommy Ray is the devil incarnate.

My phone rings again.

"Please, don't hang up on me this time," Jock says. I can tell from the slight slur of his words that he's had more than his one glass of red wine for heart-healthy purposes.

"I didn't mean to hang up. It was an accident," I say as I pull tiny bits of shattered glass out of my hair.

"Corki, you didn't really quit, did you?"

"Yes, I did."

"But you cleaned up the house, canceled the painters and dropped off a new set of keys to the business office. My accountant went to the house and everything was in order. He even said Jaws was being taken care of. If it wasn't you doing it, who was it?" he asks.

"I didn't want the fish to die."

"I misjudged you."

"You most certainly did," I say triumphantly. "I've been loyal to you for a long time, not that you've noticed. I put myself in harm's way to keep *you* from getting robbed and all you had to say was 'Mind your own fucking business.' It didn't exactly make feel valued. And then to be accused of extortion . . ."

"Corki, I'm sorry. Do you accept my apology?"

He must have had more to drink than I originally thought. Jock never apologizes. Never.

"Do you?" he asks again.

"Does it matter if I do or not?" I ask.

"Well, actually, no, it doesn't."

There! That's the Jock I know.

"I need you to help me," he goes on. "You're the only one I can trust to do this properly. I don't want my accountant in my personal affairs. Please say you will."

"Why should I?"

"I was upset. I say things I don't mean when I'm angry. Let's move on from there."

"Jock, what do you want from me?"

"Hubert, that low-life piece of triplet shit, called and left a message on my machine. He wants money to return the DVDs."

"Okay, Jock. What's on the DVD?"

"Tree. And me. Having sex." He's barely able to spit it out.

"You mean underage sex. Statutory rape. In some states it's called child molestation, right?"

"Mmmmmm. Yes."

"I see. How much money does Hubert want?"

"A hundred thousand dollars," Jock whispers.

"You're not going to succumb to that, are you?" I say, suddenly indignant. "It's going to leak out anyway."

"He promised he'd give you the DVDs and he swears he didn't make any copies. He'll even sign a paper saying that he didn't," he insists.

"And you believe that? Then when it hits the Internet he'll say that his signature was forged and he'll be raking in not only the hundred grand but also a fifty-dollar-per-view fee. You're making a mistake if you do this. You better hurry up and consult your attorney. Not me."

"This will ruin me," he says, his voice catching.

I stifle the urge to say 'You should have thought of that before you did it.'

"Well, it didn't ruin Roman Polanski. The Academy loves him even though he fled the country rather than stand trial."

"Enough, please! I don't want to hear about that," Jock interrupts. "Corki, if by chance Hubert is telling the truth . . ."

"Which he's not," I interject.

". . . it will be worth it to just wash my hands of the whole thing."

"So what am I supposed to do? Call your business office and say I need a hundred grand in cash?" I ask, exasperated. "How exactly is this supposed to work?"

"Hubert will be calling you."

"And?"

"I'll make it worth your while. I promise. Very worth your while."

"But how is it supposed to work?" I insist.

"He'll be calling you, you'll give him the money, and he'll hand you the DVDs."

"I don't think so."

"Why not?" he asks.

"I've seen too many movies where the woman who knows too much gets dumped in the sea with concrete blocks tied to her feet and a sock shoved in her mouth."

"Oh, for crying out loud, stop it! Cornelia, this is not some far-fetched movie! This is my life. There will be no concrete and no socks!" he yells.

"Can't you come back here and do it? Take a forty-eight-hour leave?"

"I am in *every* scene of this movie and cannot leave. This has to be done by you. I can't exactly ask a stranger to deliver a hundred thousand dollars of *my* hard-earned money to that shit who is extorting me. Goddamn it, woman, I'm trying to employ you but you're being so fucking obstinate I can't bear it."

He hangs up on me. I wonder if he knows he's getting off cheap at a hundred thousand.

Chapter Fifteen

"Cornelia, it is ten o'clock at night and I know good and well you're home screening your calls. This is Lucille! I expect you to pick up your phone right now!"

I hover over the answering machine wondering whether to give in to her command. I pick up the receiver.

"What?"

"What happened over here? I come home with my friends in tow and it looks like there's been a car accident in my front yard!"

"What did Tommy Ray tell you?"

"He said you mentioned Jock's name and he got a little bothered. Said he doesn't want you around here anymore while you're still working for my ex-boyfriend."

"Lucy, all I did was answer my phone. I'm not working for Jock anymore and your lover boy got more than 'a little bothered.' He blew a gasket. He totally lost it. He picked up a baseball bat, acted like he was going to kill me, then beat the shit out of your car. He called me a 'money-hungry bitch,' you a 'cunt' and both of us 'fat-ass cows'! I'm telling you, Lucy, you better leave that man before you find your ass hacked up with a hatchet."

"Corki, I love him. He's just a little jealous is all."

"A little? Lucy, you may not be alive for me to say 'I told you so,' so I'm gonna do it right now: I told you so!"

"I'm going to choose to ignore that comment, Corki. I'm actually calling with some good news," she says proudly.

"I could use some good news about now."

"We found a house! We put down a deposit and we're trying for a fifteen-day escrow. Aren't you thrilled for us?"

"Us who? Us, Lucy and Tommy? Or us, Lucy, Tommy, Thing One and Thing Two?"

"Well, the girls haven't found an apartment of their own yet, so they will be moving in with us for a while."

"I'm thrilled for you," I say flatly.

Heavens, I'm as bad at lying as Bobby Sue.

"Well, babe, if you get a chance, drive by tomorrow and take a look. Also, you can go ahead and start bringing packing equipment. You know, we'll need boxes, tape, bubble wrap, the works. But Tommy actually wants the girls to do the packing."

"But Lucy, you said—"

"I know, I know. Things just need to cool down around here. Besides, he just got a film shooting down in Mexico for six months, so you won't have to deal with him much at all." She sighs. "I'm going to miss him, but I'll be going down there as much as I can. Babe, do try to go by the new house and let me know what you think. You know how I value your opinion."

"I'll try."

She gives me the address and we say our goodbyes, murmuring all the platitudes that neither one of us means anymore.

Chapter Sixteen

"Miss Corki!" I hear on my answering machine. "It's Mrs. Shay Goode!"

Shay, Jock's financial account manager for the last seven years, calls from Maginniss, Crest and O'Leary, the business office that manages the money for Hollywood's biggest movie stars. M.C.O. sits on Ocean Walk in Venice Beach. Its serious business image is slightly eroded by the tracks of sand leading up to the front door, an ocean breeze coming in through open windows that constantly blows papers off the desks, and an outdoor shower utilized by employees who surf or swim on their lunch break. M.C.O. is also the only accounting firm I know, and I'm familiar with many, that employs forty-four women, of whom thirty-eight are black. Around town this is seen as a particularly smart hiring strategy because when the partners fire someone, it can never be attributed to color. When I hear that there are never enough blacks behind the scenes of the film industry, I want to dump that person at the entrance of M.C.O. These women manage the hundreds of millions of dollars their stars earn.

I pick up the phone.

"Top of the morning to you, Mrs. Goode. To what fortune do I owe your call?"

"Oh, brother. You need to come into the office. I have a package for you. ASAP."

"What is it?"

"Come in and you'll see."

I shower quickly, get dressed and get on the 10 freeway heading west to Venice Beach. Finding street parking immediately and giving a nod to the parking gods, I get buzzed into the office of M.C.O.

"Haven't seen you in a long time!" says Yvonne, queen of the front office. A grandmother at forty-two, she keeps the office workers on a tight leash, but still remains well liked. She's been with M.C.O. since its conception.

"Same here!" Shay announces as she walks into the reception area. "Come on back here and see my new office," she says, leading the way.

Her new office is much nicer than the last one. The top half of one wall overlooks the sea. "Hey, hey, looks like you've moved up in the pecking order."

"So have you, apparently," she says.

"No. My whole career is falling apart before my eyes and I'm hustling to get some semblance of order back to it."

"I might be able to help some with that."

"Got a new client for me?" I ask.

"Nope, better than that."

"All right. Give it up."

Shay unlocks her drawer and spreads a fan of one-hundred-dollar bills on the table.

"Damn, Shay, you're loaded!"

"No, you are. There are sixty of them and it's been requested that you count it, then sign right here saying that you've received the money," she says as she pushes a form toward me.

"Stop messing with me," I declare, praying she's not.

"This is for you, too. We received an early-morning FedEx and explicit instructions from Jock to give this to you along with the six thousand dollars in cash." She hands me a sealed, taped manila envelope. On the outside, in Jock's handwriting, is printed OPEN IN PRIVATE.

"So, tell me, Mrs. Corki, what did you do to deserve this?"

"I quit."

"You quit? So, I've been using the wrong tactics all this time by staying?"

"I'm serious. I quit *and* I hung up on him."

Shay raises her eyebrows. "Anything else you'd like to tell me?"

"Yeah. I have to go to the bathroom. I'll count the money when I come back."

I walk down the hallway with the envelope stuffed under my arm. I enter a stall, close the door and lean down to check to see if there's anyone else in here with me.

I open the envelope carefully and read the note written in Jock's handwriting.

Corki,

Please accept the $6,000 Shay will be giving you as a token of my appreciation. I talked to Jerald and he pointed out I have not given you a Christmas bonus or birthday present for six years.

This is in no way an attempt to persuade you to help me, but if you feel so inclined . . .

Jock

Shay sits at her desk waiting for me. "Ready?"

"Yep!" I count the money, sign the paper and stuff the cash and note deep into my purse.

"Shay, thank you."

Finally, I have some work. Maybe suffering from an ounce of guilt, Lucy has loaned me out to two celebrities. This week I work for Meg Ryan while her assistant, Leslie, is on holiday in the South of France. It's only seven days, but I'm thrilled. I clean out Meg's spare garage and take her drapes to be cleaned and packed for storage. Also, I oversee the plumber who's come to fix the sewer line for the guesthouse and I help her housekeeper, Eva, figure out a dinner menu. Calling my favorite company, Dave the Window Washer, I schedule them to come clean the panes throughout the house.

The next week, I work for actress Rebecca DeMornay, while her assistant, Charlotte Pepper, is off for a week in—of all places—Antigua. A sudden rush of sorrowful feelings for my lost husband surprises me. I quickly squelch the thoughts of loss and get to work.

Rebecca is a personal assistant's dream come true. She writes out clear instructions and thanks me profusely for everything. We get along so well I find myself dreaming that Charlotte will fall in love in Antigua, the way I did, and I could be a permanent replacement.

During the week I do the usual: grocery shop, drop off the dry cleaning, take her golden retriever in for a "fluff and fold" and nail clip at the groomers, then to the vet for a "forty-thousand-mile checkup." I finish the week having obtained one cool peacoat that Rebecca never wears and an application for a 529 plan for Blaise's college education.

I also take Rebecca's Volvo in for service.

Volvo is *the* car of choice amongst stars, especially stars who are new parents. They cost a pretty penny but not as much as some other cars, so no one can call a Volvo driver ostentatious. In L.A., they are also often outfitted with Yakima or Thule-brand bike racks, roof racks and bumper racks. Liam Schwartz once asked me if perchance Yakima made a shotgun rack for his Volvo. I was politely informed they do not.

Chapter Seventeen

I sit out on my balcony with a cup of coffee and my neighbor's plundered newspaper. After two weeks of being deliriously happy with Meg and Rebecca, by week three I'm jobless again. My funds are all but gone and I only have those nagging porn pictures in my safe to keep my hope of survival alive. How long will I have to suffer financially before I cave in? I am clueless as to whether Lucy and Tommy got the house. I have no idea if Jock received my thank-you note and acceptance of the mission at hand. I haven't heard from Esther and Liam, and Veronique must be on a "tour of love," because she has slipped out of sight.

I hate the thought of Jock being lily-livered and just giving Hubert the cash. I'm not sure why I didn't think of it before, but there just might have been enough cameras and tape recordings playing to beat Hubert at his own game.

I make a mad dash to Jock's house and gather tapes and DVDs from the surveillance system, Jock's bedroom safe/camera and the camera/video recorder in the range. After obtaining the list of numbers dialed from the fax machine, I make a quick call to a security specialist who works specifically with celebrities and politicians.

With all my heart, I know that Hubert has every intention of selling the DVD of Jock and Tree out to the media. I don't care what he promises to sign, he's the one triplet of Concepcion's who has always wanted to screw folks over and make a quick buck. Even when he was younger, he would quickly disregard someone if it meant gaining something for himself. Not lacking in intelligence, he constantly talks about how he's going to make his first million, and this hundred thou will be his grand start.

Before heading home, I cruise down Sunset Boulevard and stop at a spy equipment shop and am instantly transported back in time.

After UCLA, when I was still youthful and full of worldly ambition, I filled out applications for the CIA. They were very interested when they learned I had taught myself Greek, French and Italian through tapes borrowed from the Beverly Hills public library, as I had once dreamed about a job in the Secret Service or in overseas espionage work. I'd seen way too many episodes of *Mission Impossible* and had formed romantic notions of what it would be like to live abroad looking over my shoulder at all times. The crick in my neck would mean nothing—I would be an international spy. Music from spy-themed movies would be pumped over invisible speakers and I would wear black turtlenecks with a mysterious medallion hanging around my neck that established me as a member of a secret sorority organization of female CIA agents.

I watch the geeky, techie-looking guy working behind the counter. He looks like a two-year, prepaid subscriber to *Wired* magazine.

"Sir?" I call out.

"Yes, ma'am, can I help you?"

After I describe what I want, he brings out a $795 pen that records audio and has video capabilities, too. He waxes on about its lovely features. Then he shows me how easy it is to use and how stylish and sexy it is as a writing implement. I haven't exactly cleared this purchase with Jock, but have decided that under these conditions it will save him money in the long run and that it will most certainly be a tax write-off. Paying for the pen with the remaining petty cash, feeling smart and, I must admit, sexy, I leave the shop.

A friend of mine is a production editor and he agrees to help me with my Hubert video. He'll put everything I need on DVD and will lend me his portable, battery-operated DVD player. I finally feel ready to meet Hubert on my playing field, having the home team advantage . . . if he'd hurry up and call.

I'm on my way home when my cell phone rings.

"Mrs. Brown?"

It's Principal Davidson. I haven't spoken to him in so long, I was hoping I never would again.

"Yes?" I say tentatively.

"I have Blaise in my office."

His voice is straining against rage. Whatever happened, it's big trouble, I can tell.

"It seems, Mrs. Brown, that your son was testing the hypothesis that flatulence is truly a gas."

"Oh no!"

"It *is* a gas, so your son found out. His classmate is being treated right now for first-degree burns to his buttocks and groin region. I ask that you come in immediately and pick up your son. He is being suspended for a week."

I hang up the phone, do an illegal U-turn on Sunset Boulevard and head out to Santa Monica.

The beginning of the ride home is quiet. I don't know where to start with Blaise, and until I cool down, I wouldn't know where to stop. I breathe deeply and try to remember that he's only ten, in an Advanced Placement chemistry class with seventeen-year-olds readying themselves for college.

"It was just an experiment, Mom. And I proved my hypothesis. I thought you'd be proud."

"Proud? You damn near burn a boy's testicles off and you want me to be proud? Try horrified. That's what I am, Blaise, I'm horrified."

"But he said he could fart on command! He swallowed a bunch of air and could really do it. He volunteered, Mom. He backed right up to the Bunsen burner."

"God, Blaise, don't you feel *any* remorse?"

"Mom, I'm not a psychopath! Of course I feel bad. I mean, I thought the gas would evaporate *before* it reached the Bunsen burner, so *that* part of my theory was wrong."

I'm losing it.

"Blaise! Think about the poor kid who got burned, not about whether your theory was right or not!"

We fall into silence.

Finally, Blaise breaks the hush.

"That kid called me a 'statistic.'"

"Why?"

"Because you're a single mom."

"I am *not* a single mom," I say indignantly. "I am a *married* woman."

"Come on, Mom. You were married for three days almost eleven years ago. You were scammed. This whole marriage thing is a farce—it's like a charade you keep playing."

"You should have told that boy that you had a father and he died in a boating accident."

"Did he?" Blaise asks.

I refuse to lie.

"I don't know," I say quietly.

"I hope he did."

"How can you say something like that about your own father?"

"It's better than thinking he just doesn't care."

While Blaise starts on a week's worth of Algebra II assignments that night, I listen to my messages.

Lucy calls to tell me that she has been cast in a fantastic historical epic with the part of the queen. She'll be in Vancouver for the next two months, and Tommy's gone, so she'd like to speak to me about moving. She also wants to know if I've seen the house. The next call is my car-loan company demanding my payment that they hope I've mailed out because the next one is due and once you get into the habit of letting things like this slip they tend to continue. Next is Fabrizio, a service technician at the Italian Stallion Ferrari place. Lucy's windshield has been replaced; however, broken glass tore holes in the leather headrests and they should really be replaced, and do we plan on claiming this through insurance, and who is the new blonde that oversaw it being dropped off, because she forgot to leave her number.

"Mom?" Blaise calls out. "What's a cosine of an angle?"

"I don't know. Isn't there an index or something?"

"It's a glossary, not an index. How did you graduate from UCLA?"

"I didn't, remember?"

"I see why. . . ." he says, going back to his work.

"You know what, Blaise? I've had just about enough of you for one day. I don't need a smart mouth on top of everything else that's going on. If you don't know what a 'co-sign of an angle' is, look it up! Dictionary, Internet, figure it out."

I go to my room and call Jock, figuring he's probably awake. I'm right. He's awake *and* drunk.

"Hubert hasn't called me yet," I say. "But I've figured out how to get you out of this mess."

"You're a godsend," he slurs.

"Where and how am I supposed to get the money?" I ask.

"I have it in a floor safe, in the range."

"That much in cash?"

"The range used to be a bomb shelter for a very paranoid family in the late fifties. It's safer than Fort Knox and I wanted to be prepared."

"For what?" I ask.

He takes a rather large and loud gulp of tonight's vintage. "Nuclear war," he chugs. "You'll need a code and keys. The keys are taped inside the metal frame of the bed in the guesthouse. Now the code . . . the code . . ." He trails off.

"What's the code?" I ask.

I wait while he sips and flips through his address book. He keeps *everything* in there. Finally, after a few minutes of mumbling, he gives me the code.

"One more thing. What color was the case for the DVD?" I ask.

"Hell if I know."

Lucy isn't home, so I leave a message telling her that yes, I saw the house, but only the roofline (since it's behind such a tall fence) and it looks extremely secure. I also tell her about the Ferrari's seats being cut and ask her if she wants to claim the whole fiasco as an accident, but I don't bother asking for Jolene's number because, quite frankly, I need the work.

The next day, Blaise and I go to Clafouti's, a French café on Sunset, where I let him write with the surveillance pen. We drink iced tea and change seats so I can take notes on the best seat for lighting and clean pictures. Blaise doesn't mind doodling and swapping seats, it's all fun to him. I know he should still be under house arrest for the Bunsen Burner Debacle, as we now call it, but the way he opened up to me afterward moved me.

Blaise doesn't know he's helping my grand plan. I try to figure out how I'm going to carry one hundred thousand dollars and pass it to Hubert inconspicuously. He hasn't called and I wonder what sneaky things he's got up his sleeve.

. . .

A week goes by and I take Blaise back to school. Before he goes to class, he asks me to come close.

"Mom," he whispers into my ear, "I forgot to tell you . . . I need a cell phone."

"For what?"

"Everyone has them . . . in case of an emergency."

"An emergency?" I ask, incredulously. "I made it through college and half of my career without a cell phone."

"Everyone carries one except for me."

"And has that argument ever convinced your mother of anything?"

"Sometimes."

"Star and Eden don't have cells, and anyway, if Johnny jumps off a cliff are you going to do it, too?" I ask.

"Okay, drop it, Mom. You're becoming an embarrassment."

"I'm so sorry I embarrassed you!" I say as he walks away.

I shake my head in disbelief. A cell phone at ten years of age . . . what is he thinking?

I drop in the school office to make an appointment with Mr. Barba, Blaise's counselor.

Mrs. Leigh, the school receptionist, is a matronly woman who looks as if she's wiped many a runny nose and tear-streaked cheek. She wears a wool plaid suit with flat, black oxfords. She has a round face, ruddy cheeks and a slight moustache in desperate need of plucking.

Mrs. Leigh leads me down a hall plastered with notices of clubs to join and swim team tryouts and then gently pushes me through a door and points to an office on the left. "Take a seat out here and he'll come get you in a minute or two."

I wait until a man comes out of the counselor's office, followed by another man. The second man, who now approaches me holding out his hand, is of medium build with large brown eyes and salt-and-pepper hair. His demeanor exudes kindness and patience.

"Mrs. Brown, is that right?"

"Yes, I'm Blaise's mother."

"Please come in and take a seat. May I get you something to drink? I think we have bottled water, Coke, Diet Pepsi or juice."

The tone of his voice is distinctive and soothing.

"A diet soda would be great, thanks."

He brings me one, then sits down at his desk.

"What brings you here today?"

"Well, I don't know if you have met Blaise or not. . . ."

"I most certainly have."

"Then I suppose you heard what happened a week or so ago?"

"I most certainly did."

I can't read his expression.

"Blaise used to be such a good boy. He never got into trouble; he was the quiet one, respectful and decent. Now he's doing things like burning people."

"That was an accident," he replies.

"I know he said it was, but I just don't understand why he would do such a thing."

"Mrs. Brown, there's a very simple biological explanation for his behavior. He's a boy. You wouldn't know that his behavior is completely normal because you're a woman. Do you have a brother?"

"Yes, sir."

"Do you remember the scrapes your brother got into when he was Blaise's age?"

"I remember he drank a bottle of lighter fluid on a dare and had to be rushed to the hospital."

"And?"

"There was the time he and his friends somehow got a beehive in the back of his teacher's hatchback."

"And?"

"The time he and his friends decided to see if you could really dig a hole to China and the hole collapsed on one of them."

"Uh-huh."

"And I get your point, Mr. Barba."

"Mrs. Brown, Blaise is an exceptionally intelligent boy, but he is still a child. The portion of the brain that controls making logical decisions is not fully formed in males until about age thirty-four. There will be more calls, broken bones and stitches and you'll get through them just like you got through the last one."

"Promise?"

Mr. Barba smiles and pats me on the back. "He needs a strong mother, especially since his father isn't around. Blaise thrives on extra attention. He *needs* to *be* needed. He needs to have chores and know that without his help, the household wouldn't run smoothly. A lot of times single mothers . . ."

"I'm not a single mother, Mr. Barba," I interrupt. "I'm a widow."

"Pardon me, I should have said that a lot of times when a mother doesn't have a husband, she tends to do too much for the male children. Eventually, the boy doesn't feel integral to the family. He becomes needy and feels that his mother fulfilling his every need is equivalent to love. It makes it impossible for the little boy to ever become a man."

I walk away feeling comforted *and* disturbed by Mr. Barba's words. I now know that somehow, someway, I will make it through, but I also think of how many times Blaise has asked me to change a channel on the television for him, and I did it. Mr. Barba ushers me out of his office with a promise solicited from me that anytime I need to talk his is an open door.

"Hey, Corki, it's Hubert. I spoke with Jock and he said you'd pay me. When can we make the exchange? Call me on the cell phone."

He leaves the exact same number Tree called in Jock's office the morning she appeared half-naked.

Pondering Hubert's audacity, I think of the years he spent observing Jock's affinity for young girls. As a money-hungry graduate from USC without a speck of morals, he obviously found this to be an opportunity he couldn't pass up. Hubert provided the setup and Jock fell for it with his pants down and his libido up. I'm surprised it took him this long.

I return Hubert's phone call and tell him I'd like to meet at Clafouti's on Sunset Boulevard on Friday at twelve noon. He agrees to the date and time, but not the place. He balks and wants to meet somewhere more private.

"Look, Hubert, I'm doing you a favor. It's my way or the highway. You *could* wait for Jock to come home in three months. I have a lot to do and this is what works for me."

Reluctantly, he agrees, but I can feel in my bones that he's up to something. I hang up and make another hour's worth of calls.

. . .

I go to the safe in my bedroom, open it and sit on the floor in front of my closet and count the last of my cash. The six thousand Jock gave me was gone within an hour after I paid two months' rent and past-due bills. I balance my checkbook and figure out how much room I have left on my credit cards. My situation is embarrassing and pathetic. I'm forty years old and about to call my mama to hit her up for money. Of course, she only has her monthly Social Security check, so how much can she help me?

Thinking about how Hubert might try to trick me, I feel the need to go to Jock's house to get the money sooner rather than later.

Meandering slowly through Hollywood Hills' narrow roads to where there is a remote, little-known and seldom-used back entrance to Jock's house, I park at the back of the property. I descend a small wooden staircase, precariously perched on the side of the hill where Tito the gardener has planted tropical foliage so densely that I'm reminded of a trek through Jamaica's Blue Mountains.

Letting myself into the guesthouse and locking the door behind me, I realize how paranoid I'm being. My hands are trembling, my stomach is rumbling, and I can't seem to breathe deeply. I know my loss of breath is not from climbing *down* a hill. I'm scared, despite the fact that it's daylight and I'm right where I'm supposed to be, where I've been a hundred times before. I'm not trespassing; I'm carrying out Jock's request. Fumbling through my purse, I bring out my .38 and put some ammunition in it.

Maybe what my mom says is true. I watched too much television as a teenager. In crime dramas and soap operas, everyone is suspect and most people have an ulterior motive.

Going upstairs to the bedroom and running my fingers along the underside of the bed frame, I feel the key taped to the leg of the bed. Pocketing it, I let myself out, reset the alarm and enter the main house through the kitchen. Disarming the main alarm, I hesitate for a moment and watch the activities of the house through a monitor on the tile counter. Cars pass on the street outside. Sprinkler heads pop up for a midday watering. A lone man approaches the gate and sticks a direct-advertising mailer in the front gate, then disappears down the street.

Punching "Command Eight" to engage the alarm and have it protect the perimeter of the house, I go into the meditation room and descend the stairs to the range.

I practice breathing deeply trying desperately to calm my frazzled nerves. With shaking hands I turn the pop-out button with the key—the first part of entering the safe—but I'll never be able to enter the proper combination with the accuracy needed to do it on the first or second try. This specific safe will shut down after three consecutive unsuccessful attempts at entering the code. Then I'll have to wait another twenty-four hours before trying again.

I blow it on the first and second attempts. A safecracker I'm not! Having sixty seconds to attempt the code one last time, I breathe deeply, blow out my breath hard, then enter the code. I pull the handle down and the heavy steel door opens smoothly.

There isn't a hundred thousand dollars in here . . . there's seven hundred and fifty thousand dollars. Here I insisted that he have a thousand measly dollars in small bills for his earthquake kit. No wonder he always told me not to worry about it. There are also forty-three DVDs like the one that disappeared. They are filed and categorized by name: Angie, Bibi, Cissy, Deidre, Ellie, Farrah, etc. I was thinking that Tree was the first when she was actually number twenty in the alphabet.

. . .

As I hike back up the hill I feel a little self-conscious about carrying my gun. I haven't thought about my weapon since I took the bullets out and stored it out of sight a few days after Blaise was born. Now I'm huffing up the hill with a loaded pistol and a shitload of money and I start to laugh. I stop halfway up the hill, panting slightly, and realize how terribly out of shape I am. I remind myself that when I don't have work I also don't have an excuse not to exercise. I sit on a stone bench at the top of the hill and rest a moment, wondering how I got myself into this situation.

After safely securing my loaded gun and the money in the glove compartment, I back Betty out of the single parking space. If Hubert is waiting out front for me, and I have a feeling he is, he'll be waiting a very long time. Driving down Laurel Canyon Boulevard and heading toward home, I notice a police car pull in behind me. It stays with me whether I slow down or speed up.

Shit. My paranoia is peaking. I don't have any outstanding parking tickets, my registration is current, there are no burned-out taillights and I'm going the speed limit.

Go away!

As soon as I see an opportunity, I use my blinker and safely switch to the faster lane. The police cruiser switches right behind me. At a stop sign, I watch through my rearview mirror and see the officer in the passenger seat entering information into the computer on his dashboard. I get in the left-hand lane, using my blinker for certain, and they follow along. God, if they stop me and I have to open my glove compartment for my registration . . . do I have my CCW in my wallet? Of course I do . . . breathe.

I pull out into the intersection, waiting for the traffic to clear so I can make a left turn. The traffic thins, the light turns yellow, then red. Already out in the intersection, I cautiously start my left turn.

It's a standard way of making a left turn in Los Angeles, and it will surely help me lose the cops behind me. Thank God for red lights!

Suddenly, a driver speeds through the red light and slams hard into my passenger side. My perception goes into slow motion as my head and body jerk forward, then back, while my SUV flips over. The seatbelt locks and the force pushes Betty sideways, smashing me violently into the police cruiser that had been following. After hitting two parked cars, Betty and I come to a rest on her side, rocking precariously. Through a huge gaping hole where my windshield is now crushed and ripped from the frame, I see the driver who hit me try to drive his crumpled blue Chevy away. His front wheels are caved in and his car is so crippled that the police catch up to it on foot.

I am hanging in my seatbelt like a parachutist braced by her harness. I unlatch myself and fall down onto my driver's-side window, my knees buckled underneath me. Besides the windshield being gone, my rearview mirror is missing and the contents of my truck are strewn everywhere. I try to push myself up but when I do so, the SUV wobbles unsteadily.

"Ma'am, are you hurt?" a man's voice calls out.

"No, I don't think so," I yell. "But if I move, it feels like the truck is going to flip over again." I hear fire engines in the background and suddenly remember the money and my gun.

Taking the key out of the ignition, I stretch to unlock the glove compartment. The truck rocks.

"Ma'am, don't move. What is your name?"

"Corki."

"Corki, I'm Officer Bill Roberts with the Los Angeles Police Department. You're going to have to hold still until the fire department can get here to secure your car so we can get you out of there." He is kneeling down on the street, not two feet away from me.

"It's not going to catch fire, is it? I just filled it with gas," I say, panicking.

"Corki, you're fine. Gas isn't leaking. Are you hurt anywhere?"

"I'm not hurting, but I'm shaking and I can't seem to stop."

Officer Bill reaches through the windshield and holds my hand. Just as he takes it, a thick stream of blood rolls out of my hairline, down my forehead and down the ridge of my nose. I pull my hand away and wipe at the warm wetness streaming down my face.

"I'm bleeding from my head."

"Corki, I see it. The ambulance is pulling up right now."

"I don't want to go to the hospital. I have to pick up my son from school."

"Slow down, Corki. We need to get you out of here first and then we'll get your son situated. L.A. schools don't let out for another hour and a half. Your son's fine."

"Officer Bob, I have a CCW, sir."

"Corki, calm down."

"Please, Bob, listen to me."

"It's Bill, and I'm listening, but you need to calm down and not move around so much. Did you have your seatbelt on when you were hit?"

"Yes. Please, listen to me before anyone else walks over here. I have a CCW and a loaded weapon in my glove compartment. I also have other things in there that could have jammed against the gun. I don't want anyone to get shot. Do you hear me?"

He pats my hand.

"Okay, Corki, hold on and do *not* try to open the glove compartment. Hold still while I go talk to my partner."

I sit as still as I can.

Half an hour later, a handsome fireman leans his face close to my windshield. I smile at him and wonder if it's a requirement for the Los Angeles Fire Department trainees to be gorgeous as well as skilled. I can't recall ever seeing an ugly one in Los Angeles.

"Hi, Corki," he says.

"Hi. I'm getting cramped in here. Can I get out soon?" I ask.

"Can you move your limbs? I see a laceration on your scalp, but are you hurt anywhere else? Any numbness?" he asks.

"My legs are starting to fall asleep, but it's just from being in the same position for so long. I can move. I'm not hurt."

"Corki, tomorrow you may feel pain in your neck and other places in your muscles, so I'd refrain from making statements saying that you're not hurt," Gorgeous offers.

Legal *and* medical advice. I shut up.

"Okay, Corki, we have the truck supported. Do you have the ignition key?"

I hold up my hand with the key in it.

"Okay, I want you to put it in and turn the key on, but not the car. Don't turn over the engine."

I do so and my dashboard lights spring to life.

"Now, push the button on your console between the seats and see if it will roll down the rear window."

I do it and like a champ, the back tinted window opens effortlessly.

"Corki, do you want me to come in the back and help you out?"

"No, I can get out myself, but—"

"Corki, don't worry. I'll take care of the glove compartment," Officer Bill says.

I draw my legs up and bend over, crawling through the space between my bucket seats. I see my purse in the back along with a few of Blaise's magazines and my cell phone. I pick them up and put them in my purse and bring it out with me. Gorgeous helps me out and walks me to the ambulance. He seats me on the bumper at the rear. The paramedic who comes out looks mighty familiar.

"We meet again!" I say.

"Yes," he says. "I thought you looked familiar."

"Bank robbery a while ago in Beverly Hills," I offer. "Bloody nose."

The paramedic, Angelo, nods. "That's right. I knew the face was memorable, I just couldn't place the accident. You specialize in bloody incidents?" he asks.

"I try not to. I just seem to always be in the wrong place at the right time."

"Remind me. Your name?" he asks.

"Corki Brown."

"Okay, Corki, bend your head down so I can take a look at this cut on your scalp."

I lean over.

"Corki, we're going to have to take you to the hospital to sew the laceration on your head. It's just a bit bigger than a butterfly bandage will hold."

"No. I can't go. I have things I have to get out of my truck and I have to pick up my son."

"Corki, no one is going to take anything out of your truck, and you can use my cell if you want to call your son's school."

"I have a cell and I'll call, but I have to get a few things out of my truck. Please, talk to Officer Bill. He knows. I really have to."

"All right. Just let me wrap your head to stop some of the bleeding and then we'll go talk to him."

After Angelo's handiwork, I feel as if I've been freshly delivered from a facelift. My eyes feel swollen and puffy and the rest of my face is wrapped with white gauze. I call Envision and Shelly and arrange for Blaise to be picked up.

I walk over to Officer Bill.

"Excuse me, but did you get the glove compartment open yet?"

"No, I have someone who is about to do it," he says. "You want to show me the CCW now?"

"Yes, but I need to ask you to watch whoever does it, because I have something else in there," I say sheepishly.

"What is it?"

"A huge amount of cash. A hundred thousand dollars. I don't want it accidentally falling into someone's pocket."

"All right, Corki, let me see your license and CCW."

"I didn't do anything wrong!" I say defensively.

"Never said you did." He holds his hand out while I nervously fumble through my wallet to get him the papers he's demanding. "Stay right here." Suddenly he's more cop than friend.

I wait by the curb. I can see my glove compartment being opened, my weapon and the money being removed and taken directly to Officer Bill as he sits in his car checking out my record. As far as I know, I don't have one. But that doesn't stop my imagination from wondering. What if a police report shows I put a toilet paper roll on backward? After ten solid minutes, Officer Bill calls me over.

"Corki, is this your money?"

Oh shit, I've been sitting here on the curb for ten minutes watching the tow truck flip poor Betty upright and I haven't begun to think of what to say about the money. Did I think Officer Bill wasn't going to ask?

"Is this your money?" he asks again.

I'm not getting in trouble for Jock or anyone.

"No."

"How did you get it?" he asks. "To whom does it belong?"

"It belongs to the person I work for," I say, rubbing my now-aching head.

"Why do you have the money in your possession?"

"It's a long story and my head is starting to really hurt."

O*fficer Bill and his partner,* Officer Dan, accompany me to Cedars-Sinai Medical Center's emergency room. Cedars-Sinai is a movie-star hospital. Every room is a private suite complete with cable television, beds, a couch and a huge widow with a view of the hills or a cityscape of downtown Los Angeles. This is the place Elizabeth Taylor and other celebs frequent. This is where rock stars' babies are born and sick actors die. The eighth floor is where all stars are housed.

I'm in the ER, on the first floor, where the resident in charge shaves a nice big two-inch-by-three-inch rectangle in the middle of my scalp, then sews me up. It's so neatly shaved, it almost looks like a hairstyle . . . but not quite. Before he starts sewing, I ask him if perhaps he has a suture material that matches my scalp color rather than my hair.

"This is a hospital, not a hair salon," he says, incredulous.

"Then perhaps some transparent thread?" I ask.

"No," he says patronizingly, "then the doctor couldn't see them to take them out."

"Of course. I just figured with Cedars being located in West Hollywood that perhaps there might be something on the order of a vanity stitch. You know how casts now come in a variety of colors? There's even one that glows in the dark. I just thought that perhaps . . ." I say, letting my words trail off.

"No. Our variety is black stitches and staples. Head wounds require black stitches. That's your choice. Black stitches."

I sit still. Afterward, he gives me a mirror to check the results. I compliment him on his technique and ask if he got an A in Home Economics.

When I'm done, Officers Bill and Dan interrogate me thoroughly, then very kindly drive me home in a new cruiser that was delivered to them at the scene of the accident. As Bill drives, I sit in the backseat like a common criminal, telling them my Hubert story, minus some "minor" details, like what was on Jock's DVD.

"Why were you guys following me to begin with?"

They look at each other, then Officer Dan looks back to where I'm sitting.

"You have 'limo black' windows. People with dark windows usually have something to hide."

They drop me at home . . . minus the money.

Now, instead of one hundred thousand dollars, I have a receipt for what they've taken until my story checks out true.

Chapter Eighteen

I lie in bed feeling terrible and understanding why Mr. Gorgeous Fireman told me not to say I wasn't hurt. I can barely move. The trauma to my body has set in and I'm sorry I refused the pain medication the hospital offered. My head is throbbing. How stupid! I should have just taken the damn drugs.

When Shelly arrives home with Blaise and the girls in tow, she stays for a while and helps me by running a hot shower and covering my hair and stitches with a shower cap. She makes dinner, washes my dishes and helps the kids with their homework. We all do a gentle group-hug goodnight and I hug her extra tight even though it hurts.

The next morning, after Shelly picks up Blaise for school, I spend six hours on the phone to insurance companies, doctors and attorneys. Dr. Trabulus insists I see an orthopedic surgeon for continued care, and the attorney who was recommended to me by Jock's accountant as being an "SOB" insists I do the same. I schedule an appointment.

There seems to be a fraternal network of "son of a bitch" providers—from doctors to lawyers to photographers to appraisers. Apparently using the word "SOB" means that that particular person will win you the most money in your impending lawsuit. The dirtier the word used to describe them, the more desirable they are to have on my "team." Of course, desirability equals higher fees. It is Hollywood after all and I feel as if I'm putting together a production of sorts—a legal one to produce a picture about the terrible thing that happened to Corki Brown. All the SOBs want a piece of my lawsuit winnings, and apparently it will be more lucrative if I have *anything* broken. If it's just "soft tissue damage," I'll get a nominal amount.

Now I need a rental car. Thankfully, where I live in urban Los Angeles there is a rental agency around the corner. My car insurance will pay for a thirty-day rental, so I walk over and get one.

At my expedited appointment with a Beverly Hills orthopedic surgeon who charges exorbitantly for a full checkup and X-rays, I find myself hoping something's broken and am ashamed at my own thoughts. I'm starting to think like Hubert—what is everything worth?

One might think that a stitched head and a bald patch in litigious-crazy Hollywood, where it pays to look hot, would be worth financial damages, but I'm not paid to be sexy. I think the pain and suffering and hours wasted on phone calls might be worth something, too. They're not. And even trustworthy Betty isn't worth much.

The doctor returns and stoically slips my X-rays into the light box, showing me that nothing is broken. I schedule an appointment for physical therapy and leave.

Since it looks as if Betty will be a total loss, I drive over to the tow yard to empty her out. Catching a look at myself in a window of the tow yard office, I am surprised I was brave enough to get out of bed this morning, let alone go out in public. Besides the thick foam neck brace, standard fare for car accident victims, I have two black eyes, a swollen nose and a bandaged head. I look terrible. No one will be clamoring to ask me out on a date.

However, Blaise was sweet enough last night to tell me I looked just fine and then offered to sleep next to me to keep me safe. I think he wanted to make sure I was going to live through the night. I try not to think of the accident, but I keep thanking God that Blaise wasn't in the truck when it happened.

I take pictures of Betty with my camera and wish her well in whatever new form she takes after recycling. Los Angelenos are bonded to their cars, and true to form, so am I. She's been my loyal SUV for eight years and I feel an affinity for her. I remove all my stuff, including the cassette of Bob Marley that's been lodged between the front seat and the console for three years.

"Corki!" Lucy's voice rings out from the city of Vancouver. "Babe, are you there?"

No, I'm sorting out Betty's contents.

"Guess what?" she asks my answering machine. "We got the house! I'm so excited. I knew we would get it, I knew it! Babe? Are you there? I need a decorator with a flare for 1960s vintage charm. I know you're the one to ask. Help! Help! You know everyone who is good, with all the clients you've had. Help!" she screams out in excitement.

I've finally taken a pain pill and am having an allergic reaction. I can't stop scratching. I itch everywhere. I'm miserable. Besides itching, my thinking is a little batty. I pick up the phone.

"Hi, Lucy!"

"Oh! You're there?" she asks, disbelieving.

"Yeah. It took me a minute to get to the phone."

"Are you okay? You sound down."

"I had a car accident. I'm going to live, but Betty's dead."

"No! Not Betty!"

"Yeah," I say. "She's totaled."

"Oh, honey, that's terrible. Do you have a car?"

"Yeah, my insurance pays for a rental for a month."

"Listen, Corki," she says. "After the month, use Grace. Do not go out and spend more money, I command you. I know she isn't your typical car for running errands, but I won't be home anyway."

"Lucy, that is very sweet of you to offer, but—"

"I'm serious, Corki. Drive her until you can get a new car."

A new car . . . how could I afford a new car and how could it replace my trusty steed-ette Betty?

"Tell me about the new house," I ask in a happy tone that disguises how miserable I feel.

"Oh my God, Corki, I can't wait for you to see it. It needs a little work, but it's basically a perfect match for us. Five bedrooms, six and a half baths. We'll have enough room for Tommy Ray's kids plus ours when we start working on babies."

"You'll certainly need a big house," I say, remembering that growing up I never had my own room. I was happy to have my own bed.

"I think it would be really cute to do the house with vintage charm, but I need to be directed. I'm afraid I'll go overboard and Tommy Ray'll get upset."

"God forbid," I say.

"Stop it, Corki. He called and apologized for what he did and said. In fact he's going to reimburse me for the damage he did to Grace."

"I never got an apology."

"Is he still paying your weekly bill?"

"Point well taken," I say, even though she hasn't had enough work for me to know whether he'd pay a decent-sized bill.

"Look, Babe, while he's away, I need you to act as me. I want you to play general contractor. Sound fun?"

"Yeah, I like to play," I say as I scratch a bruise on my leg.

"Play and get paid! Okay, here's my fantasy. I want Tommy to come home from Mexico to a beautiful, finished home that is perfect in every way. I want his toothbrush waiting and flowers next to the bed. His clothes should be color coordinated in his closet and his boots in a neat row."

"This sounds time-consuming. What about the girls? Are they going to be doing some of it?"

"Jolene's in Mexico assisting him on the set and Bobby Sue is here in Vancouver with me. I really need you to do this, Corki. I have no one else."

I almost feel relieved, but I'm still worried. I remember the last time Lucy decided that I put too many hours into one of her projects. She refused to pay my invoice. Said I charged too much.

I might be able to count on a month's worth of income, then the "girls" will return and I'll become redundant once again.

"All right, give me the info," I sigh.

I get back in bed and screen my calls because there are so many I can't take. My head is still swimming from the pain pills. What if Jock calls and I need to explain that I don't have his money? What if Hubert calls and I have to tell him the same thing? Before I can get comfortable, the phone *does* ring. I let my answering machine pick it up.

"Corki, this is Officer Bill Roberts, L.A.P.D. Please give me a call at area code two-one-three, four . . ."

I scramble as fast as I can to get to the phone, which is only a little faster than a cadaver might move.

". . . I'd like you to come down to the station."

I pick up the receiver.

"Are you going to arrest me?"

"Is there something you aren't telling me?" he asks.

"No. I just don't want to come down there and have a surprise thrown on me. I haven't done anything wrong."

"We know that now," he says. "We spoke with the appropriate parties and your identity was confirmed."

"Are you going to give me back the money?"

"Sort of."

"What do you mean, 'sort of'?" I ask nervously.

"Just come down and we'll talk about it."

We arrange a time for me to go in tomorrow, once my drugged haze has worn off.

Chapter Nineteen

I live in Los Angeles and still avoid downtown like the plague. There's a part of downtown that is modern and beautiful, but it's impossible to find parking, and when you do, there's an eleven-dollar minimum fee. My yearly ritual of dropping off the Academy Award ballots on the last day of voting (because Jock and Lucy can never decide until the last moment how they'll cast their votes) is enough. My annual pilgrimage from West Hollywood to Price Waterhouse Coopers' downtown office is actually enough to set off an anxiety attack. I forever get lost because Los Angeles's streets dead-end in odd places and change names when they continue elsewhere.

The part of downtown I'm in, however, does not qualify as beautiful or modern. It's dirty, run-down and littered with skid row's spookiest occupants. The desperate faces of life's most downtrodden scare me and I don't feel comfortable leaving my car, even if it is in front of the L.A.P.D. I imagine my insurance company's reaction if I were to total Betty and a few days later get the rental stolen.

I park anyway and walk into the station in order to feel safe. It looks equally dank and depressing. Fluorescent lights cast shadows on the faded green tiled floors. The station needs a woman's touch. At least the officers earn a consistent paycheck and hopefully good benefits.

It turns out that "sort of" was bull. They don't give me back one dollar. All they do is ask me a ton of questions, none of which I feel are their business, but I answer them anyway because I want to go home. I've seen enough police shows to know they'll get the answers eventually. I'm no hardened criminal, but they're treating me like one. Just because I have dark windows doesn't mean I have anything to hide. Not that much, anyway. I feel misled and know that when Jock comes back, I won't have a job with him either.

I have trouble negotiating the rental car through traffic because I can't turn my head very easily to check the blind spots. My brace keeps my neck and head stationary while I cruise home at fifteen miles an hour behind a city Metro bus that stops every couple of blocks.

I come home to a message from Veronique asking how I am. She says she's in town for a while, then off to Italy. She leaves her world cell number and asks me to drop her a line.

The next message is from none other than Officer Bill, wanting me to continue planning on meeting Hubert and asking me when I'd like the money returned. Why didn't he ask me that while I was sitting in his office? I'm not going down there again. If he's going to mislead me and play games, he'll have to do it here at my house.

. . .

I stand corrected. He did *not* mislead me or play games. One and a half hours before I am to meet Hubert, the money is returned to me. I spend thirty minutes counting it out on my coffee table and signing a release for it.

I gather all my stuff together to nail Hubert. I have my spy pen in perfect working order, the portable DVD player and the edited DVDs. This has all been weighing so hard on me that I'm actually looking forward to seeing him. I just want it to be done and to be paid for the time I spent doing it.

I drive into the back parking lot of Clafouti's, and circle around it a number of times looking for Hubert's Mazda, as well as a place to park. I don't see his car, but I half expect him to appear out of nowhere the moment I park mine. I'm thankful, only this one time, that I have a rental and not Betty. He's known Betty since he was ten years old and won't be looking for me without her. Sitting for a moment, rehearsing exactly what I'm going to do and say, I rethink all my plans, backup plans and backups for backups. I scan the parking lot to make sure I'm not going to be hit up for money by a homeless person before I even get to Hubert.

With all the spying equipment stuffed in my purse, I calmly walk up the potato-vined arches of the exterior stone staircase. The place is packed and it's barely noon. Scanning the front sidewalk area, I see only one table left without a reserved sign. Remembering my little experience at the Four Seasons with Lucy, I ask first. It's free. I slip into the seat and order an iced tea.

I chose twelve o'clock because I knew the place would be packed with all the unemployed actors, models and singers who desire to be seen.

Clafouti's and all the top fashion stores that line what has been dubbed Sunset Plaza are perched on the side of a hill. Contractors flattened out the area behind Sunset Plaza to create a huge, much-needed parking area for the retailers. The restaurants lining Sunset Plaza are *the* places to be if you want to be seen, and I want to be seen, desperately. As I scan the crowd for Hubert, I see we have a special on well-built men today. Bringing out my spy pen, I wait.

Before the waitress can bring my tea, Hubert, along with his two brothers, Wilbert and Rupert, all plop down in seats opposite me. I guess it's payday for everyone involved. Looking at Hubert's mug in triplicate is not pleasant.

"What happened to you?" he asks in a disgusted tone, noticing my brace.

"Nice to see you, too, boys. Is that how you were raised? You don't even say hello and how are you?"

"Hi, Corki. How are you?" they all say.

"That's more like it. I'm fine. I was in a car accident. Now you're supposed to say 'Oh, I'm so sorry to hear what you've been through,'" I instruct.

"Yeah, Hubert, that was sort of callous, man," Wilbert adds. Thank you, Wilbert. At least one is promising on the manners front.

"Whatever, enough of the niceties. Did you bring what you were supposed to?" Hubert asks truculently.

"Yes. However, there's one thing more," I add.

"Oh, man, I knew this was going to happen. Why can't shit just go off as planned," he says to no one in particular. "What now?"

"You didn't think Jock was going to have me hand over a hundred grand without you signing a statement that you're returning all the DVDs, did you? I need the originals you took and any duplicates you made," I whisper.

"I didn't make any duplicates," he says flatly.

I put my hand in my purse and pull out the legal documents I had made up. I push them toward Hubert.

"What's all this shit?" he asks, growing more irate.

"You know what, Hubert? I'm not going to give you squat if you don't straighten up. I'm old enough to be your mama and don't need to hear your nasty mouth. You don't have anything on me, and I'm the one holding what you want. Deal?" I'm getting increasingly irritated with how disrespectful this twit is acting.

"Fine," he says. "What is this?"

"This is a legal document stating that what you're handing over to me is everything you took. It also states that you are handing over any copies, in any format, that you've made. It also says that I am giving you one hundred thousand dollars, in cash, for the return of Jock's possessions."

"I'm not signing that," Hubert says indignantly.

"Okay."

I stand up, gather my things and start to leave.

"Wait, wait, wait," says Rupert, startled at how quickly I got up. "Hubert, you're giving her everything you got, man. Just sign the paper. Don't be an idiot."

"Fuck off, Rup," he says. "Corki, just give me the money like you were supposed to do."

"Excuse me, Hubert. Who dictates how I'm supposed to do this? You? Or the guy who pays me?" I sit back down. "I don't have a lot of time. Sign the paper or not. I don't really care one way or the other. If you want to earn the easiest money you've ever made, sign it. If not, don't. But if you think you're going to pull one over on

Jock by getting his money, then putting this all over the Internet, it's not going to happen. Sign it or don't," I hiss.

I get the documents and spy pen back out of my purse and hand them to him. Hubert just sits staring at the paper and holding the pen as though he's frozen. I decide to pull a little trick that works with Blaise every time.

"Hubert, I'm going to count to three, then I'm out of here. One. Two. Th—"

He quickly signs the document then hands the entire thing back to me. I put the spy pen down on the table, the documents in my purse and pull out the portable DVD player.

"I want you to see something, boys."

"I don't have time for this, Corki. Just give me the—"

"You'll have time for this, Hubert," I say, interrupting him. I play the DVD player with the edited tape showing Tree calling him on the fax line, the scenes of the boys trashing Jock's room, and the tapes of them coming onto the property and leaving. Then I plug the pen directly into the portable DVD player and it plays back the scene that just took place—the triplets' arrival, the entire conversation in audio and digital.

"Now, boys, you can see I have evidence, including fingerprints, that proves what you did," I say. "If I wanted to, I could have all three of your asses strung up together. But I'm going to make it easy and give you the money. But I swear—and you'd better tell Miss Tree this, too—if so much as a peep of this gets out, I'm handing everything over to the cops. And don't think you're going to follow me to the car and swipe this from me either, because while I'm sitting here taping you, someone else is videotaping all of us. I'm also not the only one with copies of this, so don't get any ideas. You lucked out this time. All you have to do is behave yourselves. Hear?"

The three of them say nothing, but with scowls on their faces, they nod their heads.

"Do what you promised, Corki."

I look around the crowd and see my good friend Noah and smile at him. Noah, a longtime dedicated Rastafarian, has blond dreadlocks down to the backs of his thighs. His Swedish ancestry shows through his shining blue eyes and super-high cheekbones, but Noah is as Jamaican as one can get without having been born there. He walks over with a Hermès shopping bag slung casually over his shoulder.

"Hey, sister."

I stand and we kiss each other hello as he casually drops the bag onto Hubert's lap. I watch over Noah's shoulder as Hubert looks inside the bag and appears satisfied. He puts the stolen DVDs in my held-out hand, then he and his brothers get up and leave without saying a word. Noah sits down, winks and smiles wide for the spy pen.

Without any warning, four of the well-built men I'd been admiring earlier abruptly get up and lunge past us. They're on top of Hubert and his brothers before they even get to the curb. Within seconds two unmarked police sedans pull up with lights flashing in the rear windows. Six uniformed officers surround the Brothers Grimm before they realize what's happening. Hubert looks back at me with hate in his eyes and spits in my direction. I can't exactly walk up to him and tell him that I had no idea this was going to happen. I helped plan it. From parties to sting operations, I plan it all.

I pay for the iced tea and leave with Noah while watching Officer Bill and Officer Dan, doing what they get their salaries to do, protect and serve.

. . .

At home I listen to the message on my answering machine. There is only one.

"Mrs. Brown, this is Principal Davidson at Envision Prep. I need to speak with you. Please call me at your earliest convenience."

The high I've been on since pulling off a successful sting operation drops to an all-time low. He doesn't say "Goodbye" or "Good day" or any of the sign-offs that might let a parent know their kid is okay, but then again, he didn't call my cell, which indicates it's not an emergency. I call back.

"Ah, yes, Mrs. Brown," Mr. Davidson says with restraint. "I want to talk to you about your son. I'm afraid I misjudged our ability to help him with his educational pursuits."

"What do you mean?"

"It means that I don't think Envision Prep is well suited for his needs."

"What did he do now?" I ask.

"Ma'am, the question should be, what hasn't he done? He somehow got hold of the second-grade roster, pretended to be a teacher, and called the parents to inform them that their children have been showing *Homo . . . sapien* tendencies. Half the parents don't get past the "homo" part, especially when the second half of the term is swallowed and barely audible. I have thirty-two angry parents calling asking to have their kids removed from our campus. I've received threatening, angry e-mails and letters asking for my resignation. I think your son needs more . . . more discipline than we are legally allowed to perform."

"Well, where is he supposed to go?" I ask in a panic. "It's almost the end of the school year. Can't he just finish there and I'll arrange something different for next year?"

"Mrs. Brown?" he says, then pauses. "No. He will be dismissed from Envision as soon as I get the paperwork through the proper channels. That will take a week or two, tops. Please make other arrangements at your earliest convenience. Good day."

He hangs up without my response. I lower my head. My eyes are brimming with tears. What has happened to my boy?

The phone rings. I sniff back my tears and answer it.

"Miss Brown? . . . This is Mr. Barba, Blaise's counselor," he says with a deep cough.

He sounds as if he has a terrible cold, but his kind voice is a beacon in my churning sea. I let myself cry freely.

"Mr. Barba, I just received a call from Mr. Davidson and he says Blaise is being kicked out of school."

There is a pause, a sigh, then silence.

"I don't know what I've done wrong. I love my son so much and I try as hard as I can to teach him to do right, but it all seems to backfire. I would do anything I could for him, but I just can't seem to get it right."

My sobs are coming out hard.

"Miss Brown, don't worry. Everything will be all right."

Mr. Barba doesn't seem as sure of himself as he once was. Where he was so eloquent before in helping comfort me, he now only repeats that everything will be okay and not to worry. I try to feel better after we hang up, but I can't help worrying about my son. I pray that Mr. Barba can do for Blaise what I have been unable to do.

Chapter Twenty

With L.A. Unified School District still in session and Blaise expelled from Envision Prep, I telephone his old school and see about reenrolling him immediately. Dr. Castillo doesn't sound thrilled by the prospect, but we are in the district, so she can't exactly turn us away. In fact, he can start the next day.

It's been a month since my accident and three weeks since Concepcion's sons were arrested. My life has quieted considerably. My shaved hair, hidden under a plethora of different hats, is starting to grow back slowly. My stitches have been removed and my body is on the mend. Officers Bill and Dan returned the money, which I returned to Jock's safe. They never asked me to explain what was on the DVDs that Hubert turned over to me at Clafouti's. I destroyed them immediately. I'm sure Hubert gave the officers an earful about Jock's underage sex partners, but that won't come out in the rags until Hubert resurfaces, angrier than ever at the way he was trapped like a fox.

I haven't heard from Jock. I called and left a message that all was done and taken care of. I risked my life for Monsieur Jacques, saved his career and his hundred grand, and he hasn't even said thank you.

This is the last day my insurance covers the rental car. With no extra money to continue renting, I have to give it up. It's not possible to function in L.A. without a car—especially in my business—and I have no idea how I'll scrape together the funds to buy one, so I take Lucy up on her offer.

Ferrari Modena 360s were not built to run errands. In fact, I am convinced they were not built for more than showing off, Italian-style. They're almost impossible to get in and out of, and the gas pedal is as narrow as a fine pair of Italian leather shoes. My wide foot keeps slipping off the accelerator and hitting the brakes instead. After narrowly missing running down Mickey Rourke at a Beverly Hills intersection, I am convinced that I'm not suited to the flashy lifestyle expected of Ferrari Modena owners.

"Corki, it's Esther."

I pick up the phone.

"Hi! Long time no hear!" I say, as if it doesn't affect me at all that I've had no work from them.

"You're hearing from me now," she says.

"Good point. What's up?"

"Cameron Diaz and I are hosting a Celebrity Meditation Retreat here at the house. I don't need a lot, but I am going to need your help. There's a place on Montana Avenue that has agreed to donate their Oriental rugs for the retreat, and I need you to pick them up. Plus, I'm going to need padding to go under all of them. I'll give you the measurements. Also, I'm going to need . . ." She proceeds to give me a list of items—outdoor umbrellas, stands, coffeemakers, microphones, podiums, speakers and other supplies for her retreat.

With the top down on Lucy's Ferrari, I'm able to cram most of Esther's requested items into the car. Of course, that makes me look like a Beverly Hillbilly cruising down Rodeo Drive with rug pads hanging precariously out of the top.

I pull into Esther's driveway just as she, accompanied by Cameron Diaz and Justin Timberlake, says goodbye to her land-scaper, who is doing last-minute plantings. Esther points me out to them, says something, then starts laughing so hard she actually falls backward on the grass. She kicks her legs like a three-year-old having a hissy fit, tears running down her face from the hilarity. In be-tween her fits of laughter, Cameron's embarrassed smile and Justin's smirk, I explain about my car accident and not having enough work to just go out and buy a new car.

"Jesus, Corki, why didn't you just tell us?" she asks, still gig-gling.

"I just did."

"Before you were reduced to this!" she yells out hysterically, pointing to the Ferrari.

"Well, look, Esther. Someone lent me this car."

She wipes off the grass and helps me bring the new purchases into the house, followed by Cameron and Justin. The moment we enter and pass a freshly bathed Lord Ganesh, Esther bursts out laughing again. She recounts the scene of me pulling up in the loaded Ferrari to Shelly and Liam. The only one laughing is Esther.

"Did you get hurt in the accident?" Liam inquires.

"A little." I take off my baseball cap and show him my buzz-cut patch.

"Oh, it's growing peach fuzz," Shelly observes. "It's healing nicely."

My shaved head has upstaged Esther.

"Honey," she calls out to Liam, "write Corki a check so she can go out and buy herself a car."

The room goes silent and I see Liam's Adam's apple suck back into his throat.

"Okay. Corki, how much do you need?"

I say nothing.

"Give her around twenty thousand, Liam. The only caveat to this loan is that you have to buy a car that is environmentally conscious. No more SUVs or trucks. Get either a hybrid or electric, something with really good gas mileage."

Liam goes to his office and comes back with a checkbook. He scribbles out a check for twenty thousand dollars, made payable to me, Cornelia Brown. He hands it to me with a smile. "If you need more, let me know."

"Liam, I haven't been working very much and I'm worried there might be months I can't make a payment on time. I don't want there to be any weird feelings or—"

Liam stops me. "We'll work it out."

Chapter Twenty-one

Lucy pleads with me to help decorate her new house, so I call my older sister, Drusilla, who just graduated with a degree in interior design. I invite her to L.A. and she presents her ideas to Lucy and Tommy Ray via a video computerized conference call. They hire her on the spot. Drusilla stays in our apartment while she transforms their mansion into a home.

Lucy and Tommy, from opposite sides of the continent, come to an agreement with Drusilla that the design of the house should be an eclectic, modern 1950s/60s style. Retro funky. Drusilla designs his-and-hers offices that feature walls painted in Tommy Ray's favorite shade of pale gray-blue and floors tiled in his favorite combination of black and blue squares, but her trim is white, while his is black. His office features black leather chairs, hers white leather. Since the offices share a common entrance, the effect is stunning.

The whole Spanish-style house receives a fresh coat of paint, inside and out. Drusilla orders 1950s vintage wallpaper from New York for the guest room. The great room has ebony hardwood floors and creamy white walls. The ceiling has beautiful, rustic, ebony-stained wood beams that complement the floors. Even though Lucy doesn't cook, she requests a Viking stove be installed along with a double oven for me. Drusilla orders double sinks and glass-fronted cabinets for the kitchen.

The locks have been changed, a new yard planted, and a security system worthy of royalty has been installed. It's a frightening system that talks to the intruder. It spells out, in a computer-generated voice, what the intruder must do, and what will happen if he doesn't. I have also researched, recommended and supervised the setup of at least a half-dozen other gotta-have-it technical household systems such as the state-of-the-art heating-and-cooling system that can be programmed by phone to warm or cool the house an hour before the occupants come home.

I work closely with the contractor to create a panic room built in a closet off the master bedroom. It looks like a normal walk-in, but the pocket door is lined with steel and inside the closet are all the amenities one might need in case an intruder has entered the property. However, this is slightly different from other panic rooms. Lucy, unbeknownst to Tommy Ray, wants a code that will admit her but lock him out! I keep my mouth shut when this feature is requested. Why move in with a man you're afraid of? The red flags are waving wildly. Why isn't she paying attention?

After setting these advanced technological wonders in motion, I come home to my 1940s fourplex with a small front yard that is watered by turning the sprinklers on by hand. And those don't even work properly. With a broken pressure regulator, water shoots up out of the bushes so strongly a fireman could fight fires with it. I turn a key to open my door and adjust my heating thermostat manually. I don't know if anyone's been to *my* house, but I will know if someone with an access code has entered Lucy's property. If the pool man is supposed to come on Monday and Thursday between twelve and two, the system will let him in. But if he gets caught in traffic and arrives at 2:15 P.M., he is barred access until the next time he is scheduled to be there. This system gives new meaning to being at the right place at the right time.

Lucy calls from the set wanting to make sure nothing is done to the house that will offend Tommy Ray's senses, and Jolene calls from a hotel room in Mexico, trying to guarantee the same thing. Everyone wants to make sure Tommy Ray's happy. What fun! A household ruled by the threat of Tommy Ray's outbursts.

After faxing back and forth to Canada and Mexico, Drusilla and I put together a complete furniture layout, room by room.

Tommy Ray and Lucy take a brief break from their respective films to fly home for the final approval before I have their belongings moved into their new abode. Lucy loves it, but more importantly, Tommy Ray is very happy and they send Drusilla home with a hefty paycheck and a complimentary ticket to see Tommy's friend Duane Diamond in concert.

I not only have Chipman United moving Lucy's possessions out of her rented home, but I have them bringing her belongings out of storage, too. Additionally, I have Lucy's mom, Beryl Bennett, and her new boyfriend bringing a few things in a U-Haul down from Montecito the same day. The next day, Tommy Ray's stuff will arrive.

It takes a month of constant phone calls to get one of these moves to go smoothly. I have a reputation among my clients for my ability to manage the kind of complex moves common to Hollywood celebrities. I take responsibility for all the details—large and small—so they are free to focus on demanding production schedules or a postproduction fling with a costar. I've handled over twenty large-scale moves dealing with everything from boarding the household pets to carpeting, tableware to toilet paper, and window coverings to wine cellar placement.

As I pass out floor plans with furniture arrangements to each mover, I also greet the furniture companies making deliveries from their custom-design showroom floors.

My new car, a VW Jetta wagon TDI that Blaise has christened Bella, gets fifty miles to the gallon. She is parked on the street in front of the new house as movers and delivery companies file in and out. I'm directing the flow of traffic as I stand leaning my back against the driver's-side door. The U-Haul truck containing Lucy's mom arrives, with her newest guy behind the wheel. They pull up precariously close to me.

"Hi, sugar!" Beryl calls out.

"Hey! You guys made good time," I yell out above the clamor.

"Well, with this gorgeous hunk of a man behind the wheel, how could we not make good time?" Beryl asks.

Beryl always looks good. I've never seen a blond hair out of place or her full lips not perfectly done with a tone of lipstick that complements her outfit. She dated a lot after her divorce from Lucy's dad, but never seemed to find a partner to suit her wildness. Lucy is always a little embarrassed by her mother's crazy ways, but I happen to like her eccentricities. Beryl has no shame about stating what she likes, wants and feels. I always know where I stand with her, even when she's "mad as a hornet."

Beryl squeezes her young hunk's thigh as she wrinkles her nose and blows him kisses. "Cornelia"—she refuses to use my nickname—"honey, this is David, and David, this is Cornelia Brown, my daughter's assistant. Where can we park this tank?"

"Actually, the delivery truck that was here just left. You can back into the spot directly behind my car," I say.

David the Hunk, who looks closer to my age than Beryl's, turns the steering wheel to parallel park. I look down at the papers in my hands when I feel the side of the truck's front bumper on my stomach and the wheel running over my toes.

"Ahhhh!" I scream. "Whoa! Beryl! Stop! I'm getting run over!"

Beryl connects with the look of anguish on my face and grabs the steering wheel out of Hunk's hand. She yells at him like he's her employee.

"Holy Jesus! David, you're crushing Cornelia! Put your foot on the fucking brake!"

She jumps out of the cab and rushes over to me.

"My God, Sugar! Are you okay? Is anything broken?" she asks, holding me more tightly to her than the truck did when it was crushing me.

"I'm fine," I say, barely able to speak as she holds my face tightly to her bosom.

"I'm sorry, sugar," she says over and over.

"I'm fine, really. It just gave me a hard squeeze," I insist.

"Cornelia, you listen to me. I have a very fine insurance policy for just this type of thing. You promise me that you'll let me know if you start hurting or if you need to go to a chiropractor. Send me the bill and I'll pay it right away," she says, still holding my shoulders tightly.

"Beryl, I'm fine. Don't worry. Why don't you let one of the Chipman drivers back the truck in and we'll get it unloaded," I say, trying to calm her.

One look at David the Hunk and I understand he's been emasculated in front of the whole crew of moving men. He steps from the cab and lets Tony, a professional driver, back the truck up. Everyone quietly goes back to work.

It takes ten hours to move Lucy's possessions into the new house, arrange everything and haul away the packing material. Shelly drops

Blaise off at five o'clock and he spends the next two hours running up and down the truck ramp. Most of the Chipman guys are dads and they seem much more tolerant of this behavior than I. After eight hours of being on my feet, nonstop, I have to contain my mouth. I want to go home and rest, but the fun seems to be just starting for Blaise. Fifty-two-foot tractor-trailers mix very well with ten-year-old boys.

After the movers leave, Blaise and I continue to unpack boxes. Since it's a Friday, we work late into the night. At midnight, we go home. When I take my shoes off, I find that my toes are bruised, but they all move.

On Saturday morning, Tommy's move is done in six hours. Unpacking and organizing takes me a solid week of eight-hour days. Blaise helps since he has become a master at folding underwear, socks and T-shirts. With five hundred T-shirts between the two of them, he gets a lot of practice. I color-coordinate the clothes and stack cooking pots from biggest to smallest. Blaise organizes the library, puts logs in the fireplaces (I put the long matches on the mantel) and hangs curtains. We make six beds, organize bathroom drawers, and stock soaps, shampoos and conditioners in all the bathrooms.

The house is ready, but no one comes. Lucy goes to Mexico while Jolene and Bobby Sue fly back to Tennessee. Lucy and Bobby Sue return to Canada and Jolene goes back to Mexico. Everyone is flying everywhere, but no one comes home.

. . .

I sit at home trying to drum up work. I call Veronique but am informed that she is out of the country until further notice. She must be cruising the Mediterranean aboard Roberto Tratelli's yacht.

I give my apartment a good spring cleaning, move furniture and vacuum underneath, wash curtains, clean out cupboards and go through clothes and toys that are outgrown. My house and car and life have never been cleaner or more organized. However, I find myself falling into a funk.

"Coooooorrrr—kkkiiii! Are you there?" I hear Lucy cry out in excitement. "Honey, answer the phone!"

I drag myself out of bed and pick it up.

"Hello," I say.

"Corki, honey. It's Lucy. You sound so sad."

"I'm fine. I was asleep."

"Honey, it's one o'clock in the afternoon! What's wrong? I know you well enough to know something is wrong if you're in bed at this hour," she states.

"I'm fine. Late night."

"Well, get some good rest because I'm about to give you the job of planning my wedding!" she proclaims like a circus announcer.

I wake up immediately.

"Your wedding!"

"Yours truly will be walking down the aisle with Tommy Ray Woods, whose divorce was finalized three days ago. He is a free man and we are getting married!" she screams.

"Lucy, I know absolutely nothing about putting together a wedding," I warn, thrilled about the idea of a big project and slightly frightened of publicly botching the whole thing. "I'm no wedding planner."

"You are now," she says in her Memphis drawl.

"Lucy, when is all this supposed to happen?"

"Corki, babe, you have four weeks. I'll take care of invites from here, but I can't do it until I know you've secured a location."

"Where do you want it?"

"We want to have it where we met."

"On the set of *Live with Regis and Kelly*? New York?" I ask, panicking.

"No, where we *originally* met," she says.

"But you told me—"

"No, honey. Atlantis," she says.

"Atlantis?" I ask, confused. "Lucy, you're making me work too hard."

"Atlantis. Our first recognized life together. Greece. We want to be married in Santorini, our original home and the home of Atlantis."

She's going crazy.

"Babe, are you still there?" Lucy asks.

"Yes."

"Are you up to it?" she asks. "Tommy says he'll pay you handsomely if you can set it up. Bobby Sue doesn't know her ass from a hole in the ground, and Jolene's out of here. Tommy promised."

"Lucy, I—"

"Corki," she interrupts, "you're the only person I know who can do this for us. You spent that year in Santorini as a foreign exchange student. You speak—"

"I spoke, not speak. I haven't practiced in over twenty years!"

"It's like riding a bicycle. You just have to get back on. I don't even know how to say hello. You do."

"That might be all I remember," I claim. "Tell me how you see the wedding."

She gives me the broad outlines of what she wants and the number of people attending.

"I know it'll take a couple of weeks' planning from L.A., but I'll also need you there a good ten days ahead of time to secure and set up everything," Lucy says emphatically. "I want this to go off without a hitch, as if I planned it myself. I'll FedEx two tickets for you and Blaise overnight. He'll love Greece and we'll pay for everything: the prep, the ten days in Santorini plus all the rest of the time you'll need afterward to wrap up. Plus, we'll give you both per diem for food. I beg you, please, I need you, Corki."

"Okay, Lucy, I'll do it."

"Oh, honey, I knew you wouldn't let me down." She starts crying. "Thank you so much. You don't know how much this means to me."

"I do, Lucy. That's the reason I'll do it."

Lucy spends a minute crying and mopping up tears.

"Babe, there's one more thing. Tommy has a request. He really wants his mama to be at the wedding."

"His mom?" I ask, incredulous.

"Yeah, it's real important to him that Luella be there," she says.

I jot down a note to call Lufthansa and Olympic Airways to check out their policy on transporting human remains. I have a sense Tommy Ray won't want his mama riding in cargo.

Chapter Twenty-two

"We call them 'cremains' in the industry," he says to me over the phone.

Cremated remains. Cremains. Every business has its "speak," but this one strikes me as cold. Luella can come with us as far as Athens, according to the man on the phone at Lufthansa.

"It's fine for you to carry cremains on board. They're considered part of your carry-on luggage. However, you should call Olympic Airways and make sure you can carry them all the way through to Santorini," he suggests.

I call Olympic and confirm that I can indeed carry Luella on board with them, too. I ask both airlines to send me a faxed statement of this policy. The last thing I want is to get stuck with Luella in Frankfurt, Germany, trying to change planes and unable to board.

I spend the better part of two weeks on the phone making reservations with airlines, private jetliners, hotels, caterers, florists, photographers and musicians. According to my phone company, I have racked up six hundred dollars' worth of long-distance charges to

Greece, Germany, Mexico and Canada. I fax birth certificates, divorce decrees, passports, death certificates, copies of blood tests and marriage licenses back and forth between the four countries. In addition to all the paperwork involved, I make four trips to the Greek consulate to get documents translated into Greek and authenticated.

While doing research to line up the appropriate clergy member to perform the ceremony, I discover that for twenty-five bucks I could become a minister through the Church of All Peace and marry them anywhere in the world without all this red tape. I approach Lucy about this option, but she declines. I go ahead and submit an application, just in case.

I call Jock, Liam and Esther and let them know I'll be out of the country for a couple of weeks. I call Dr. Trabulus and ask for a prescription for sleeping pills so I can make it through the ten-and-a-half-hour flight. Blaise seems to do just fine flying, sleeping, changing time zones and maintaining good health. I'm the one with a more delicate constitution—I stay up all night and then fall apart as soon as I get to my destination.

It takes me a full day to pack Lucy and Tommy's luggage into the Louis Vuitton trunks she takes on every trip, and half a day to pack our clothes and traveling items. I've rerented tapes that teach Greek from the Beverly Hills library and it *is* like getting back onto a bicycle. The language returns to me in waves. A few nights before we leave I even have dreams in Greek. I start to feel the warmth and familiarity I felt when I lived in the Greek Cyclades.

To treat Blaise, who has been a quiet angel as of late, I take him to my favorite Greek restaurant/store in Los Angeles. Papa Cristos on West Pico is an institution to all Angelenos looking for authentic

Mediterranean goods. They specialize in Greek food, but have items from all the countries bordering the Med. Blaise happily munches through gyros, Greek salad, spanakopita (spinach pie) and tzatziki (yogurt sauce).

I schedule a van, minus the backseats in order to accommodate all of Lucy's trunks, to pick us up at her new house, where I've brought our suitcases. At the airport, I stuff as much into our carry-ons as humanly possible, including Luella, and we set forth on our trip to Santorini, Greece.

Chapter Twenty-three

Our taxi and the one behind us, which carries our baggage, pull into the Hotel Plaka in Athens's old town. The Hotel Plaka isn't the Four Seasons, but we are greeted more warmly here. The other guests look at us questioningly with our ten pieces of luggage, eight of which cost more per piece than a week's stay. I rent two connected rooms—one for the luggage, one for us. Thankfully, I don't remember enough Greek to even try to explain the reason a mother and child would need this many trunks.

We take hot showers, then we walk through the Plaka, where I buy Greek fisherman sweaters for Blaise and me and eat a dinner of *choriatiki salata* (Greek salad) and *pastitsio* (pasta casserole). After a small treat of baklava for dessert, we retire to the hotel and fall into a much-needed, much-deserved sleep.

At six-thirty in the morning, I wake up to feel the room shaking. I sit up straight. Blaise doesn't even twitch in his sleep. I get him up and we stand in the doorway awaiting an aftershock that happens a minute later. I thought I'd left earthquakes behind in Los Angeles, but Greece rocks even more than L.A.

The hallways are littered with tourists not quite sure what to do in a situation like this. Feeling like an old professional, I'm able to calm some of the travelers, but knowing that Greece's building standards are not the same as L.A.'s, I'm not truly comforted by my own words. We dress quickly and leave the hotel. After standing in line for five hours in an uninspired government building to ensure that Lucy and Tommy can indeed get married here, we gather our luggage and get on the first plane to Santorini.

Adonis, our taxi driver, meets us at the island's airport. He's a short, squat man with hands the size of T-bone steaks. Adonis is rather overwhelmed when duplicate trunks keep appearing out of the cargo hold. Finally, he calls his brother, appropriately named Hercules, to come help him out. Hercules easily loads the remaining trunks into his van and off we go to set up Lucy and Tommy Ray's nuptials.

"Hercules? Where's Xena?" Blaise cracks himself up.

"Enough," I say with a warning tone in my voice.

"What's his real name?" Blaise asks, stifling a giggle.

Thankfully, Hercules pretends he doesn't speak English and therefore can ignore Blaise's rude comments. Following Adonis, he drives the minivan through the hilly streets of Messaria and the main town, Fira.

We are staying in a "cave," a house sunk into volcanic rock in the town of Imerovigli overlooking the caldera, where legend has it that Atlantis sank into the water after a terrific volcanic explosion. The deep sea waters between Thira, Santorini's other name, and the island of Thirassia across the caldera look warm and inviting. It is from here that I will set up camp to organize the wedding and reception.

. . .

We've been here over a week, but with all the work of arranging the wedding, we have yet to step foot on the beach. Lucy's private jet arrives at four-thirty and finally we've got most of the day to ourselves. Blaise and I have breakfast on the stone patio, then gather our beach supplies, jump in the rental jeep and head out for a day of exploring. I show him where I lived, worked and played during my year here.

Lucy walks down the stairs of her private jet in stiletto heels that make her six feet four inches tall. A yellow peasant blouse stops just below her breasts, and her very, very short skirt is Mediterranean blue. This must be her Hollywood version of fun-in-the-Greek-sun beachwear.

Behind Lucy is her mother, Beryl, dressed sedately in navy-and-white linen with smart, flat sandals and looking the part of the mother of the bride-to-be. David, Beryl's emasculated boyfriend, comes out next, but he's not looking terribly emasculated at the moment. Right now, he fits in perfectly with all the other dark-haired Greek-god types. Lucy's agent, Jay, and his lover, Michael, her manager, follow closely behind. They try surreptitiously to touch each other to express their awe at the beauty surrounding them.

I'm surprised to see Burt Reynolds come out, followed by George Hamilton and Jerry Lewis. This is going to be Beryl's shining moment and she wants all her friends to witness it. Following Jerry is Beryl's ex—Lucy's dad—Luke, and his latest flame, Tina, who was last seen all over the rags on the arm of a certain married multimillionaire.

Arriving in separate private jets are Daryl Hannah, Lucy's past castmate, as well as other past cast members Penelope Cruz and George Clooney, who has flown in from Lake Como. Angela Bassett descends, followed by Meg, Courteney, Halle, Lisa, Winona and Lucy's whole posse. I can already see that she gave me a very inaccurate head count as to how many people were going to attend. As I watch them descend the aircraft, I get on the horn trying to find extra rooms around Fira with the superior service to which these stars are accustomed.

What was I thinking to have accepted this mission? If this many people come off Tommy Ray's plane, the island won't have enough rooms to house them.

At the huge prewedding dinner on the cliffs of Fira, Lucy explains to me that the only person missing is Tommy Ray. He had to do an extra day's worth of shooting in Mexico. Blaise and Jack, Meg's son, can't wait for the meal to end so they can duel each other with Yu-Gi-Oh cards. After dinner, Beryl gives me another once-over and then announces to the people at her table that I was the one David ran over with the U-Haul. I look across the table at David, who peers down the side of the cliff, embarrassed. I don't know whether he wants to pitch himself down to splatter on the rocks, or pitch Beryl, but when he looks up, I mouth the words "I'm sorry."

The wedding will be on a stone balcony overlooking the caldera, the volcano and what is described in every travel publication as "the most breathtaking view on the planet." Today is the big day. The actual nuptials will take place with the sun setting in the background—one of the most highly admired sunsets ever. Every night, tourists and locals alike dot the rim of the island's volcanic peak, cramming into restaurants, onto cave rooftops and on tops of cars, then for an hour the world stops. A hush falls over the island population in order to watch nature put on a scene-stealing show.

I make calls checking for the thirtieth time that all will go off without a hitch. If I succeed, I might consider a second career as a wedding coordinator, but only for the rich. Only the wealthy could pay me enough to repeatedly subject myself to this amount of prewedding torture.

I double-check the estimated time of arrival for Tommy Ray's jet and reconfirm with Hercules that he will have a sedan (not an easy find on this island), and he assures me he will be there to meet Tommy Ray. He already has the sedan gassed and washed. It will be there at 3:30 P.M., or 15:30 as they say in Europe, as planned.

I'm a little upset that Tommy Ray is cutting it so close and pray that he's clean, shaven and ready to pour into his wedding suit the moment he steps off the plane. At least I don't have to meet him at the airport myself, after our last encounter.

Driving to the caterer's home kitchen myself, I see an entire lamb stuffed with herbs and smelling mighty good roasting on a spit in the backyard. The trays of appetizers I requested are ready and taste spectacular. Huge platters of moussaka, *keftedes* (meatballs) and *vleeta* (greens) are prepared and ready to go. *Tiropitas* (cheese pies) are cooking in the oven and the wines are chilling as we speak. An array of Boutari, retsina, Metaxa and ouzo will be available for imbibing.

I drive back to the hotel worried, wondering if my choice in wedding drinks was wise. The side of a steep Santorini cliff is *not* the place to get stumbling drunk. With Tommy Ray's fondness for boozing it up and getting rowdy, Lucy may be a widow before the night is over. During the wedding, Blaise and I will be in the back row, as far away from the cliff's edge as possible.

Holidays in the Cyclades have been known to bring out qualities in folks they never knew they had. Men who have never looked twice at their own gender wake up the following morning with a splitting Metaxa-inspired headache next to some dude named Costas who swears he herds sheep for a living. Women who are considered modest souls back home find themselves stripping down to almost nothing, skinny-dipping in the warm waters of the Med, then lying topless under the sun so as to not get a tan line. I did the latter the last time I was here, and no one was more surprised than I, except for the goat that unexpectedly walked onto the beach and began licking my face.

Back at the hotel, I iron clothes for the big night while Blaise studies the volcano and late-day nude sunbathers through the left-over binoculars Lucy gave him after the New Year's Eve party. I get Luella out of my luggage and undo the bubble wrap in which I have her safely packed. It is 3:30 P.M. right now and Tommy Ray's plane should be landing any moment. Blaise and I get dressed and drive to Fira to oversee the last moments of decorating.

When we first walk onto the hotel balcony, I am stunned to see just how beautifully the place is turning out. Sweet scents of scattered flowers mix with the lusty deep herbal smells of sage and oregano. The indigo blue waters of the Mediterranean contrast nicely with the flapping umbrellas of pure white. The seascape is blue with white boats bobbing on the waters as far as the eye can see.

The deep reds and oranges of bougainvillea blossoms complete the clean, crisp color palette. The chairs are covered in pure white linens against the whitewashed walls, and the dinner area is pure white with painted blue tables covered in starched white linens. Tropical fish swim up and down the length of the tables in long rectangular aquariums—an idea I borrowed from the walled aquarium in Jock's house.

Waiters and busboys move about, setting up the tables and readying the hotel for the guests who will begin arriving any moment. Pulling Blaise aside, I give him one of my lectures on proper behavior. I don't want Lucy's wedding ruined by the sudden outburst of a Juvenile Hall–prone child.

"Mom, we don't need to have this conversation. I wouldn't want to ruin Lucy's wedding any more than you would."

Studying Blaise's face, I see his sullen expression and tension seem to have been left in Los Angeles. He actually seems happier. I certainly am. In fact, this just might be the happiest I've been in a long time—on a paid vacation of sorts, in Greece with my son. He hasn't been any trouble whatsoever; in fact, he's been a big help. I am ready for the festivities to begin.

The guests start to arrive and take their seats as I stand back by the bar eyeing the wine. Retsina, made with the essence of pine tar, is a wine either loved or considered best when used by painters to strip wallpaper. I think it's heavenly.

The musicians start exactly on time, playing bouzouki, fiddle and oud. When they start to play music from *Zorba the Greek,* I breathe in the surroundings deeply and pour myself a glass of retsina. The combination of the music with the sea in front of me, the warmth of good wine in the country where it is made, and the blue-and-white Greek flags whipping around in the constant breeze that cools the island makes me happy. When the bearded Orthodox priest walks up the road with Lucy in her unbelievably gorgeous white gown, followed by additional musicians blending their tunes with the ones playing here at the hotel, onlookers cheer. It's so beautiful that I can't help it—I take another sip of wine and cheer, too. People line the road, clapping and whistling as she follows the priest into the hotel.

The photographer and videographer are eating up her presence. They photograph her beauty from all angles and she knows how to bask in the moment. Finally, the musicians start the quiet, low music reserved for Tommy Ray's arrival.

The guests begin turning their heads and a low murmur emanates from the gathering. Lucy looks at me with a question on her face. I instruct Blaise to wait right where I put him and then run out the front of the hotel. As I make my way through the crowd, I see the sedan with Hercules behind the wheel pull up in front of the hotel.

Thank God! Better late than never.

Hercules spills out from behind the wheel and pulls me aside. He speaks so rapidly in Greek I catch only a few words: airplane, airport, wait, hot. I can't understand. I push past him and throw open the door to the back of the darkened sedan.

It's empty.

"Hercules, where is the man you were supposed to bring here?" I ask in broken Greek. "Speak to me slowly," I command.

He raises his shoulders. "I don't know."

"What the hell do you mean you don't know?"

"His plane never arrived," he explains. "It's hot. I can't wait forever. I wait one hour, that's it. I want to be paid for my time."

"Don't move!" I demand in my best Greek.

Rushing to the hotel lobby and grabbing the phone, I call the airport to speak with a supervisor, who says they're closing the airport for the night. No more planes are expected. I ask about Tommy Ray's plane and the supervisor says that it never showed up, never canceled its arrival and never responded to communication.

"Did it crash? Did it ever leave Mexico City? Did it refuel in Miami? Can you tell me anything?" I cry.

"Nothing, ma'am." He hangs up.

I push my way through the guests and approach Lucy.

"Lucy, Tommy Ray's not here. His plane never arrived!" I whisper. "They're closing the airport for the night. Can you call his cell and see if they got delayed somewhere?"

Lucy stares at me without uttering a word. Her beauty transforms into horror and ugliness before my eyes. She reaches her hand up to her head as if she's going to faint, and brings it down as hard as she can, openhanded across my face. My cheek burns.

"You witch!" she screams. "You've ruined my wedding, you horrible, vile witch." She lands on me, pelting me in the face as the crowd gathers around to watch. I'm horrified when I hear Blaise screaming out for me. Lucy scratches me with her freshly painted nails, leaving marks down my arms and neck.

I can't hit her in front of her mom and dad and a priest! This crazy woman is supposed to *pay me,* and I'll surely never get paid if I hit her.

"Have you lost your mind, Lucy?" I growl. "Get off me!" I grab one of her flailing arms and bite her as hard as I can. She wails in pain, then hits me even more viciously across my back and head.

Jesus, why isn't anyone helping me?

Finally, pushing his way through the crowd, Blaise jumps on Lucy and pulls her head back. She screams at him to stop and he clinches his jaw and pulls harder. Clumps of hair and flowers are coming out of her head and into his fists. He straddles her and cranes her face back to meet his.

"No one hurts my mom!"

"Get off me, you little brat!" Lucy cries out.

Suddenly, Luke, Lucy's dad, intervenes and pulls Blaise, who's yelling and punching, off Lucy, and Lucy, who's screaming bloody murder, off me.

"You bitch! You're fired," Lucy screams, pointing at me.

"You can't fire my mom!" Blaise yells out with equal fervor. "She quits!"

"Forever, Corki. I never want to see you again! How fucking dare you ruin my wedding! What are you? Jealous? Jealous of my relationship with Tommy Ray because your own husband left and never came back? Huh?" she screams as she kicks her dad away.

The guests suddenly gather around Lucy.

Unbelievable! I get attacked in front of everyone for nothing I've done and they go to rescue her! Beryl sweeps by me. "You better go on home now, honey. You've done enough for one day."

I gather up Luella from her crazy son's wedding, grab Blaise and get the hell out of there. Blaise is furious and I can barely see straight to drive back to Imerovigli without plunging down a hill.

Íts six A.M. and I haven't heard or seen Lucy or any member of her entourage for twelve hours. Blaise and I rest our luggage on the tarmac as we wait to board the flight out of my favorite island; I doubt I will ever return. My eye is black and aching. I've had enough of movie stars to sate me forever. The faster I get away from these people, the faster I can begin to create a normal life for us.

I'm mad at myself for not punching Lucy into the stone pavers and really angry that she brought up Basil, something I told her once in confidence. Still, I'm hurt that I worked harder than I ever have to create a truly lovely wedding and then got treated like her whipping boy. The venom with which she attacked me has jarred me to the bone.

Our plane lands on time in Athens but the outbound Lufthansa flight is full. I show the woman behind the counter our full-fare tickets and we are put on an Alitalia plane bound for San Francisco via Milan. San Francisco is close enough. Five hundred miles from home will be more comforting than being halfway around the world with a bunch of maniacs.

On board the Alitalia flight, Blaise quietly watches the screen at the front of the cabin, which shows where our plane is in midflight against a map of Greece, Italy and the Adriatic and Ionian seas. Our plane hugs the Greek coast heading north before crossing the sea. I lean on the window watching the sea and wonder how this event has affected Blaise. He hasn't spoken one word since last night. I put my arm around him for the remainder of the trip, and this one time, he doesn't remove it.

We arrive at Malpensa Airport in Milan, potentially the most poorly named airport in the world. *Malpensa.* Bad thoughts. Bad thinking. It's apropos at the moment, but I don't want to get on a plane with anyone else who has bad intent.

As Blaise stands with the Italians at a *tremezzini* stand munching on a broccoli-and-shaved-Piave-cheese sandwich drizzled in garlic-laced olive oil, I get out the world cell Lucy provided for me in time of emergencies and use it—all I want. I call my mama and tell her everything. I call my sister Prudence in Menlo Park and tell her we're headed her way and can she pick us up at the airport. I call Veronique's world cell and tell her the whole story.

"Corki," she says with compassion in her voice, "this is one of the worst things I've ever heard!" I can hear Roberto in the background talking to her. Before I can respond, she continues. "Corki, there's a bus at Malpensa that will take you to the train station in Milan. Why don't you guys come to Portofino for a few days? Roberto has a small apartment that isn't being used right now. You're welcome to stay there. Come! We'll take you out on his boat."

I think for a moment and accept her offer. We gather our bags and head toward the airport bus stop. On the bus ride into the city, I call my sister again and cancel the pickup at San Francisco.

Portofino, with all its beauty and solitude, beckons so strongly I can taste it.

Chapter Twenty-four

Five hours later we sit on Roberto's docked "boat," as Veronique called it. I call it the biggest yacht I've ever been on.

"It's one hundred and fifty feet long, Mom," Blaise beams. "That's what Mr. Tratelli told me. This is so incredibly cool."

I sit in the hot tub sipping a diet soda that tastes similar to the sea in which we're floating. I'm being pelted, not by Lucy, but by six jets of pulsing water beating every knot I've accumulated in my back over the past four weeks. I feel my tension floating away.

"And he said that if I want," Blaise goes on, "when we go out to sea, I can steer the boat. He'll even tell the captain to teach me about navigation by the position of the stars. Is this cool or what?"

I can barely find the breath to answer.

"Mom, are you listening to me?"

"I am, Blaise. It's cool," I say nonchalantly.

Blaise looks bored for a moment. "I'm going off to explore," he says and scampers off. I watch him go until he grabs hold of the doorframe and swings into the cabin.

The waiter, a small effete Armenian man named Teymour, approaches me with drinks balanced on a tray.

"Ma'am, would you like another drink?"

I smile at him and shake my head. "No thank you, Teymour. I've had enough."

He bows slightly and leaves.

Veronique and Roberto join me in the hot tub, where we all sit quietly taking in the Italian sun. I ponder the graciousness they showed in inviting us here on a real vacation, and break the silence.

"I can't thank you two enough for this. Can I please cook you dinner tonight?"

"I was hoping you would," Roberto says, smiling without opening his eyes. "Marcello, one of the cooks, can take you to market in Santa Margherita Ligure if you'd like."

"I'd love that."

After a dinner of lobster, pasta with mussels, and white beans with roasted tomatoes, Roberto proposes a toast. Blaise loves this tradition and stands to meet all the other clinking glasses. Out of the dark galley comes candlelight. A brightly lit birthday cake is suddenly in front of Blaise, much to his amazement. With all the excitement, we both forgot that today is his eleventh birthday, but apparently Veronique did not. He shrieks with childish joy and surprise and blows out all eleven candles with one breath.

As we eat the delicious almond-flavored cake with vanilla gelato,

I admire Roberto, who, I must confess, looks devilishly handsome with his tanned Italian skin and white linen shirt.

"Corki," Roberto says my name with a roll of the *r* that I wish was part of my everyday accent. "My lovely Veronique told me of your struggles this past week." He raises his glass of champagne. "Here's to freedom and starting life anew."

"Here, here!" we all say and I take a sip.

"Thank you," I say, nodding. "This is very kind of you to invite us here. This has all been lovely. Thank you so, so much."

"You are most welcome," he says.

I tuck Blaise into bed at the "small apartment," a three-bedroom, three-bathroom villa overlooking the harbor of Portofino. A flickering bulb resembling a candle's flame softly lights the room. Blaise pulls my arm so I'll sit down with him. He sleepily stares at me.

"Mom, you remember when Mr. Barba called?"

"Yes."

"It wasn't Mr. Barba."

"Yes it was. I talked to him. He had a cold."

"No, Mom, he didn't," Blaise looks down, embarrassed. "It was me."

"But I—"

"Mom, I'm so sorry I made you cry. I never knew I was hurting you like that. You didn't seem to care about me that much. It seemed like your work was more important than me."

"That was you, Blaise?" I stare at him with my heart pounding rapidly. I reflect back on "Mr. Barba" coughing and not being quite as eloquent as he was the first time I'd spoken with him. I think of how I poured my soul out in a steady stream of sobs.

"I was just going to pull a trick on you, that was all. I wanted to see what you'd tell Mr. Barba, and then, well . . ."

"Well, you found out," I say, smiling and embarrassed.

"I sure did."

"Blaise, I'm doing the best I can. I know sometimes it doesn't seem to be enough, but you mean everything to me."

We're silent for a moment, then I run my hand through his dreadlocks.

"Mom . . . we'll be okay, right?"

"We'll be more than okay, Blaise," I say, trying to forget that I now have no idea how we will survive financially.

I kiss him on the forehead and sit with him until he falls asleep.

Chapter Twenty-five

Home isn't quite as sweet with a throng of reporters and photographers sitting on my front steps eagerly awaiting our six A.M. arrival. I prepare Blaise for the onslaught of questions about to be thrown at us as we sit in the sedan that brought us home from the airport.

"Blaise, you see those guys in front of our house?"

"Yeah."

"They're the paparazzi. They're going to shove cameras in your face and yell taunting questions. Remember how we play blind? Now we're going to play deaf, dumb *and* blind. No matter how they try to provoke us, we'll walk through them like Moses parting the Red Sea, understand?"

"Yeah. Why are they here?"

"They're waiting for us because they want to ask me questions about Lucy. Since I'm not going to lie for my clients anymore, I'm just going to keep my mouth shut . . . at least until Lucy and Tommy Ray pay me what they owe."

Before I can prep him anymore, Blaise bolts from the car,

whizzes past the crowd and disappears around a corner of our four-plex. He darts to the left where there's a storage room under the stairs rather than going up the staircase to our apartment.

Good for him; he got away!

The driver gets our luggage out of the trunk and opens the door for me to get out.

I've never in my entire career as a personal assistant been asked to sign a confidentiality agreement. I don't know why; most assistants are asked to sign immediately. But I took my own unspoken oath twenty years ago. I swore to protect my clients' personal information and never reveal anything about them to anyone . . . especially the press.

I put on my sunglasses—a defensive tool. I won't have to look anyone in the eye and no one can see my blackened one. I'll walk straight on through, just as I told Blaise to do.

I get out of the car and the paparazzi are on me within seconds.

"Are you aware of the breakup of Lucy Bennett and Tommy Ray Woods?" one calls out.

"Is it true that Tommy Ray Woods was last seen in Mexico City with his costar, Damienne Beauté?" another asks.

If *that's* true, it will be a stab in the heart to Lucy. She used to baby-sit Damienne!

"Did Tommy Ray dump Lucy Bennett at the altar? Is it true?"

"Is it true Jock Straupman is moving to Paris permanently?"

That's a new one. I'll have to check. I'll pick up the *National Enquirer* when I go to the grocery store. They know half the goods on my folks before I do!

"Are you aware that Lucy Bennett was seen yesterday on the island of Pantelleria with the singer B. C. Collins?"

That's another new one, but it wouldn't surprise me. She doesn't mess around when it comes rebounding. It's her specialty.

"Corki, are you aware of any of this?"

The paparazzi quiet as I turn around to face them. Suddenly I hear a hiss, then a spurt, and a geyser of water shoots straight out of the bushes, drenching the cameramen and forcing them backward to protect their equipment. I look over toward the room under the stairs.

Blaise has turned our unruly, good-for-nothing-until-now sprinklers on the sharks.

As I stand in the water, getting thoroughly soaked, the cameramen dash out to the street to avoid the wild jets of water shooting everywhere. Blaise peeks out from behind the door and gives me the thumbs-up. Smiling at my son, I pick up a magazine from the ground and look at the front cover.

"Can you explain that?" a reporter calls out.

There I am on the wet cover of a popular weekly magazine, standing next to Lucy on the balcony overlooking the caldera. The picture was taken two seconds before Lucy attacked me.

It's seven A.M., but with the paparazzi circling our apartment like a pack of dogs circling their kill, I can see that today, even though it's the last day of school, would be a very good day for Blaise to be there.

I make espressos for us both, a once-in-a-great-while treat for Blaise, who would probably fall asleep without one. By eight A.M. we are sneaking out the back door, firing up Bella and burning rubber out of the backyard without bothering to get out and close the gates after us.

. . .

Dr. Castillo greets Blaise with a smile. Besides being a fine principal, she's a good actress.

"Welcome back, Blaise."

"Thank you, Dr. Castillo. I'm happy to be back."

Dr. Castillo and I raise eyebrows at one another.

As I pull away from the school, Shelly calls on my cell.

"Corki, I was hoping you were home."

"We just arrived. I have so much to tell you, it's crazy."

"Same here. Atom's in the hospital," she says. "The doctors say he'll be okay, but apparently it was shaky for a while."

"My God, what happened?"

"Well, let's just say the drugs we were so afraid the big, bad wolf was going to give to the kids didn't come from Compton. They were sitting right here on Esther's kitchen counter. She left her Xanax out and Atom swallowed a bunch of them. He's not talking yet, but they've stabilized him. They had to pump his stomach."

"Oh no!"

"Esther's been so busy with her event planning, I think someone needed attention and someone got it! Handyman Dwayne found him on the floor in the hallway. Liam's in pieces. You know him, Mr. Best Dad in the Universe. He hasn't been back to the studio since. He's at the hospital, hasn't left Atom's side and has no intention of leaving. Esther, on the other hand, is falling apart. She's crying one minute, screaming the next, all from her bed, all in a tranquilizer haze. I can't work hard enough to keep her happy, which sort of leads to the good news in all this."

"Which is?"

"Which is that I won't have to much longer."

"Why?"

"I've received a scholarship and I'm going back to school to get my master's degree."

The moment I get home, I type out my invoices on the slim chance that I'll actually get paid. To Lucy, I also submit my six-hundred-dollar phone bill that's been outstanding for a while. Thank God her business office gave me her credit cards to pay for hotels, flights and per diem, otherwise I'd be out way more cash than I already am. Within five minutes of faxing my invoices, I get a call from Debbie, who pays Lucy's bills. She is sorry to tell me this, but she has been given specific instructions not to pay any of my invoices.

That bitch!

So, not only am I out my six hundred for the phone bill, but two weeks' worth of pay. I'm fuming. An hour later, I get a call from Harvey, who pays Tommy Ray's bills.

Same thing.

I pace my living room, trying to figure out a way to get the money that is owed to me. Finally, my neighbor calls to ask what I'm doing up there. Trying to wear a path in the hardwood floors? And why is the front yard flooded?

I explain the situation. "Are those the same folks you just moved into that place in Beverly Hills?" she asks.

"Yep."

"Sounds like you need to go on a 'shopping spree' and get what's due you."

Hmmmm. Interesting perspective. I lie in bed and think some more. I don't realize I'm asleep until the phone wakes me.

"Hello," I say, groggily.

"Corki Brown?" a male voice asks.

"Yes?"

"Bob Caplan, *National Enquirer*," he states. "Looks like you might be out of a job, huh?"

"What?"

"Judging from the cover of *Peo*—"

"Yes, I saw the cover," I say.

"Have you seen the layout?"

I sit up in bed.

"No, just the cover."

"Well, it's just on the newsstands this morning. You were caught, on film, being . . . well, it looks like, assaulted by Lucy Bennett."

"No!" I say in disbelief.

"Yes, that's what it looks like." Bob is quiet for a moment. "I hope you have a nest egg."

"Why?"

"Well, the cover and inside story is all speculation. To be frank, Corki, I'd pay dearly for the whole story told from your perspective."

"I'm sure you would, Bob. But I can't do that. You know I can't." If I talk, I know I'll never be hired as a personal assistant again. I suddenly wonder if he's taping the conversation.

"It could be worth twenty-five thousand dollars, especially with pictures," he says, tempting me to forget my morals.

"Bob . . ."

"Thirty. I could go up to thirty if it's juicy. It looks very juicy. Do you have any bruises or anything like that? If it's visible, I might even be able to squeeze out thirty-five."

I'm silent as I think of the money owed me.

"Listen, Corki, all this will be forgotten when the next scandal hits the papers. Lucy and Tommy will find solace in someone new, and you'll have a little nest egg for yourself."

I feel as if my soul is up for auction.

"Bob, I'm sleeping. Can you call me another time?"

I gently hang up, knowing good and well that I just openly invited him to figure out what my soul is worth.

I cogitate on the stories I have sewn up inside of me: Jock and his proclivities—all of them—young girls, guns, child porn passed off as art, secret rooms; Lucy and her endless fodder for front-page stories—the sex pictures, the romps, the wedding fiasco, her secret code to the panic room, her past affairs with married men, her attempts at purchasing people—her punching and scratching and lies and deceit.

I have to call Bob back and tell him that he should never, ever call me again. I pick up the phone and it is dead. I call the phone company from my cell and am told that my phone has been cut off for nonpayment of $633.19—the $633.19 I spent arranging the wedding—Lucy's wedding.

Chapter Twenty-six

"Corki, it's Veronique. I tried calling you at home, but . . ."

"It's been cut off," I say into my cell phone.

I explain what happened with being refused payment for all my services rendered.

"I'm on an express train to ruin."

"Stop it! You are not. Look, we're home in L.A. Would you like to come over for dinner? Say about seven?"

"You're cooking?" I ask, surprised. She never cooks.

"Believe it or not, yes. Roberto will be helping, though."

"I would love to."

I drop off Blaise at Shelly's house with his strict promise, made in writing, that he will not start any fires or do *anything* destructive. Blaise even offers, with a mischievous smirk, that he will be happy to sign it in blood.

He kisses me goodbye and I drive from Baldwin Hills to the Hollywood Hills, giving myself a stern lecture about honor and values and morals—all of which are teetering dangerously on the verge of destruction. I can't help considering Bob Caplan's offer. Thirty-five thousand dollars could last me to the end of the year, even if I had no work whatsoever. Then, if I add in the porno pictures of Lucy, Tommy Ray and the girls in their romp, that could bring in even more money—maybe another thirty or forty. Even more.

I park in front of Veronique's house and sit in my car for a moment trying to remember who I am. I'm not Hubert, willing to take advantage of someone's lack of character. I'm not . . . or am I?

I knock on Veronique's door and she opens it with a big hug.

"You look better, Corki," she says, examining my face. "At least you can open your eye now."

"I feel better."

She takes my hand and leads me through her home, which is decorated with antique Italian, French, Mexican and Spanish crucifixes adorning the walls. Religious figurines, saints and icons compete for space with petite brass bells and Buddhist gongs. Smoky incense fills the air.

We cross the room to her outdoor balcony overlooking the hills and canyons. Roberto joins us and we drink Italian wine and watch the last of the sun dipping down into the Pacific Ocean. In the distance, coyotes start their nightly ritual of howling to one another, readying themselves for their dinner hunt. Through the back door, we hear a kitchen timer ring.

"Roberto?" she asks, "can you get that?"

"Most certainly."

. . .

We eat a dinner of pan-seared scallops with pasta and spinach out on the Mexican-tiled deck of Veronique's four-bedroom, four-and-a-half-bathroom home. In the distance, over the din of the Hollywood freeway traffic, we can hear the heavy clanging of church bells striking eight times.

"So, Corki," Roberto says with that roll of the *r*, "what now?"

"Well, quite frankly, I don't know."

"Are you tied to Los Angeles or will you be looking for work elsewhere?" he inquires.

"I've been an assistant for twenty years. It's the only thing I'm qualified to do, and L.A. is the only place I could do it. There's New York, but I don't know the city well enough to start up a business there. I'm not qualified to do any other type of work. I suppose I'd better start looking for other clients, but I'm not sure that's what I want."

"I see." Roberto leans back, retrieves a cigarette out of his pocket and lights it. He offers one to me and I kindly refuse. We sit in silence, mosquitoes buzzing us, for a while longer.

"You can cook," he offers.

"That's true, but I don't know of anyone who's going to pay me to consistently cook for them. I'm not exactly a trained professional."

"What is the largest number of people you've cooked for at one time?" he asks.

I look over at Veronique, pondering the question.

"Was it the time you did my Oscar party?" she asks.

"Yeah, I was thinking about that. How many were there?"

"At least a hundred. Probably more."

"I think that's the tops. We'll call it one hundred."

"Can you do it again?" he asks.

"If it pays the bills, I could do it every night."

"That was what I was thinking." Roberto leans back and balances carefully on the two back legs of his chair.

"I'm sorry, I missed it. What were you were thinking?"

"Cooking for a group of people. Have you ever been to St. Bart's?" he asks.

"Oh yes, years ago. In fact, I went with yours truly!" I say, pointing to Veronique. We laugh at the memories.

"I was shooting a Dutch film in St. Martin with Rutger Hauer," Veronique says, "and Corki and I went to spend the two days we had off from shooting in St. Bart's. It was gorgeous, but the flight over was harrowing."

"To put it lightly," I say, and we both laugh again as we remember the scariest flight of our lives. "Over the open sea, in a nine-seater, a red light started flashing in the cockpit, followed by a loud buzzer. Everyone in the plane looked at each other as if knowing it would be one of our last moments alive. Veronique even screamed, which scared the pilot more than the buzzer!"

"I own beach property over there," Roberto says quietly.

"Nice," I say, fantasizing about asking him if he wouldn't mind loaning me that someday. If it's as big as his "small apartment" in Portofino, I'd be a very content vacationer.

"It was a waste of space when I purchased it," he says, shaking his head. "It had an auto repair shop on it. Can you imagine *that* on the beach?"

"Sort of bizarre!" I agree.

"Very close to the Hotel Eden Roc. You know it? Lovely beach, shallow for swimming and close to the airport."

"We stayed at Eden Roc," Veronique announces.

"What kind of home did you build on it? Is it gorgeous?" I ask, readying myself to ask to borrow it.

"I didn't. I bought it twelve years ago and have done absolutely nothing with it."

So much for my vacation dreams.

"So, what do you think, Corki?"

I couldn't afford the ticket anyway.

"About what?" I ask.

"It's a prime piece of property."

"Um, okay," I say, still not sure what he's getting at.

"I'm an investor. I have a spectacular property in one of the best locations on the island. It's being wasted as a garage. I am willing to put money into fixing it up to be something of better use, but it would have to be executed quickly because I lose money in downtime. Renovation would be downtime," he says thoughtfully.

"What are you going to build, a small hotel?" I ask. Maybe Blaise and I can get a discount at the place if we know the owner.

"Yes. Seven beachfront rooms and a small, forty-seat restaurant. I could invest the capital to get the place renovated and in working order. I could also invest two years' worth of what would be rent for the converted structure," he says.

"It sounds lovely," I say dreamily.

"Corki, for you!" Veronique says, incredulously. "You open the restaurant. Your menu, your ideas, your future. *This* is what you're qualified to do, not slave away for us for the rest of your life. And the parts you aren't qualified to do, you do your research and *get* qualified for."

My mind is spinning.

"It will be more work than you think," Roberto goes on. "But if you're as smart about money, cooking and business as Veronique makes you out to be, you could make some very good money in that location," he says, shaking another cigarette out of his pocket and lighting it.

"I don't have any formal training. I just cook what I like and what I think other people will like."

"I very much enjoyed your cooking," Roberto says calmly, inhaling deeply, then blowing out billows of smoke into the air. "I'm not doing this just for you, Corki. If this is done properly—and I suspect it would be—I stand to make money, too, you know."

Chapter Twenty-seven

I notify all the clients I still work for—Liam, Esther and Jock, although he's questionable—that I'm done. It's a bit of a laugh, but I give my two-week notice.

Esther says now that Atom's well, she'll take Bella and use it as a third car to drive to their beach house in San Diego. She plans on taking Atom on more mini-vacations where they can relax and get away from all the stress of renovating their new home.

There has been no response from Jock. Figures. I haven't heard from him since the day I put myself on the line. I called and told him that Hubert and the Brothers Grimm were arrested and I had possession of his DVDs, which I subsequently destroyed. I also told him that I returned the one hundred thousand dollars to his safe.

Not one call.

I know he's still alive and thriving, because I read about him in the tabloids. I know he still checks his answering machine, because it takes four rings for it to pick up, which means he has listened to his messages and the machine is empty. I don't know if he's mad because the police got involved or because I directed it in the way that I saw fit, but as far as I'm concerned, it's over.

I sort through what's left in my garage of horrors. I have had two garage sales. I'm getting rid of all the stuff I don't want anymore and, more importantly, the stuff I've been holding on to for "when"—when I get a house of my own, when I get nice boyfriend, when Blaise grows up, when I have company over for dinner. All the "whens" are sold and I'm going to live for the now.

I'm down to a sordid selection of my clients' pasts. Liam's guns for which he never took lessons. Liam's gun safe to hold the guns for which he never took lessons and Liam's ammunition that goes in the guns. I have every diary and memory of Lucy's past that could have started a potential war under the domination of Tommy Ray. I have the wide array of liquor and wine from Lucy's cabinets. I call Mary at Almor Liquor on Sunset. She gives me the vintages, histories and prices of all the wines and liquors I have and tells me how I can ship the load of them to the French West Indies. She says I can sell the Rémy Martin Louis XIII for $150 U.S. *per shot* at the restaurant's bar.

Then there's the matter of the sex pictures in my safe. Bob Caplan from the *National Enquirer* got hold of my cell phone number and calls me every day. He says we have to "strike while the iron's hot" and if I keep stalling it will become yesterday's news. He says that time is of the essence, but I think sex is timeless. Movie stars embroiled in foursomes will be hot forever. He's upped the ante to forty thousand if I call back today and spill my guts.

Forty thousand could help with my moving and survival expenses. Even though things are starting to turn and life is looking way, way up, I'm still tempted. I've started to dial Bob's number again and again, but I've yet to do it. If only I was raised differently and could base my decisions on what feels good instead of on what my mother taught me. Mom always says, "Two wrongs don't make a right." If only I didn't have to live with myself after I cashed that check.

I can't even deal with the contents of the safe right now. However, there's also the matter of Luella, who is not in my safe anymore. She's on my fireplace mantel. How can Tommy Ray refuse to pay me when I have his mama? Did he stop caring about her because he's found himself a new honey? Or has he forgotten all about her?

I sit at my desk, writing down notes of how to get all this stuff back to the rightful owners, when my cell phone rings.

"Cooorrrkiii, it's Lucy! Hey, honey!"

The nerve. She sounds as if Santorini never happened. What can she possibly have to say to me?

"Yes?" I ask, cautiously.

"Corki, my dear, you must be so mad at me for my bad behavior," she says.

"I am."

"Can you forgive me?"

"Why would I want to?"

"Because I love you and need you," she says, playing the victimized child.

"Lucy, I want to be paid what I am owed, and after that I want you to pick up your stuff that's in my garage."

The line is silent.

"In fact, I'm calling your business office right now. I want to go get my money and then we'll see about continuing this conversation. I'm giving you three minutes, then I'm calling Debbie." I punch the button and hang up.

I don't need to wait three minutes, because Debbie calls me in two.

"I have your check waiting for pickup," she announces, as surprised as I am.

"I'll be in the office in thirty minutes," I say.

I throw on some clean clothes and walk out the door. As soon as I lock the door and spring down the steps toward Bella, my cell phone rings again.

"Corki, it's Shay, Jock's business manager," she says jokingly, "in case you've forgotten."

"Very funny. I haven't been able to call you."

"Don't start lying, missy. Your fingers ain't broke!"

"You got me. I could have called. I've been so involved trying to stay afloat I haven't touched base with anyone."

"Well, you might want to touch base now. You're doing something right again 'cause I have another check for you," she announces in a way that lets me know she enjoys being the deliverer of good news.

"Hallelujah! What did I do to deserve this? I haven't heard from Mr. Straupman in so long I thought he forgot about his lowly little assistant."

"Girl, shut up and get in here," Shay says, laughing as she hangs up.

Two money runs in one day. Now, if I can get Tommy Ray to cough up his part, I'll be paid up. I think once I explain to Harvey that I have Luella, Tommy will rethink his tight fist. I swing by and pick up my check from Debbie and cash it immediately before Miss Lucy changes her mind. Shay's office is next.

Yvonne, office queen, stands up as I enter. She holds in front of her the magazine with me on the cover.

"Care to give the scoop?" she asks.

"Uh, no. What's the saying? A picture's worth a thousand words. Is Shay in?"

"You know she is. Hold on a second." Yvonne rings Shay's line and announces my arrival. I am summoned back to her office.

"Miss Corki, this is too much dirt!" she says as she waves the magazine around.

"Who you telling?" I say in agreement.

"Girlfriend, I'm telling you, you need to write a book. Anyway, on to the here and now. Jock called out of the blue and asked me to cut you a check for fifteen thousand dollars. Said you'd know what it was for."

"Maybe it's a going-away present!"

"Maybe," Shay says. "Maybe he's just realizing how much you know. . . ."

On my trip home, I call Harvey and leave him a message that Luella wants to go home to her son, but her son still owes me money and Luella doesn't feel good about that and neither do I. I also tell him I'm leaving the country and I've had enough of this. I'm ready to put a lien on the house Tommy Ray and Lucy just purchased if this doesn't get straightened out quickly. I don't know if I can legally do this, but at least it lets Harvey know that I have Tommy's mama and I'm sick of playing games.

At home, I put Liam's guns, ammunition and gun safe in the back of Bella and drive to his and Esther's home in Pacific Palisades. I walk into the house and yell out hello. Shelly comes out of the dining room.

"Hey, Shell, you alone?" I ask softly.

"Yeah, you don't have to whisper," she says.

"I'm just cleaning out the last of the stuff and thought I'd drop off Liam's guns."

"Yeah, I heard," she says. "Here it is my last week, nice and quiet, and then you call announcing you're bringing the guns back. She threw a fit. She said you could drop off the safe, but the guns and bullets are not to enter this property. She said to donate them to charity."

"Yeah, right! 'Oh hi, Save the Children, would you guys like a shotgun complete with three hundred rounds of ammunition?' What the hell am I supposed to do with a .357 Magnum and a pump shotgun? Donate it to the L.A.P.D.?" I ask desperately.

"I don't know. Call the police?"

I do and am surprised. The L.A.P.D. gives me money for them, which I promptly donate to the Save Corki Brown Fund. Liam's not pleased with his stuff being sold, but given the alternative (his wife being pissed off), peace in the house seems to be a better offer. I sell my gun, too, as I don't think I'll be needing it anymore.

Lucy calls me again and again.

"I need you, honey. Bobby Sue isn't worth the birth certificate that was issued to her, and what am I supposed to do with this house? You and your sister did a beautiful job, but I need my stuff out of there before Tommy Ray gets back from shooting in Mexico. He'll be back in two weeks. Help! Forgive me please. I lost control. I know that and I promise it will never ever happen again. For God's sake, Corki, when I come home to L.A., I'll be homeless. I'm going to have to live at the Four Seasons, do you have no sympathy?"

Tommy Ray has Jolene call and ask me for Luella.

"I want my back pay first," I say.

"Are you holding his mother hostage? This is extortion, Corki."

"Bug off! I've taken very good care of Luella. I even hand-carried her to Greece and back when he couldn't bother to show up for his own wedding. I could have left her in her urn on a cliff overlooking a volcano. I could have had my own little ceremony and spread her ashes out at sea, but I didn't do any of that. I brought her all the way back here and I expect to be paid what he owes me. Tell Harvey that I want the money in cash tomorrow morning because I'm leaving the country on Saturday. And if I don't have it, Luella, whom I've become quite fond of, is coming with me for a proper burial at sea."

"Luella was terrified of the water!" Jolene says in a panic.

"Tomorrow morning then. In cash."

I disconnect and wait.

Saturday morning is here. I have sent the few possessions we want to arrive ahead of us by U.S. Postal Service. Blaise and I each have one large suitcase and a carry-on.

I hear a knock on the door and Shelly stands in the doorway.

"Ready, Freddy?"

"Ready!"

We haul our bags down and load one big one into the trunk and the rest into the back of her old broken-down convertible Mercedes. Blaise squeezes into the tiny bucket backseat next to the luggage.

Just as I go upstairs to lock up, a car screeches around the corner. Harvey pours out, in a huff, with an envelope in his hand. I can tell he's not used to being commanded to work on Saturday mornings. His pudgy face is unshaven and an aroma of coffee lingers on his breath.

"Here's your money. Count it, sign here"—he shoves a paper toward me—"and give me the urn."

"Good morning to you, too, Harvey," I say.

"Good morning. Sorry for the lack of civility, but I was told to deliver this to you on the double," he says breathing heavily.

"Thank you, Harvey. I'm sorry Tommy Ray only came to his senses this late in the game and had to wake you up on a Saturday morning."

I dig Luella out of my carry-on and hand her to him.

"Bye, Harvey! Bye, Luella! I'll miss you!"

I stand at the front door, sorting through my keys. I lock the door, but can't leave. I stand there for a long time.

Shelly toots the horn.

"C'mon, sister, the plane isn't going to wait," she yells.

"I'm sorry," I yell down. "I forgot one thing."

I open the front door and come back in, get the key to the gas starter in the fireplace and light it. Flames jump up wildly in the brick encasing. I dig in my purse, gather all the sex pictures of Lucy, Tommy and the girls and toss them in one by one. I watch my ties to the past go up in flames and wait for them to disintegrate into dusty ashes, then turn the flames off.

I'm hopping down the front staircase, taking two stairs at a time, when my cell phone rings.

"Corki, it's Bob Caplan from the *National*—"

"I know where you're from, Bob."

"The public is dying to hear the real story. It's over three weeks old. It's becoming yesterday's news. If you're going to change your mind, the time to act is now. What do you say, Corki? You want to tell what really happened? Warn others interested in becoming an assistant what it's really like? It could be like a public service announcement."

I like his new spin.

"A PSA, huh?"

"Yeah."

I'm silent for a moment as I negotiate my way through the gate and into Shelly's car.

"Call me in an hour," I say. "I'll think about it."

Acknowledgments

Thank you, God!!!

I thank my mom, Patti, and sister Melissa for six long and drawn-out years of reading, re-reading and editing my book again and again. And then, just when you thought you couldn't edit it one more time, doing it again. Your editing skills and dedication are astounding. I couldn't have done it without you! *Merci beaucoup, grazie mille, mucho gracias and efharisto poli.* I also deeply thank my sister Laura for having a fresh pair of eyes to look at my book and fine-tune it. And of course, my wonder boy Cayman, thank you for encouraging me to "hurry up and write."

I owe a very big and grand thank you to my editor, Josh Behar, for believing in me and having a vision that I hope I stepped up to the plate and delivered. You're brilliant.

My attorney/agent and friend, Martin Groothuis—thanks for the "papa" lectures, reality chats and your encouragement.

A huge thank you to my publicist, Seale Ballenger, who steps lightly, eyes wide open with kindness and insight. You provide fabulous guidance!

A round of applause from me to the crew at HarperCollins Publishers: Michael Morrison, Libby Jordan, Will Hinton, Judith Stagnitto Abbate, Betty Lew, Shubhani Sarkar, Julia Bannon, Susan Kosko, Tim Bower and Susan Sanguily. I truly cherish all you've done. Thank you.

A special round of applause to Andrea Molitor at Harper for explaining the process, the "word of mouth" and your kind spirit. You're an angel.

To Kristen Green, thank you for starting me out with your "fishing" techniques. You rock!

To one of my best and most courageous friends ever, Dan Rastorfer, I owe you tremendously. Thank you for every ounce of your love, help and friendship. Viva Jamaica!

My super good friend Stacy Cheriff—you've rescued me innumerable times and I value you. Our dinners at Spumoni on Montana—unforgettable!

I thank my dear friend Marla Rubin, you're a pillar, unstoppable, and you brought Paris alive. The food, God, the food! Marilyn and Bob Goldman, very clever you two are!

For Twyla Heckard—thank you for the times you've let me just write! You're a good friend . . . and your fried chicken ain't bad either!

Michelle Forbes and big sister Danielle Forbes, you're great friends and troopers and your mothering skills are right on the mark. I've learned a lot from you two. Papa John—you've done well!

Dr. Judith Perez, thank you for your professional insight. I appreciate the time you gave me.

Laura Kulsik and Bart Yasso, thank you for reading the book in the middle of the L.A. Marathon!

To Cheri Mancuso, who set me straight and instructed me on making the most important decision of my life, a big hug.

A special note of gratitude to the folks at Chipman-United Moving Lines—Bob Ensign, Amalia Espinoza, Mike Foreman and of course, Ron Quinn. You move me! Over and over. Nelson, I miss you!

A big hug to my Beverly Hills "family," Virginia Hirsh, Barbara Barrett, Arnold Clements, Kevin, Beth and Hannah Hirsh, Brian, Cathy and Liah Hirsh, Dean, Tammy and Brooke Clements.

Kelly Gouldrick, thank you for your cheerleading.

To Morgan Stevens, the original, I send my best love.

A special thank you to Joseph Barba, a teacher, coach and friend. You're an extraordinary human being and inspiration.

Jeanne Tripplehorn, Leland Orser and your gorgeous baby boy, August, I have deep gratitude. I treasure your honesty and trust.

Michael Abrams, thanks for your kindness, advice and peace.

To Mary Michiels at Almor Liquor, thanks for being a lifesaver during the holidays and every time I needed you to be one.

David Silberkliet, master chef, thanks for the foodie talks and friendship.

A huge thank you to Rebecca DeMornay, your generosity and insight astound me. At the wildest times, I pull your pearls of wisdom out of my memory banks. Sophia and Veronica—you're lucky!

Barbara Birnbaum, Karen Hollis, Cecile Cabeen, Kathy Smith, Kate Mackie and Louise Wechsler, thanks for taking on the challenge!

To my neighbors and nighttime chat friends, Anika Jackson, Shirley McNair and Mark Berry. You're good neighbors.

To Elaine Young and Barbara Eisner—you're great friends! Café Roma at one?

My niece Joelle Wagner, brother Hollis Howard and my bro-in-law, Robert Caplan—I love you all.

Boyd Schulz of Victoria, B.C., your antics make my life look boring. Long live Milano!

The kidlets—Todahtiyah and Sundiata Forbes, Simeyon Forbes-Mays, Kobie Lee, Drew Cheriff, Miles Kneedler—you keep my place rocking!

Dr. Joshua Trabulus and Dr. Myles Cohen—thank you for keeping me functioning!

Thank you for being in my life! Elsa Lopez, Lina Parrillo and Pasquale Fabrizio of Pasquale Shoe Repair, Arthur Amaral, Robyn, Kennon and Andrew Pearson and Bob, Libby, Debbie and Ian Roseman, Imelda Colindres, Kristine and Eirick Haensheke, Rosalyn Myles, Marija Krstic-Chin, Shelby Marlo, Ann Martin, Karen Michaels, Hugo Nathan, Richie May, Lisa Nicholls, Laura and Melanie Parker, Marina Schlesinger, Mike Shen, Don Spina, Norma Snyder, David and Tor Strawderman, Edy Foglino, Cheryll Roberts, Linda, Josh, Dylan and Maeve Almos, Frank Galassi, Jeff Haas, Joan Howard, Michael Flynn, Shaunse Neighbors, John, Gloria, Veronica and Yvonne Wehrmann, and to Kate Svoboda-Spanbock thanks for the name suggestion. Good choice.

Tallia and Michael Amos, thanks for being the beautiful, insightful people.

To all the Quaker folks at the Visalia Friends' Meeting—your community service and spirituality deeply inspire me.

My special thoughts and prayers go to those who have passed: my father, Melvin Howard, grandparents Florence and Harold Pimlott, my UCLA professor and good friend Dr. Erskine Peters, my client Anton Furst, friends Tony and Nancy Artley and my bro-in-law, Klaus Wagner—I love you and miss you all.

And thank you to the fifty-plus celebrities—actors, singers, musicians, producers, writers, directors and presidents—who have kept my life very, very interesting and busy for the past twenty years.